A Match to Remember

By Helen Hawkins

A Concert for Christmas
A Match to Remember

a&b

A Match to Remember

Helen Hawkins

Allison & Busby Limited
11 Wardour Mews
London W1F 8AN
allisonandbusby.com

First published in Great Britain by Allison & Busby in 2024.

A CIP catalogue record for this book is available from
the British Library.

First Edition

ISBN 978-0-7490-3120-6

Typeset in 11.5/16.5 pt Adobe Garamond Pro by
Allison & Busby Ltd.

By choosing this product, you help take care of the world's forests.
Learn more: www.fsc.org.

Printed and bound by
CPI Group (UK) Ltd, Croydon, CR0 4YY

For Matt

Chapter One

'Where could it have possibly gone?' Lizzie flung open the bottom-most of three drawers and pulled everything out. Among the pile now on the carpet was a selection of old clothes, unworn and unfolded; two pairs of skiing gloves, despite having never gone skiing; an unopened box of AA batteries; and her birth certificate hidden amongst a couple of Sky bills and her rental agreement. At least her birth certificate was in a folder. She could almost hear her older sister, Kirsty, scolding her for not having important things like her rental agreement and birth certificate alphabetised in a plastic wallet somewhere safe.

She was certain she'd taken her DBS check out and left it on the counter in the kitchen, ready for the big day. But it had since disappeared and she could only surmise that it had sprouted wings and flown away. Things had a habit of doing that in this flat.

It wasn't unusual for Lizzie to be awake in the early hours. She hadn't slept properly in years. But last night, sleep had evaded her. Entirely. It was her first day as a trainee teacher at Cranswell Primary and she was buzzing with excitement. And now, also panic.

She grumbled under her breath and kicked the drawer shut, before padding through to the kitchen and pushing down the plunger on the cafetière; the rich, fresh aroma of coffee was welcome after her failed search. After pouring herself a mug, she cracked open the window in the living room, the day already warm, and sat with her feet up on the sill, looking out over the town. A few deep breaths would usually help. The view looked out onto the busy shopping street below, but at this hour, it was just the delivery man who brought great big bags of flour to the bakery each morning. He whistled a jolly tune. Lizzie took another deep breath and brushed back some of her frizzy hair, heated from the stress and exertion.

A movement from the door made her jump and she turned, the sudden motion spilling coffee onto her pyjama shorts.

'Why are you creeping up on me?' Lizzie said, standing up to brush the hot coffee from her legs.

'How long have you been awake?' Tom asked.

'A while.' She refilled her mug and passed a second to Tom.

'Thanks.' He took a sip and a deep breath. 'We shouldn't have stayed up that late on a school night.'

Lizzie shook her head. 'Especially not on the first school night.' She rubbed a hand over her face, conscious that she probably looked hideous. She could only imagine the size of the bags under her eyes.

Tom drew a circle in the air towards Lizzie's face of unremoved make-up and crazy hair. 'This does not look like the face of a trainee teacher about to embark on the first day of the rest of her life.'

'No, Tom, it does not. This is the face of someone who stayed up way too late and was sabotaged by her flatmate, who didn't think to put a stop to the *Sex and the City* marathon.' She crawled onto the sofa and pulled a blanket around her.

Tom put up his hands in defence. 'You are a thirty-year-old woman, Miss Morris. You need to learn to take care of yourself, which includes choosing a reasonable bedtime.'

'But while I'm learning to take care of myself, you need to help me,' she whined, pulling the blanket up further.

Tom laughed.

'What time is it?' She propped herself up and downed the last of her coffee.

'Seven-fifteen,' Tom said, holding up and pointing at the clock from the sideboard.

'Oh God, I need to get showered and dressed!' Lizzie jumped off the sofa and snapped into action. 'Like now. I'm going to be late for my first day. What am I going to wear? And where is my DBS check? I swear I left it here with my lunchbox and bag.'

'How have you not thought about what to wear yet?' Tom asked, incredulous and oblivious to the more serious issue of the lost DBS check.

Lizzie shrugged.

'I'm telling you now Lizzie Morris, you will get nowhere as a teacher unless you get yourself a little more organised – lesson number one from a teaching assistant who's seen it all. Have a shower and I'll pick out a couple of options for you for when you've finished. Your DBS is on the side of the bath, by the way.'

Lizzie opened her mouth to ask why and then decided not to bother. She didn't care how it had got there; she just cared that she'd found it. She reached up and kissed Tom on the cheek as she passed him.

'Love you!'

Stepping into the shower, Lizzie could feel herself frowning. She'd been so prepared for today. She knew where she was going and how long it would take her to get there; her lunch was prepared and in the fridge ready to go – and had been carefully thought out to ensure it was easy to eat in public and wouldn't stink out the staffroom. She had visited WHSmith to get herself a new pencil case, and stationery for every possible stationery requirement. Never in the history of readiness had anyone been so ready for their first day. And yet she'd not slept – worrying again – and her DBS check had somehow made its way into the bathroom. She shook her head, moving it onto the shelf before turning the shower on.

Letting the water from the shower run down her hair and back, she closed her eyes and took some deep breaths. Everything would be fine, she thought. She withheld the nervous urge to throw up that was beginning to wash over her in stronger and stronger waves.

When she returned to her bedroom, she saw Tom had hung two outfits up on her wardrobe, including accessories, which hung down from the coat hangers. On the floor, he'd laid out some shoe options for her. On top of that, he'd replenished her mug of coffee.

Where had she got so lucky with a friend like Tom? Bizarrely, they'd not met until they were both at university, but it hadn't taken them long to realise that they'd both grown up in this same sleepy little market town, just at opposite ends of the high street. And now they'd met in the middle, sharing a flat above the bakery near the village green.

Lizzie blow-dried her unruly hair and straightened it in front of the mirror. The June sun, having already risen for the day, reflected off her fiery red locks, emblazoning the colour even more than normal. It was going to be another scorching day. By the time she'd added a thin layer of make-up and pulled her long hair up into a ponytail, she was beginning to look half human again, if a little bedraggled by the heat.

Tom's outfit choices were perfect, as always. His 'leaving the rest of her wardrobe tidy' was not. Lizzie stuffed a couple of pairs of shoes back into the wardrobe and slid the sleeve of a corduroy blazer and the skirt of her bright red Jessica Rabbit dress back through the crack in the door. Not that she'd wear either of those items of clothing again – one was hideously out of fashion and always had been, and the other was only appropriate for a twenty-year-old – and a skinny one at that.

Lizzie's phone buzzed and she removed herself from the wardrobe to see who had texted her. It was from Kirsty:

Hey! Hope today goes well! Can't wait to hear all about it at practice later! xxx

Lizzie smiled. Her sister's jolly text messages were so unlike her real-life Eeyore demeanour. In reality, Kirsty was nearly a decade older and far more serious than Lizzie was. After their parents died, Kirsty had become something of a mother hen to her.

She padded over to her dressing table and pushed around the necklaces and bracelets that clung together like spaghetti.

'How are you getting on?' Tom asked, his head popping round the door.

'Better, but your regular check-ins are starting to stress me out!' Lizzie said, placing a long silver necklace over her head and pulling on a thin-knit oversized cardigan. 'Do I look like a teacher?' She held out her arms and gave him a spin.

'You look great. Are you ready to go? If we leave now, we can still walk instead of driving,' he said, looking at his watch.

Lizzie nodded. 'I just need to find Mum's ring.' She rifled again in the chaos that was her dressing table and pulled out the ring – silver with two starfish at either end of the loop of metal that spiralled around her finger – memories of a holiday to the Isle of Wight as a child growing only slightly less vivid than the occasion itself. She slipped it on and took a deep breath, holding her finger and the ring with her other hand. 'I promised I'd get here,' she said quietly, remembering her determination to become a teacher and how proud her parents would have been to see her walking over the school threshold as a trainee.

'Lizzie!' Tom's voice brought Lizzie back to the present, and she took a final breath in the hope it would remove her urge to cry.

'Coming!' she said. Lizzie took one final look in the mirror and left her bedroom.

Lizzie and Tom lived about a fifteen-minute drive away from the school, but to walk it would only take forty-five minutes, with less traffic and fewer roadworks. Despite her excitement, Lizzie was keen to put off arriving for as long as possible. Nerves were creeping in and the butterflies in her stomach were having a rave.

Grabbing her ready-made, aroma-free lunch from the fridge and putting it into her new school bag, Lizzie set off with Tom as if she were fifteen again and it was the 1st of September. In reality, it was the 1st of June and today was the first day of the rest of her life – the start of her dreams finally coming true. Thanks to Tom's role as a teaching assistant at Cranswell Primary School (and her own unemployed status), she'd managed to bag half a term's paid work experience before her official placement started after the summer. Her mum and dad would have been so proud and Lizzie couldn't wait to get started.

Chapter Two

The nostalgia of arriving at the front gate of the school was tangible. The smell of the playground's warm tarmac, the laminated wall displays in primary colours, the abundance of Comic Sans. It was like no time had passed since she'd been here with her mother, since she'd been here herself as a child.

'I'll take you through to reception,' Tom said kindly.

It might have been the primary school she'd attended as a child, but the memory was so distant, it was like a white rabbit's warren of corridors where everything was a third of the size it was in the adult world. She wouldn't have been surprised to see the Mad Hatter having afternoon tea in the library.

'Here,' Tom said, indicating the door. 'Good luck!' he added, with a kiss on her cheek.

Lizzie signed in at reception and sat down on a squishy, carpet-textured chair.

The displays in the foyer were clearly there to present a good impression to visitors of the school. There were environmental awards, enlarged smiling photos of children playing outside or looking studious over science experiments; a wall of recognition identified students who had done particularly well in their schoolwork, or who had demonstrated one of the school's values in their conduct around the site. And it smelt really clean, like newly hoovered carpet and air freshener. Lizzie smiled to herself. This was definitely the type of place she wanted to work. She just hoped that the laminated photographs were a true reflection of what she'd let herself in for. For the first time since she'd sat down, nerves crept in again and she twisted her mum's ring around anxiously.

'Elizabeth Morris?' The sound of her name made her jump. A young, dark-haired woman came through into the reception area and Lizzie stood up to shake her hand.

'Call me Lizzie,' she said. 'Nice to meet you.'

The woman smiled and tucked her hair behind her ear. 'I'm Sophie – Miss Lawson. I'm going to be your mentor while you're training here with us.'

Lizzie returned the smile. 'Yes, I remember you from the interview,' she said. 'I'm so excited to get started!'

'Excellent! Come this way.' Sophie led her back through the labyrinth to a classroom.

Lizzie tried her hardest to walk tall, her long legs helping her to achieve the sure-footed stride she was after, but inside, those butterflies were still partying. She knew that her confidence could come across as arrogant at times, or at the very least, like she was in control. But she wasn't; not really. If anything, she was out of control. She rubbed her temple, willing the edge of a headache that was creeping in to go away.

Sophie showed Lizzie where she could leave her bag and coat (a tiny cupboard in the corner of the classroom that was filled with neatly ordered art and craft supplies) and then took her on a quick tour of the classroom. It was a large, square room and so organised that Lizzie could see straight away that she'd need to up her game. This wasn't a classroom in which people lost things. There were drawers and cupboards everywhere, and little baskets and tubs. Everything had its place and a laminated label with an image to accompany each of the words. The displays were immaculate, each looking like they'd been refreshed only yesterday. Out on the tables, there were pots of pens and stationery, each item labelled with a child's name. Things suddenly felt very real and Lizzie took a deep breath, willing her heart to slow down. There weren't any children here yet; she still had time to get herself together.

'Let's get a cup of tea before the children arrive,' Sophie said, taking Lizzie along the corridor to the staffroom. She continued to talk as they walked. 'So today, and probably the next couple of weeks, will really just be about observing the lessons and working with small groups of children on their tables, if that's OK? It'll give you a feel for the environment and the class. They're Year Six mind, so they can be a little big for their boots,' Sophie said. She was making their tea and pouring boiling water into the mugs on the work surface.

'They'll soon lose that when they become small fish in a big pond at secondary school,' added another teacher who had appeared in the staffroom.

Sophie poured a cup for the new teacher too. 'This is Kate,' she said, handing it to Kate.

'You're going to love it at Cranswell,' Kate said, taking the mug.

'Here,' Sophie said, passing Lizzie a cup.

Lizzie looked down at the mug, which was only half full.

'You're going to want to add cold water to the top, otherwise you'll never drink it in time,' Sophie said, as if reading her thoughts.

Lizzie did as she was told and gulped the tea down in its entirety (it turned out Sophie's trick worked perfectly) before following Sophie and Kate back down the corridor. They were clearly good friends and Lizzie followed them feeling like a third wheel. Her nerves surfaced again and she felt suddenly out of her depth. How would she cope fitting into somewhere that was clearly already so tight-knit? At least she had Tom.

'I normally greet students as they come in,' Sophie said when they'd returned to the classroom. She struggled to wedge a doorstop under the door.

In the distance, the hum of children floated on the air.

'Here they come,' she added, as if a tsunami or typhoon were on its way down the corridor.

Little did Lizzie know, Sophie was spot on. Before she knew it, they were surrounded by children, who, at ten going on eleven, weren't really that small any more. A couple of them were on a par with Lizzie's stature.

'Good morning, Benjamin,' Sophie said as a short, round boy waddled into the room.

'Morning, Miss Lawson.'

'Morning, Lyndsey.'

'Morning, Miss,' Lyndsey said.

Next, a tall girl came in with what looked like two sidekicks. They were in school uniform, but the kind of uniform that had been modified between leaving their parents and walking through the school gates.

'Morning, Miss Lawson,' they chorused as Sophie frowned

and all three of them lengthened their skirts with a roll of the eyes. The adjustment added a good three inches to the hems.

'Morning, girls,' Sophie said.

Lizzie found herself smiling and nodding in acknowledgement as the girls passed. She recognised something of herself in the girl gang.

'Good morning, Nigel.' As he passed, Sophie turned to look at Lizzie as if to say, *Whoever calls their child Nigel?*

'Morning, Misses,' he quipped, strolling past.

Lizzie smiled at his cheekiness and felt herself relax a little.

'Morning, Miss, morning, Miss,' another child said as she passed the two of them waiting at the door.

Eventually, the steady stream of children came to an end, and Lizzie followed Sophie through the classroom door. All the children were hanging bags up on pegs, or were at various stages of gathering pencil cases or workbooks. Sophie clearly had them whipped into shape and working within a routine. But what Lizzie found most overwhelming was how many of them there seemed to be, like a well choreographed dance troupe. For the first time, and probably not the last, Lizzie wondered whether she'd taken on more than she could handle.

Sophie pointed out a chair for Lizzie to sit in. Unfortunately for Lizzie, it was one of the children's chairs and about a third of the size she needed it to be. When she sat in it, she was all scrunched up and could feel her organs wrestling for space. This was going to get spectacularly uncomfortable in roughly less than a minute. She stretched her legs out under the table to give her insides a fighting chance.

Sophie began with literacy, and Lizzie's interest piqued. This was what she'd studied at university – well, English. She knew what Sophie was talking about and could definitely help

18

the children if called upon. Although, with a class of ten- and eleven-year-olds, she hoped that would be the case with most of the lessons. Maths would be a blip; she knew that, but she was mentally prepared for that one. She breathed a sigh of relief and settled into her tiny chair. All she had to do was watch the lesson and gather tips from Sophie's teaching practice. She could absolutely do this.

'Miss, have you got a ruler?' one girl asked. She seemed much smaller than all the others in the class and had blonde hair so light it almost seemed translucent.

Stationery was the kind of problem Lizzie could deal with. She took out her shiny new pencil case and passed a ruler to the girl.

'Thank you.'

'No problem,' Lizzie said, feeling pleased with herself.

'Audrey, can I borrow it too?' Nigel asked, all legs and arms and scrunched into his chair as much as Lizzie was with her grown-up frame.

'It's Miss's,' said Audrey, her tongue poking out as she concentrated on underlining the title in her exercise book.

'That's OK, Audrey,' Lizzie said, committing her name to memory.

Audrey passed the ruler to Nigel, who borrowed it and returned it.

'What's another word for walk?' Audrey asked, chewing on the end of her pencil as she thought for a moment.

'You can't use walk,' another student chimed in. It was Benjamin, who had entered the classroom first earlier. 'It's a banned word,' he added, gesticulating excitedly at a display on the wall.

Along with 'walk', words such as 'nice', 'good', 'bad', 'scary' and 'lovely' were all banned in Miss Lawson's classroom, it seemed.

'Well, what's your character doing?' Lizzie asked, trying, and failing, to think of another way to help Audrey without simply giving her a list of alternatives.

'He's creeping up on a baddie.' After a second, Audrey's eyes widened. 'What about crept?' She almost shrieked in her excitement.

'See? You don't even need me. You did that one all by yourself,' Lizzie said with a smile, and she realised that her nerves had eased with the good cheer of the children.

'Can you read mine, Miss?' Benjamin asked, holding his exercise book out as an offering. It looked like it had seen better days, with dog-eared corners, a damp, wrinkly edge and the faint smell of nicotine absorbed into the pages.

'Of course, Benjamin.' Lizzie took it from him, being careful not to touch the suspiciously damp area on the cover. She read his work and the entire table held a breath as they waited for her appraisal of it.

Lizzie remembered something vaguely from her pre-reading – something like start with a 'what went well' and come up with an 'even better if'. Her mouth was dry and she wanted to say the right thing. It felt like the entire classroom was anticipating her appraisal. She had to remind herself it was only a handful of ten-year-olds and they didn't have a clue who she was or what she was doing in their classroom. What went well . . . even better if . . .

'I think you've used punctuation really well, Benjamin.' She started with more certainty than she felt in the nauseous pit of her stomach. She swallowed. 'Your exclamation mark to show that the man is shouting is excellent. Can you think of a different way to start your second sentence though? They both start with "He went" and I think you can come up with something more exciting than that.'

She waited for Benjamin's response.

'Thanks, Miss,' he said brightly, taking his book back and focusing on improving his sentence straight away.

The others carried on with their writing too and the lesson descended into a quiet buzz of concentration.

Perhaps she might just be able to pull this off.

When break time finally came, Lizzie was ready for it.

Sophie led the way into the staffroom, immediately disappearing into the crowd of people. There must have been twenty different teachers and staff crammed in the office-cum-kitchen space and suddenly Lizzie was alone in the mêlée – the eye of the storm. It was OK. She would just sniff out the coffee and busy herself with that. It was only twenty minutes before lessons recommenced. She would be fine navigating her way through break time alone. Wouldn't she?

'How's it going?' a familiar voice asked.

'Tom, thank God!' Lizzie breathed a sigh of relief and held her stomach. 'It's going really well. But I was getting a bit concerned that I'd have to find the coffee all by myself.' She made a show of looking around the staffroom for it.

'Over here,' Tom said, linking arms with Lizzie and pulling her over to the kitchen counter, revealing a wholesale-sized tub of Nescafé. He patted the top of it affectionately.

'So you guys really like coffee.' Lizzie looked the gigantic tub up and down.

'Lizzie, you know as well as I do that coffee is the only thing that will get us both through this day, and the many days to come.'

'Good point,' Lizzie said, spooning the granules into two mugs that Tom had readied for their drinks.

'So,' began Tom. He stirred his coffee and topped it up with cold water from the tap. 'Shall we celebrate your first day of school with a takeaway tonight? My treat.'

He sounded genuine, but Lizzie knew 'my treat' meant he'd end up borrowing the money from her, or using her laptop so the default card was in her name.

'Sounds lovely,' Lizzie said. 'I've got football training tonight though, remember, so it'll be a late one. You could order it ready to arrive at eight forty-five?'

'It's a date.'

As quickly as break time had arrived, it ended. The bell went, and Lizzie looked down at her barely touched coffee with disappointment.

'Just top it up with tap water and down it,' Tom said. 'It's the only way to get caffeine in you when you're at school.'

Lizzie laughed at the strange coffee-drinking ritual that everyone at Cranswell's seemed to have adopted. She followed his advice but still scalded her oesophagus. Perhaps practice made perfect?

The fractions projected onto the board terrified Lizzie upon her return to the classroom. Maths had never been her strength and the problems on the board were just that: problematic. They looked like runes or Sanskrit, whatever they might be.

Sophie stood at the front of the classroom and explained the task with a demonstration, while Lizzie sat at the back of the room in her tiny chair, trying to keep up. Luckily for Lizzie, the children around her seemed to know their stuff when it came to maths, so she found herself checking a few workings and picking up plastic counting cubes that had magically 'fallen' from the table. Interestingly, Nigel always seemed particularly buried in his work when the cubes mysteriously skipped between the children. Hmm . . . she'd need to keep an eye on him.

Before Lizzie knew it, the bell rang for lunchtime and the children flew out the door, racing to join the canteen queue or get outside for a game of tag. As far as Lizzie was concerned, it couldn't have come any sooner.

'We're on duty during the second part of lunch,' Sophie said as they collected the children's books. 'So go and grab your lunch from the fridge, make yourself a quick cuppa and come back here. We'll go out in about twenty minutes.'

'OK.' Lizzie sighed, feeling bitterly disappointed that she couldn't just sit for the forty-minute lunch break and wondering if her feet could even cope with only twenty minutes of rest.

She wandered down the corridor, hoping she was heading in the right direction for the staffroom – everywhere in this place looked the same.

From the fridge, Lizzie picked out her sandwich and flopped down on one of the staffroom chairs. It was one of those in a hideous seventies orange-brown colour. Another teacher she recognised as Kate came in just as she bit down into her food.

'I wouldn't set up camp there,' Kate said, reaching into the fridge for her own lunch. 'That's Ged's seat,' she added, and left as swiftly as she'd arrived.

Yes, Tom had warned Lizzie about staffroom politics. Apparently, there were unwritten rules all over the place. She was just glad that Kate had mentioned it before Ged had come in and she'd unwittingly caused a scene.

'Thanks,' she called after her.

With only ten minutes before she needed to be out on duty,

Lizzie settled down into another chair on the other side of the staffroom. She really didn't want to be upsetting anyone on her first day. She wondered where Tom was, then toyed with the idea of making a cup of tea and realised that she probably wouldn't have time to make it, let alone drink it. School, it turned out, was a very busy place. She would need to plan for this in the future – maybe a flask she could prepare in the morning before school . . . ?

'Ready?' Sophie asked brightly, popping her head around the door.

Lizzie swallowed what was in her mouth, feeling it slip uncomfortably down her throat, and mourned the other half of her sandwich after throwing it into the bin.

'Yep,' Lizzie replied, sounding far cheerier than she felt. An immense wave of exhaustion swept over her, like an extreme afternoon slump. It was just a bit earlier in the day than Lizzie would have expected. After all, she'd only just eaten lunch. Maybe a walk outside would blow away the feeling of tiredness and she'd be back on it for art and PE that afternoon. She wondered how Sophie appeared to remain so enthusiastic all day.

'So I'll let you into a little secret,' Sophie said as they walked in a figure of eight around the school site.

Children tore around their legs, and they dodged flying footballs.

'I'm supposed to be positive about all aspects of teaching,' Sophie said. 'Especially with trainees. But duty is, without a doubt, the most hideous part of my job.'

Lizzie laughed. 'How come?'

A child raced past them and splattered Lizzie's legs with the mud from a rogue puddle. She bent down to brush off as much of it as she could, failing miserably.

'Partly because of things like that,' Sophie said, handing her a tissue. 'You either get cold or wet, or like today, you get sunburnt. And if nothing happens, it's really dull. And if something does happen, you have to follow it up with phone calls and meetings. It's just not the part of the job I signed up for.'

Giving up with the mud on her tights, Lizzie continued to walk with Sophie around the school site. As they talked, Sophie kept her eyes crawling over the playground, watching the children to make sure that they were all safe and behaving.

'It's nice to be outside, though,' Sophie said.

The slight ache in Lizzie's feet and her scrunched-up toes begged to differ.

Lunch sailed by and the less said about art, the better.

'We're really lucky,' Sophie said at the end of the session, coming over to drop a couple of paint pots and glue pasters into the sink. 'We've got a PE guy who comes in to do our PE lessons for us, so we would normally get planning time. I think for today though, and maybe for a few lessons, it might be worth you staying in there to observe what goes on – especially with your background in sport. Miss Davies said you play football?' She phrased it like a question.

'Just the local football team,' Lizzie said, placing the paint pots upturned on the draining board. 'We've had a good season, though. We've made it to the final of the local cup tournament for the first time in over five years. It's been something like twenty years since we won it last. I'm crossing my fingers I'll get picked for the squad.'

'Impressive,' Sophie said. 'Then you should definitely get involved in PE more than I normally would.'

'I'd be interested to see how teaching PE is different to

coaching it.' Lizzie lifted the final glue pot out of the sink and left it to dry.

'Shall we get this lot through to the hall then?' Sophie said, gesturing at the gaggle of children in various stages of undress. Most of them were ready, but even at ten years old, some of them had an interesting interpretation of what 'ready' meant. The ones who had managed to put on their shorts or leggings and official school Aertex tops made those wearing one of their dad's baggy T-shirts or a too-short hand-me-down from a sibling look dishevelled and not quite prepared.

'Right, let's line up, everyone,' Sophie said.

Dutifully, the students went to the side of the room nearest the door and lined up. Lizzie looked at the children and saw that strangely, they had chosen not to stand next to their friends. Hang on! They were in alphabetical order. How was Sophie doing this?

Lizzie followed them down the corridor through to the hall, which had been cleared of the lunchtime tables and chairs. She stretched as she walked through the door – her back was in bits after crouching over children, tables and sinks all day. Her feet weren't faring much better, either. Her headache, at least, had subsided. She was looking forward to sitting down with Tom and a takeaway, even if she had to find the energy to endure football training as well before then.

'Hi everyone!' said the PE teacher, whose freshness clearly told the story of someone who hadn't already spent the day looking after children.

The class raced in and surrounded him in a perfect circle. Routines again, noted Lizzie. She took off her necklace and bracelets, and slung them onto a chair against the wall, before joining the rest of the class. Her mum's ring stayed where it was. It could go in her pocket if she absolutely felt the need to remove it.

'Miss Morris is with us today,' Nigel said, waving his arms excitedly towards the PE teacher, who, until now, had been facing the opposite side of the circle.

'Hi.' Lizzie waved self-consciously. 'I'm just observing today.'

'Hi . . .' There was a pause as a look of recognition passed over the PE teacher's face. 'Hi, Miss Morris,' he said, recovering.

Lizzie's breath caught in her throat and she forgot to exhale.

It was Noah Hatton. The PE teacher in front of her was Noah Hatton.

Noah. Hatton.

Chapter Three

She stared foolishly at him for far too long. He was taller than she remembered, but still lean and athletic. His dark hair was dishevelled, like he ran his hand through it all day and didn't care about the consequences. He locked his dark eyes with hers – as mesmerising as Lizzie remembered. When he flashed his perfect smile at her, he caught her off guard for a further moment. And then she remembered that she hated him.

'Mr Hatton . . .'

'Nice to see you,' he said, recovering much more smoothly than Lizzie had managed to.

The children began to fidget, bored with waiting to begin.

'Join in if you're up for it,' he challenged before turning back towards the children. 'Right.' He turned to face another side of the circle and put a stop to their moment. 'Warm-up time first.' He clapped his hands together – all energy and enthusiasm – and the children moved their attention away from Lizzie to Noah and what he was about to say.

Lizzie suddenly became very aware of the fact she would now be exercising in front of Noah Hatton. Not only that, but she would be exercising in tights and a cardigan that she'd bought specifically because it made her look like a teacher, and definitely not because it made her look particularly good or like someone who was prepared to participate in sport. She suddenly grew very warm. She would need to ditch the cardigan, anyway. She shrugged it angrily from her shoulders and laid it over the back of a chair.

The children and Noah were doing star jumps. Lizzie kicked off her boots and flung them over to the edge of the room, ready to join in. It was warm in the hall. The sun had shone through the windows all day, creeping across from one side to the other, making a greenhouse of the space. And now Lizzie was doing star jumps in a jumper dress. Although she wasn't entirely convinced that all of her sweat was coming from the exercise alone . . .

As she exerted everything she had through the warm-up, she noticed that on the other side of the hall someone had pulled the climbing frames out and a sort of circuit had been set up. Lizzie focused, trying not to worry about what was to come, intent on completing each part of the lesson and helping the children around her.

She hadn't seen Noah Hatton for over ten years. She wasn't about to start worrying about what he was thinking now. It turned out to be difficult to feel tense and annoyed at the same time as running through a series of yoga-esque moves. Lizzie relaxed her face, aware of the frown that must be pasted across it.

'OK guys, let's head over to this week's circuit. Line up in your colour groups.'

The children dutifully did as Noah asked and, after a few

moments of bustle, lined up perfectly where they knew they should be.

'Today,' he began, stepping back into the alcove that the climbing frame produced, 'we've added in the ropes.'

It was clearly a big reveal. There were a couple of 'yesssss'es, and an air grab from one child. For half a minute, they descended into a chaos of whispers and excitement.

'They've been wanting to do the rope climb for ages,' Noah said to Lizzie while he waited for the noise to die down.

She couldn't think of anything witty to say, so just threw him an awkward smile and kept quiet.

Once the children were listening again, Noah explained how to go about climbing the ropes safely, and told them that the aim was to scramble to the top and back down carefully when they were on that part of the circuit. 'Now, can I have a volunteer?'

Every single hand shot up.

'Miss Morris. What about you?' Audrey's tiny voice came from nowhere and seemed to rise above the rest of the crowd.

Noah looked directly at her, a mischievous smile playing at his lips.

'I'm not really dressed for . . .' But her response was drowned out by nearly every single child jumping up and down and cajoling her into saying yes. Fine, she would show Noah Hatton that she could do it. Besides, it would get the entire class on side if she was successful, which was important for when she taught them properly. That was definitely why she was about to agree to do it. Definitely not because of some odd notion that she needed to impress Noah Hatton.

'All right,' she said finally, stepping towards the ropes – stepping closer to Noah.

'OK, here you go.'

He passed her the rope, which she took. Then, he held it still as she reached up as high as she could to grab it, and jumped up to clamp the end with her feet. Noah steadied her, using his free hand on her hip. The rope swung around wildly. Noah's touch had Lizzie struggling to concentrate for a moment. She couldn't place the emotion, but felt an underlying hum of rage . . . or passion? She lost her footing and landed again on the floor.

'Let me try again,' she said defiantly.

Noah pulled a face that implied he didn't think she'd be able to do it, but held onto the rope again anyway. And they went through the same process. This time, Lizzie did everything she could to ignore Noah's touch and focused on gripping the rope tightly with her feet instead. Slowly, she shuffled her hands and then her feet up the rope as the children cheered for her from below. She began to feel more confident and move a little faster.

Then, it suddenly dawned on her that Noah probably had a spectacularly interesting view from where he was standing directly below her. In the moment that her mind wandered, her concentration slipped and so did she, suddenly finding herself a metre lower than she had been. The children gasped like it was a pantomime, like she was the damsel in distress being saved by Batman above Gotham City. Damn it! She wanted to be Batman, not saved.

Looking down, she could see that Noah looked a little fraught. Then he smiled.

'Are you ready to come down?' he asked.

Lizzie was tiring of his thinly veiled challenges and low expectations. 'I need to touch the top, don't I?' she shouted, refusing to give in.

'It's OK, you've done great all ready. Just shimmy back down.'

Lizzie hung there for a moment – trapped between potential

danger and humiliation of her own creation. Nope. She had come this far, and the children were still cheering. So on she went, climbing to the top in only three more moves and touching the highest of the climbing frame bars before shuffling down, much more quickly that she had shimmied up. The class erupted into rapturous applause.

Lizzie jumped off the bottom of the rope and turned to her audience to bow dramatically, before glancing at Noah, who stood there speechless for a moment. She smiled smugly.

'Very good,' he mumbled.

She shrugged as if it was nothing and returned to where she'd been standing.

'Seeing as you're such an expert,' he said, his voice laced with frustration, almost like he'd wanted her to fail, 'you can man the ropes. Help the kids reach up to get a hold and steady them so they're braced and safe.'

'Will do.' Lizzie padded her way triumphantly over the crash mats to the ropes section. Except triumphing felt somehow anticlimactic. There was an odd feeling in the pit of her stomach.

She spent the next twenty-five minutes giving children a leg up and cheering them on as they climbed, making it look far more straightforward than Lizzie had done. She supposed they were nimbler and lighter – they didn't have to carry the load Lizzie did. And they seemed to have zero fear of death.

When she wasn't engrossed in supporting the children, she was trying not to glance in Noah's direction, despite feeling his eyes on her almost constantly.

As the session came to a close, the children circled around Noah again, ready for him to finish the lesson.

'So, as always, I'm looking for three volunteers for the end of lesson challenge.'

Instantly, every single child's hand went up.

'Hmm,' he said, making a show of thinking carefully about whom to choose. 'How about Audrey, Ella and . . .' He looked around the circle. 'Miss Morris, care to take on the challenge?'

Lizzie didn't know what the challenge was, but while she initially feigned a modest refusal, she was champing at the bit to challenge Noah again, whatever it was. Just the fact he'd called on her was enough to increase her irritation, and beating him at something would make her feel much better.

The problem, she discovered a little too late, was the challenge was a three-legged assault course race. Noah flipped a coin and let Audrey choose whom she wanted to pair with. Traitor. After all the effort she'd put in with her earlier in the day. But you would choose the PE teacher, wouldn't you? With Audrey choosing Noah, Lizzie felt like he'd already won the first round before they'd even properly started the challenge. She sighed and consciously tried not to fold her arms. She didn't want her body language to give her away.

Lizzie was left with Ella, a tall, thin girl with fiery red hair similar to her own. Each pair's legs were tied together, and they were off. Ella, it turned out, was ridiculously clumsy, and she and Lizzie were left wobbling around near the starting blocks straight away, as Audrey giggled her way with Noah through a tyre hop and over a seesaw. Lizzie took some deep breaths and reminded herself there were children present – including her partner Ella – and it was just a Year Six PE lesson. It was the taking part that counted. Not.

'Come on, Ella. Let's do this!' she said, cheering her on, a smile painted across her face.

Ella stood up from where she had become a crumpled heap on the floor and they tried their best to catch up, but Noah and

Audrey had long since crossed the line and were doing a victory dance as Lizzie and Ella finished the race.

Red-faced and breathless, Lizzie and Ella came to a standstill. Noah reached for her hand and held it high. 'Girls and boys, our worthy runners-up!' he announced, and the class erupted into a cheer.

Lizzie scowled, pulling her hand away. His touch burnt.

She was glad to see that it was nearly three o'clock. And even happier to see Sophie creep in through the hall door.

'Right, Year Six,' Sophie announced. 'Let's get back to the classroom and get changed.' Which, of course, they all did without a fuss.

Lizzie struggled not to roll her eyes, irritated that everyone around her seemed to be perfect at whatever they did.

'Lizzie, wait.' Noah called after her as she followed the last of the students out of the hall.

'Not now, Mr Hatton,' she said. 'I have to go with the class.' She walked out of the hall without glancing backwards.

As the door closed behind her, she heard Noah Hatton kick a football across the room.

Chapter Four

By the time Lizzie arrived back at the flat, she only had twenty minutes to get changed and get out again for football training. She'd always known that Mondays would be a rush, but football was everything to her and she was happy for it to be a bit crazy if she could still train with the team. Although this definitely felt like a bit of a push. Imagine how tired she'd be once she was in school and teaching properly. She threw the thought away to the back of her mind and shoved what she needed into her bag.

'Kirsty!' Lizzie waved at her sister from across the car park – one of the highlights of football training. 'Am I glad to see you!'

'Rough first day?' Kirsty asked, pulling her in for a hug and kissing her cheek.

'Interesting first day.' Lizzie linked arms with her, and they went into the leisure centre to book onto their pitch.

'Tell me more,' Kirsty said. 'I could do with cheering up. Every day's a rough day with me.'

'Trouble with Steve again?'

She didn't nod, but Kirsty's face said it all. Lizzie squeezed her a little tighter, their sisterly roles reversed when it came to Steve.

'And how are the boys?'

But Lizzie didn't have time to hear Kirsty's answer because when they pushed through the heavy double doors into the hall, the warm-up had already begun. They both shed their bags and other belongings and joined in.

Lizzie welcomed the breeze on her face as she picked up her speed, while Coach Zoe instructed them to jump and reach and complete stretches at several points during the warm-up. Her trainers squeaked on the concrete floor, painted green and criss-crossed with the boundary lines of various sports in different bright colours. The sports hall at the leisure centre had a very particular smell. Lizzie couldn't put her finger on what it was exactly, but there were notes of dust and sweat despite the tall, airy vastness of the room.

Coach Zoe blew her whistle. 'Right, come on in then, ladies.'

They all ran and huddled around her, recovering their breath. Some leant forward, their hands on their knees; others stood with their hands on their waist, or wiping sweat from their brow. The warm-up was always the toughest part of practice.

'So, next stop is the final.'

The girls whooped and cheered. Kirsty and Lizzie shared a smile.

'Well done, ladies. Saturday was awesome. Today, I'm going to start thinking about who I want for the squad on final day, so make it count,' she said, before dividing them up into five-a-side teams.

'Reckon you'll make the team?' Kirsty asked as they made their way over to one of the pitches painted out in primary red.

'Maybe.' Ordinarily, Lizzie would be wholly focused on the endgame and playing for the team that would lift the trophy if they won the cup final, but her mind was elsewhere. She rubbed a hand over her face, exhausted from the day. Her body still felt scrunched up from the child-sized chairs. 'I mean, I'd like to, but I guess it's up to Coach. You?'

'I think I might be past it,' Kirsty said, a note of sadness in her voice. Ten years ago, she'd been at the heart of the team, but now that she was one of the oldest, Lizzie knew Kirsty only came for the exercise and to get out of the house once a week. She needed a break from Steve and the three boys.

At half-time, they moved to the side of the hall. Lizzie pulled her water bottle from her bag and took a long, cool drink.

'Why was your day so rubbish? You never did say,' Kirsty said.

'I bumped into Noah.'

Kirsty snorted and choked on her own water.

'What?' She wasn't often speechless.

'Noah.'

'Noah Hatton?'

'Noah Hatton. It turns out, he's the guy who comes in and teaches PE on a Monday,' Lizzie explained.

'Wow. That must have been awkward,' Kirsty said. She was only too aware of Lizzie and Noah's past – having been there for her when it all went wrong the last time. When their parents had been killed in the fire and Noah had broken up with Lizzie, all in the same week, it had been an awful time and Kirsty, as the older and wiser sibling, had needed to step up and take care of things.

'It wasn't ideal seeing him again, no,' Lizzie said, taking another swig from her bottle.

'What happened?' Kirsty looked at Lizzie and then watched as some of the girls worked on shooting from the penalty spot.

'Well, besides showing him my bum while I climbed a rope . . .'

Kirsty snapped her attention back towards Lizzie.

Lizzie continued, 'We got into a stupid three-legged race and he won.'

'That sounds like a pretty strange dream,' Kirsty said, her eyebrows crinkled.

'Not a dream, Kirs, a nightmare.' Lizzie rolled her eyes and redid her ponytail.

Kirsty looked like she was thinking about what to say next. 'Was he still . . .'

'Hot? Yes. But he's also still an idiot,' Lizzie said quickly.

'So, still not forgiven?'

'Nope,' Lizzie said defiantly. She would never forgive him for what he'd done. 'Most definitely not forgiven. People can't change. He will always be a selfish, arrogant, cruel human. So, I'm just going to accept it and try to keep clear.'

'Is that really your plan?' Kirsty asked, a note of disbelief in her voice. Lizzie supposed that having seen them together last time, she couldn't quite believe that there were no feelings there any more. Although, after a moment of contemplation, Kirsty looked slightly relieved that Lizzie wasn't thinking of going back there. Lizzie guessed it was probably because she couldn't bear to be there to pick up the pieces when it all went wrong again.

Lizzie nodded and chewed on a fingernail.

'But won't it be awkward, having to see him every week?'

'Maybe.' Lizzie shrugged. 'Sophie said that we normally have that time set aside to plan lessons while he teaches the class, so I'm hoping that I'll maybe have to observe him a couple of times and then I'll be done. I don't need him in my life any more.'

'No,' Kirsty said, thoughtful. 'Definitely not. How was the rest of your day?'

'You mean the teaching part?' Lizzie said. 'It was fine, I guess. Just observing is pretty boring, but also terrifying when you see what Sophie has to do minute by minute to get the class on side.'

'You'll be great,' Kirsty said. 'Mum and Dad would be really proud.'

'I know,' Lizzie said, a lump sticking stubbornly in her throat and taking her by surprise. Her hand went to twist her mum's ring instinctively. 'I have learnt one thing, though.'

Kirsty nodded in anticipation as Lizzie side-stepped the awkward topic.

'Flat shoes are a must for tomorrow.'

Kirsty smiled. 'Did you find that out the hard way?'

Lizzie nodded. 'How's Steve? You didn't say earlier,' she asked, changing the subject.

'OK, I guess,' Kirsty said. She sighed.

'Go on,' Lizzie said, prompting her to continue.

Monday was technically football practice, but unofficially, it doubled as therapy for Kirsty. She'd been with Steve for as long as Lizzie could remember – childhood sweethearts – and it was not good for her. And now, she had three boys under five to compete with too. Lizzie was fairly sure that Kirsty had had the children to save what was left of their marriage, but she would never say it to her sister. The irony was that it was now the boys that meant she couldn't leave. Lizzie only hoped that one day, Kirsty would realise how awful Steve was and decide to leave him for her own good.

'We fight every Monday when practice comes around. It's

the only thing I ever do by myself, and he complains about having to look after the boys every week for a couple of hours.'

'I know,' Lizzie said softly, reaching for Kirsty's arm and giving it a squeeze. It was the same grumble she heard every week.

'I mean, he knew this about me before we got together. I've played football since I joined secondary school. I think it was what first attracted him to me and yet, it's the one thing he always chooses to get angry about,' Kirsty said, incredulous despite it being a decade-old argument.

'Doesn't it bother you that he's out every weekend and too hungover to parent the rest of the time? Surely you've earned your Monday off,' reasoned Lizzie, and added, 'at the very least.'

'You'd think,' Kirsty said. 'Come on, let's get you in that football team,' she said, grabbing Lizzie by the arm as the whistle went for the second half. Saved by the bell.

They ran over to the pitch, Lizzie half worrying about her sister's dysfunctional relationship and half drifting back to the confusion that bumping into Noah had brought into her life.

Why had Noah Hatton rattled her so much?

She missed a shot on goal, and then another.

'Wake up, Lizzie!' Coach Zoe yelled across the pitch.

If Noah Hatton became the reason Lizzie lost the opportunity to play in the cup final, he'd live to regret it. She wouldn't let him ruin her life now – not like he had then.

'So you weren't excited to see him at all? Or curious about him? Anything?' Kirsty asked, still fixated on the reappearance of Noah as they walked together to their cars at the end of practice.

'At first maybe. I was definitely thrown by him being there. But then I remembered how hideous it all was, how he stopped me from being there.'

'It wasn't your fault.' It didn't matter how many times Kirsty said it – or anyone said it – Lizzie couldn't help but tie her break-up with Noah to her parents' deaths.

'I know.' A lie. 'It's got nothing to do with that. I just didn't feel anything for him and I would never go there again.'

Kirsty looked disappointed, as if she wanted there to be more to the story. Lizzie wondered for a moment whether she was hoping to live vicariously through Lizzie's romantic escapades, in a bid to distract herself from the hideousness that was Steve.

'Kirs, Noah's not your ex. He didn't treat you like shit. I'm telling you, there's nothing exciting about Noah Hatton turning back up in my life.'

That seemed to shut her down, Kirsty's inner matchmaker shrivelling away to nothing. 'Ignoring any reappearing feelings is probably for the best,' she said after a moment.

'Agreed.' Lizzie wondered if her sister was onto something. Had her feelings resurfaced? She'd not mentioned having feelings for him again to Kirsty. Had she given that impression? The headache she'd been repressing all day threatened to resurface. She pressed the button on her key fob to unlock the car. 'Noah's not in my life any more for a very good reason.'

'Understood,' Kirsty said, pulling Lizzie in for a hug and continuing further on to her own car. 'See you on Sunday for lunch,' she yelled across the car park.

'See you then.' Lizzie threw her bag across to the passenger seat and jumped into the driving seat after it.

She got out her phone, swiped to engage it and wrote a quick text to Tom: *There best be wine and pizza ready when I get home Xx.* Before she'd even turned the key in the ignition, he'd sent her a photo of the 'order out for delivery' screen from the pizza website and in the background was a bottle of red, open and breathing next to two glasses. She'd lucked out with Tom as a flatmate. Why would she ever need another man in her life? Especially if that man was Noah Hatton.

Lizzie arrived home just as the pizza did. Thanking the driver, she went upstairs to the flat and dumped it on the coffee table before flopping down on the sofa.

'Hi,' Tom said, walking through from the kitchen and passing Lizzie a glass of wine.

'Thank you,' she said, taking a sip. 'I've never needed a drink more.'

'Tough day?' he asked. 'I bet school was a bit of a shock.'

Lizzie nodded. 'Yep. But school isn't the bit that made it tough. Not really.' She stood up and placed her wine down on a coaster. 'I'm going to have a quick shower, and then we need to talk.'

Tom's face lit up at the prospect of gossip. 'I can't guarantee that there'll be any garlic bread left when you're done,' he said.

'I would expect nothing less from you,' Lizzie said as she made her way through to the bathroom.

The shower went some way to removing the grubbiness of the day from Lizzie's skin. Her back and feet ached from all the standing and bending during the school day, and her muscles were sore from the exertion of training. The water didn't remove the ickiness she felt at having seen Noah again, though.

'Come and tell me all about it,' Tom said, patting the space next to him on the sofa as Lizzie re-entered the living room.

'God, where do I start?' She rubbed a towel over her hair before casting it to one side and reaching for her wine.

'How was your first day?'

'Good really. I could see lots of the stuff from my pre-reading in practice and the children are adorable. Except Nigel, but I've got my eye on him. Seriously, everything went much better than expected. And they'd already copied my DBS at the interview, so this morning's drama was totally unnecessary.'

'Annoying.'

'Yep.'

Tom took a bite of pizza and a string of cheese flopped down onto his chin before he wound it round his tongue to pull it back towards his mouth. If he'd not been Lizzie's flatmate for what felt like a hundred years, she would have been grossed out. As it was, this was the tip of an almost too comfortable iceberg.

'Sophie said she thought you knew the PE guy, Noah.'

Tom had guessed it in one, and Lizzie's face gave her away instantly.

'Do you?' Tom asked, clasping his hands in excitement.

Lizzie nodded, taking a slice of pizza from the box. 'Yep, ex-boyfriend,' she said, taking a bite, slightly concerned that Sophie had sensed their past. She had been going for nonchalant but clearly hadn't pulled it off.

'Ah,' Tom said, sipping his wine. 'I sense drama.'

'You sense right.'

'What happened?'

Lizzie wasn't being cagey on purpose. She just didn't really know where to start.

'We went out during sixth form.'

'And . . .'

'And then we stopped going out a year or so later.'

'What happened in between?'

Lizzie stalled. She hadn't expected the pain of going back

43

there, but she suddenly found it difficult to catch her breath. She put her pizza down and crossed her legs up on the sofa.

'Me and Noah. It had been on the cards for a long time. We'd been friends for ever – all the way through secondary school – and no one was surprised when we got together.'

'Did you love him?' Tom asked, tilting his head sympathetically.

Lizzie nodded. 'That's the problem. I really did.' She reached for her wine glass again and took a large glug. She didn't know why she felt suddenly sad, a strange nostalgia drifting over her. Noah had treated her appallingly, and she hated him.

'Oh.' Tom wasn't often speechless but he seemed to grapple around for the right thing to say next. 'What went wrong? Did you not go to uni together?'

Lizzie shook her head. 'We stayed together for a bit, long distance, but not for long.'

'What happened?'

Lizzie opened her mouth to reply and then changed her mind. She wasn't ready to think about it. It was so much more than just a break-up and no one at the time, not even Noah, realised. It was only Kirsty, whom she'd eventually reached out to, who understood the impact of their relationship ending.

Tom reached out and touched her arm, his bottom lip poking sadly out in solidarity. 'You don't have to tell me, love.'

'It still makes me sad to think about what happened, even after all this time. He really meant something, so treating me like he did – that hurt.'

She was grateful that Tom didn't push it any further. Instead, they sat in silence, sipping their wine every now and then. By now, the pizza had taken a back seat to the conversation and was going cold on the table.

'But you're hot. And you were even hotter ten years ago, you know, before you got all old,' Tom said with a smile, in an attempt to lighten the mood.

Lizzie appreciated the joke but still threw a cushion at his face.

'I guess there was something about me that he just didn't find lovable,' she said, focusing on her feelings about the break-up rather than the days afterwards. Lizzie wiped a drop of wine off the rim of her glass, staring sadly into it as she spoke.

'I'll get another bottle,' Tom said, jumping up off the sofa to run to the kitchen.

Lizzie picked a piece of ham off a slice of pizza and ate it. She suddenly didn't feel very hungry and instead felt quite emotional, which surprised her.

'Actually,' she said as Tom came back in and flopped down on the sofa, 'I think I might call it a night. I don't want to feel like I did this morning when I wake up tomorrow. I need a good night's sleep,' she said, knowing full well that with the events of the day and Noah's reappearance dredging up the past, sleep would be elusive at best.

'Are you sure?' Tom asked as she stood to go to bed.

'Yes, I'm sure.'

Tom smiled sympathetically, with a tilt of the head.

'I'm fine,' she said, reading his mind.

'As long as you're sure. I don't want to hear muffled pillow crying through the wall.'

'You won't, I promise.' Lizzie bent over and kissed him on the cheek. 'Walking tomorrow?'

'If your lazy bum is out of bed early enough.'

Lizzie smiled.

'That's better.'

'Thanks for today, Tom. I really don't know what I'd do without you sometimes.'

'That's what I'm here for,' he said, lifting his wine glass for a 'cheers'.

'Night, Tom.'

Lizzie sloped off to her bedroom, refilling her wine glass and taking it with her just in case. She drank it down as she slipped into her pyjamas before crawling under the duvet and shutting her eyes. But her brain wouldn't let her relax. As soon as her eyes closed, there he was again. Noah Hatton. Was he really going to haunt her until the end of time?

Chapter Five

It was in the early hours of the morning that Lizzie found herself seated once again on the windowsill, looking out over the town as people began to rise. The recycling lorry had been past at about 4 a.m. and now there were mothers taking their newborns for early morning naps, businesspeople grabbing coffees from Greg's café before catching the bus into the city, and elderly shoppers hoping to hit the supermarket at 6 a.m. when it opened to avoid the rush.

Lizzie had dreamt of the fire again last night. It was the first time it had crept into her unconscious for a while. And it was another thing she hated Noah for. She was certain that if he'd not reappeared in her life, she wouldn't have woken up in the middle of the night gasping for breath, as though the whole flat was engulfed with toxic smoke.

She yawned as Tom shuffled into the living room.

'Lizzie! It's five-thirty. Why are you up?'

'I couldn't sleep. What's your excuse?'

'I finished that second bottle of red and I'm parched.'

Lizzie smiled. 'I'm about to jump in the shower if that's OK?'

'Course. I need to rustle up something greasy and find some caffeine.'

'Good luck.'

Lizzie disappeared into the shower and tried not to think about Noah or the fire. She was ninety per cent certain that he wouldn't be at school today. Her rational side told her she shouldn't worry about it. But then if anyone had asked her yesterday morning, she'd have been one hundred per cent certain that Noah Hatton wouldn't have been at school. She sighed, attempting and failing to relax her shoulders.

More of the children said hello to Lizzie at the door that morning. Nigel attempted a fist bump, which Sophie shut down straight away.

'I'll allow a handshake but that's the best you'll get,' she said.

'I'll take it.' Nigel grinned and shook both of their hands enthusiastically, like a Wall Street businessperson in the body of a ten-year-old.

'Morning, Miss Lawson, Miss Morris,' Audrey said shyly as she wandered in.

'Morning,' said Benjamin and smiled at them both.

Lizzie smiled at their acceptance of her. Today was going to be a good day. She could feel it. Well, that and she was mostly safe in the knowledge that Noah wouldn't be appearing from anywhere by surprise today. In fact, it was Lizzie's sincere wish that he wouldn't surprise her anywhere ever again.

In literacy, the children were looking at their stories from the day before and explaining why they'd chosen particular words and their effect.

'I chose it because it's another word for walk and you said it was a good idea,' Audrey said, wrinkling up her nose.

'That's not what she means,' said Nigel unkindly. 'Duh!'

Ben snorted with laughter.

'Thank you, boys,' Lizzie said. She'd heard teachers say it on the TV and it seemed to convey a sense of disappointment in their comments. Wherever she'd seen it, now it worked, thankfully. They both shot their heads down and carried on with their own work.

'What Miss Lawson means, Audrey, is why is that word better than any others you could have chosen? Now let's look at yours.' Lizzie shuffled closer and tilted Audrey's book to get a better look at what she had written. 'See here,' she said, pointing to the page. 'Where you've used the word crept. What does that mean?'

'It means he's creeping,' Audrey said after a moment.

'Now try to explain it without using the word creeping or creep.'

Audrey chewed on the end of her pen. 'He's, like, sneaking up on the others.'

'Great. And what kind of person does that make him seem like?'

'Like, sneaky and mysterious,' Audrey said triumphantly as she realised that she'd managed to explain her choice.

'Perfect!' Lizzie said. 'So you need to write "The verb 'creep' suggests the man is . . ."'

'Sneaky and mysterious?'

'Exactly! Great job!'

Audrey high-fived her and got straight on to writing her sentence down before she forgot.

Nigel, who had been watching quietly from under his floppy

hair, looked up. 'Can you check mine?' he asked.

Lizzie sensed that he merely wanted her approval. His work was excellent – and he knew it.

'It's fantastic, Nigel. I really like that you've come up with two alternative ideas as to what effect the word might have. Nice one!'

Nigel smiled, pulling his book back towards him. 'Thanks.'

For once, in maths, Lizzie understood what they were doing. Today's lesson led on from yesterday's, so she had that to build on fortunately. Again, she was impressed to see her table of children were quite adept at their maths work, making it far easier for Lizzie to do her job without looking foolish.

'Are we on duty again today?' Lizzie asked as the children filed out for lunch.

Sophie shook her head. 'Not today. Go and enjoy your lunch. We're digging for fossils followed by music and composition this afternoon. You're going to need the rest!'

Lizzie wasted no time making her way to the staffroom, determined to get in a decent break time before everything kicked off again.

'Ooh, Lizzie,' a voice said as Lizzie hurried down the corridor.

She turned around to see the headteacher, Miss Davies, poking her head out of her office door.

'Miss Davies.' She took a couple of steps back in the direction she had come.

'Oh, call me Florence,' she said, gesticulating manically, a bundle of energy. 'Have you got a minute?'

'Of course.'

Florence (it felt weird calling her that; Lizzie would forever have to call her Miss Davies – she was the headteacher, after all) stepped back, and gestured for her to come into her office.

'Have a seat.'

Lizzie stepped in and sat down on one of five squishy leatherette chairs surrounding the large round table. If King Arthur were the leader of a school, his office would probably look just like this. A large panoramic window looked out onto the gardens that the Year Five and Six gardening club tended every Thursday after school. The grass was lush and green, and several varieties of flourishing vegetables had been planted out in rows, alongside several strawberry plants with ripe berries, ready to be picked.

Miss Davies poured Lizzie a glass of water and sat down in a chair on the opposite side of the table.

'Thank you.' Lizzie took a long sip. The last time she'd sat here was during her interview and the memory of her nerves returned rapidly.

'So, I just wanted to catch you and float something by you,' Miss Davies began, her arms outstretched on the table.

Lizzie nodded, bracing herself for what was coming.

'As part of your official training next year, you need to participate in the wider school community and collaborate and contribute to something whole-school,' she explained.

Lizzie could vaguely see where Miss Davies's speech was leading and her heart started to beat loudly, full of anticipation, excitement and fear. The clock ticked, deafening in the silences between speech. It both made the conversation feel awkward and also reminded Lizzie of her lunchtime break ticking away from her.

'I just thought it might be easier to get that bit of business out of the way this side of the summer, seeing as you'll have a hefty teaching load, and planning and assessment and the like come September.'

If Lizzie had known Florence Davies better, or if Miss Davies weren't effectively her boss, right about now she'd be telling her to hurry the hell up and say what she wanted to say. The ticking clock marked further seconds of her time floating away. Of course, instead, she sat quietly, listening to the big build-up which seemed to go on for ever, with her hands folded angelically in her lap. She reached for another sip of water as Miss Davies continued to rationalise the task she was about to set for Lizzie. It was clearly a marathon and not a sprint.

Lizzie glanced again at the clock behind Miss Davies's head as the minutes of lunch hour continued to tick away and the chaos of fossils and composition crept ever closer.

Finally, Miss Davies got to the point she was trying to make. 'So, I wondered whether you might be up for planning sports day this year? Sophie said that you play football outside of school, and from what I've heard from the children about the PE lesson you took part in, you've got quite a competitive streak – just what we need!' Her voice had taken on the quality of a military leader, and she thumped the desk enthusiastically at the end of her speech.

Lizzie blushed to think that someone, somewhere (and potentially a ten-year-old at that), had already called her out on her competitive nature. But actually, organising sports day sounded right up her street – and Miss Davies was right, getting the wider-school bit ticked off this side of the summer was a sensible idea.

'That sounds great,' she said, much to Miss Davies's delight.

A million questions already raced through her head, though. When was it scheduled for? How had it worked before? Did she have or need a budget? Who did she need to talk to, to get the things she needed? Waves of nauseous excitement and trepidation washed over her, almost uncontrollably. Lizzie knew this about herself, though. What she needed to do was to go home, have a coffee and write a list; so she kept her mouth shut.

'Excellent,' Miss Davies said, clasping her perfectly manicured hands together in delight. Her large red earrings danced uncontrollably. 'I'll let Noah know,' she added.

'I'm sorry?' Lizzie said, nausea becoming the overriding feeling at the mention of his name.

'Noah Hatton,' Miss Davies explained, as if Lizzie genuinely needed it spelling out to her. 'He ran the PE lesson yesterday for Year Six. He does all of them and also coordinates sports day for us, so he'll help you out. You'll be working together.' She said it without an ounce of realisation of what the revelation meant to Lizzie.

Lizzie opened her mouth to protest and then closed it again, through fear of involuntary vomit escaping and covering the round table. She twisted her mum's ring and then pulled her sleeves down over her hands.

'I'll email him this afternoon and copy you in so you have his contact details. Then, I suggest you two meet at some point later this week to discuss what you need to do. Most of the organisation will be on the day, of course, but Noah will help you with the preliminary stuff. There's not a great deal of money available, but you can raise a little extra budget if you need it at the school fundraiser next Friday.'

'The fundraiser?' Lizzie had a vague recollection of Tom mentioning something about a school thing on a Friday. In reality, she'd asked the question in lieu of having nothing else to say. Her mind was reeling and thoughts weren't volunteering themselves coherently.

'Yes, a week Friday. The PTA organises it mostly. It's a hog roast, bar, live music – that sort of thing. But if you and Noah want to set something up to raise some money for sports day, you'd be welcome to. In any case, it would be good for you to come along so you can see what the school is all about.'

Miss Davies was still talking. Lizzie could see her mouth opening and closing, and her bright red nails flashed in front of her eyes as her hands gesticulated all over the place. But she couldn't hear anything any more. It was probably because she'd just been catapulted into a state of shock. Her ears were ringing, deaf with the thump of pumping blood.

'So, I'll check in with you both in a couple of weeks. It's only four weeks away, so you'll have to get cracking,' Miss Davies said, as Lizzie's consciousness came back to the room.

'Of course,' she said weakly. 'I'll start thinking about it today.'

'Excellent.' Miss Davies stood to show the meeting was over. 'I know that I've left it in expert hands.'

The subtext didn't go amiss. This was a big deal, and the entire school would be involved. Lizzie couldn't mess it up, even if it meant dealing with Noah.

She left the office and nibbled at the corner of her sandwich. She might have enjoyed the quiet of the staffroom if she hadn't been thinking about both sports day and the organising of it alongside Noah.

Before long, her thoughts were interrupted by the bell to indicate afternoon lessons. Lunchtime had disappeared and Lizzie had fallen through it as though it were quicksand.

History and music were as terrifying as Sophie had said they would be and by the end of the day they had left Lizzie with a headache and a bruised foot, from where Benjamin had dropped a glockenspiel on her toe. She tried to tell herself that she wasn't feeling crappy because of Miss Davies's lunchtime Noah revelation, but she knew she was fooling herself.

Flopping down in one of the staffroom chairs (not Ged's), she finally got around to eating the rest of her lunch. She still had little appetite, but the problem seemed to be the tightening of her throat rather than already having a full stomach. It gurgled loudly in protest. She would sit and eat, maybe make a cup of tea while Tom finished his work for the day, and then they would both walk home. It would be lovely and relaxing, she thought, forcing her shoulders to lower and realising just how tense she was feeling.

Lizzie unlocked her phone and scanned a couple of messages from the football team on WhatsApp and another from her sister, asking how her second day had gone. Then she checked her emails and her breath caught in her chest. Noah.

The message in her inbox was from Miss Davies, explaining that further to their conversation earlier today, she was delighted to say that Lizzie had agreed to help Noah in the organisation of sports day, and that from this point she'd leave it up to them. In the 'cc' address line, there was Noah's email. Lizzie's heart jumped to her throat.

After a long moment, as she contemplated replying to the message while ignoring Noah's virtual presence, another email popped up. Noah had replied and cc'd Lizzie in:

Sounds great. Lizzie, are you free on Friday after school to discuss what we need to do moving forward? I'm in for Year 1&2 PE anyway, so I can meet you in the office afterwards? N

Ugh. 'N.' For some irrational reason, his sign-off really annoyed her.

55

She was free on Friday after school, and it made sense to meet him then, but she really didn't want to. For a second, she considered responding to his message. Then she decided that because he'd irritated her yesterday and because sometimes she simply enjoyed being petty, that she would wait and reply later, opting to put the kettle on instead. Avoidance seemed to be the best tactic until she'd thought more about what to say.

'Are you making one for me too?' Tom asked, wandering into the staffroom. 'I can hear you stomping about and clattering all the way down the corridor. Why such angry tea making?'

'No reason.' She hadn't realised she'd been taking her irritation out on the kitchenware.

'No-ah reason?' joked Tom.

'Ugh.'

'Do you want to talk about it?'

'No-ah. Not really. Shall we just drink tea and then head home?' Lizzie said, feeling thoroughly fed up.

Tom nodded. 'Course. Shall we go via the milkshake shop?'

'Yes, please. Let's do that instead of tea,' she said, flipping the switch on the kettle to stop it from boiling.

'Great. I'll just grab my stuff from the office.'

The walk home from school went some way to lifting Lizzie's mood. She shared with Tom what had happened and he sympathised. The problem was, there was really nothing anyone could do about it. Lizzie was going to have to suck it up and get on with it.

Milkshakes purchased, they headed back to the flat. Tom unlocked the door, having laden Lizzie with all his belongings.

'Thanks,' he said, putting down his milkshake and taking his stuff from her. 'Fancy lasagne tonight?'

'Sounds great,' Lizzie said, flopping down on the sofa and

rifling through the post. 'Don't put as much chilli in it this time though, please. It nearly blew my head off last time!'

Neither of them were known for their culinary skills, but Tom in particular had some interesting tastes – if you could call them that. Let's just say that they had made it onto the Christmas card list of several takeaway establishments in the local area.

'There's a letter here addressed to both of us,' Lizzie said, turning it back and forth. 'There's no stamp.'

'You know, you could solve the mystery by opening it,' Tom suggested.

'Good point.' She slid her finger from one end of the envelope to the other, tore it open and began to read.

'Oh no!'

'What is it?' Tom asked, putting down the onion he was chopping. He came around from behind the breakfast bar and into the living area. He leant on the back of the sofa, reading the letter over Lizzie's shoulder.

'It's Stanley,' she said.

'Stanley . . . ?' Tom thought for a moment. 'Oh! Stanley, the landlord Stanley?'

'Yep. Stanley, the landlord Stanley,' Lizzie replied, giving Tom the time to read the letter for himself over her shoulder.

'He's selling the flat?' Tom was incredulous.

Lizzie nodded. 'And we have to be out. Look, it says here,' she said, pointing. 'Thirty days' notice. That only takes us to the 2nd of June. That's not even the end of term.'

'Crap,' Tom said, staring at the page as if hoping it might show something more upbeat. He took it from Lizzie and turned it over, as if it might reveal some secret get-out clause.

'I guess we'd better get house hunting,' Lizzie said.

'Yep,' agreed Tom. 'Fancy a takeaway?' he asked. 'I'm far too stressed now to cook.'

'Yes, takeaway sounds good,' Lizzie said.

Her thoughts and attention slipped to the Rightmove app. Noah was annoying, but he had paled into significance now that they were going to be effectively homeless within a month.

Chapter Six

Lizzie spent the whole of Friday worrying. She knew this because by the time they reached Golden Time on Friday afternoon, one of her nails was bleeding from where she'd chewed it down so much.

She'd not slept well again either. Twice she'd fallen asleep and woken gasping for breath, having dreamt of the fire. It always got worse when she was anxious about things in her conscious world. Noah Hatton and an eviction notice should just about do it. And that didn't even include the general stress and exhaustion that came with being in the classroom with thirty ten-year-olds every day.

Golden Time perked her up a bit, though. After a week of watching them work so hard, it was lovely to see the children choosing to do different activities and genuinely enjoying themselves. Lizzie had helped Sophie set it up at lunchtime, so that the children could choose from a variety of craft activities, sports and games outside, or playing games on the computers.

When given the option, Lizzie had opted to man the craft table, assuming that Noah would likely be outside doing the sports side of things. She knew she had to meet him later to talk about sports day, but she wasn't ready to volunteer to spend time with him for any longer than necessary.

Little Audrey was fast becoming one of Lizzie's favourite pupils. Despite every teacher everywhere claiming not to have them, Lizzie couldn't for a minute believe it. Audrey was sweet and kind, and she was happy to ask Lizzie for help, which meant they'd spent much of the week working together.

During Golden Time, Audrey spent her hour making a mug out of air-dry clay for her dad. Lizzie didn't have the heart to tell her that air-dry clay wouldn't hold water, so she sat and helped her and another little girl to make their mugs.

'I don't think we'll be able to test them until they're dry,' Lizzie said, as Audrey picked up her mug and was left with just the handle in her hand for about the fifteenth time.

'I might go and play outside for a bit,' she said, slightly deflated.

'Me too,' said her friend, scraping her chair back and heading towards the open classroom door.

Lizzie watched them go and saw Noah greet them outside. His hair was dishevelled from entertaining the children in the June sunshine and he was wearing shorts again, showing off his muscular legs.

Lizzie looked away in the same instant as he looked up and locked eyes with her for a brief second. He raised a hand to wave, but Lizzie ignored her peripheral vision and tidied up the mess the girls had created.

After the children had packed up and left for the day, Sophie came over to where Lizzie was cleaning paintbrushes and clay-moulding tools in the sink.

'Why don't you head off?' she said, standing next to her to wash the pile of things in the other half of the sink. 'I've got this.'

'It's OK,' Lizzie said, suddenly not wanting to leave the classroom and see Noah a minute before she absolutely had to.

'No, go on. I know you've got a meeting with Noah, which is always rubbish on a Friday. Maybe if you go now, you can get it over and done with and then you'll be able to call it an early night.'

With no alternative, Lizzie said, 'As long as you're sure you don't mind.'

'Not at all.'

Lizzie pulled her hands out from the sink full of water and dried them on the towel next to it.

'Thanks for this week,' she said to Sophie. 'I've had so much fun. Your class is great.'

'They are pretty special,' Sophie said, smiling. She clearly had a genuine tenderness towards them. 'You've done a great job, too. I'll think next week about how you can get more involved in the teaching side of things, if you're up for it? I remember when I first started teaching, the observations were really dull. The best thing is to go right ahead and get stuck in.'

'That sounds great,' lied Lizzie, suddenly feeling a little terrified.

'Have a good weekend.'

Lizzie reached for her bag from inside the craft cupboard. 'And you.'

As she walked down the corridor, she could feel her palms getting clammy and under her fringe, her forehead was suddenly very warm. Her throat was tight, but she struggled through a swallow and scrunched up her hands into fists, attempting to find her inner strength before she went into the office where Noah would be waiting.

She knocked on the door, even though it was a communal office space shared by the whole of the primary school staff. There was something about Noah that made Lizzie feel smaller somehow, her normal confidence worn away to tatters.

'Come in.'

His voice made her bristle.

Lizzie pushed open the door. 'Hi.'

Noah sat at one of three circular tables in the room, scribbling furiously on a sheet of paper. Lizzie assessed the seating situation and pulled out a chair from the opposite side of the table; then she sat down. Noah finally looked up.

'You know you don't have to knock, right?' He laughed.

Lizzie felt like he was laughing at her and didn't really know how to reply. She fidgeted in her chair, pretending to get comfortable.

'How's your week been?' he asked after a moment, smiling across the table at her.

Lizzie was thrown by his now seemingly pleasant nature.

'Exhausting,' she answered honestly. 'And full of surprises.'

Noah smiled. 'Working here is great. You're going to love it.'

It annoyed her he presumed to know her well enough still to make that kind of judgement.

'I hope so,' she said, emotionless. She rifled through her bag and pulled out a notepad and pen.

Noah took the hint. 'Shall we get started then?'

Lizzie nodded. 'Let's.'

'So, Flo wants us to plan sports day together. I've printed out the plans from last year as I thought it'd give us a good place to start.' He slid a pile of two or three sheets over for Lizzie to look at.

She flicked through them, scanning each one briefly.

'Unless there's any other ideas you have, or anything that you'd like to see that's not there?'

Lizzie shook her head. 'No, this all looks good. Shall we go through these lists then and divvy up the jobs, that way we can each get on without bothering each other and catch up in a couple of weeks to see where we've got to?'

She attempted to pretend that it was a suggestion driven by workload concerns and efficiency; she hoped it wasn't obvious that really she was trying to come up with anything she could to avoid spending more time with Noah than absolutely necessary.

He ran a hand through his hair and chewed on the end of his pen, considering her idea. 'Let's go through the list and see what the jobs are first, and then we can decide how to go about getting them done,' he said, avoiding Lizzie's suggestion and taking the lead.

He always did that. She hated it.

'I just think it might be better if we worked together on things rather than separately,' Noah said. 'That way, if anything goes wrong, we'll pick it up before it becomes too big a problem to resolve.'

Of course, he thought she'd mess up. Trust had always been one of their issues.

'OK.'

Lizzie only said OK in that tone when she wasn't OK about something, but didn't want to fight about it. As the receiver of far too many 'OKs' over time, it was likely that Noah knew exactly what she was doing – but he didn't flinch or take the bait, irritating Lizzie even more.

'So,' he began, his eyes flicking to Lizzie's and then back down to the page. 'Basically, there are three sets of jobs – ones that need to be done before the event, jobs for the day and then all the tidying up and social media stuff afterwards.'

'Great,' Lizzie said, not taking her eyes off the page for a moment, despite feeling Noah's eyes burning into the top of her head.

'Before I knew you were helping, I put the date on the calendar and booked the field from the secondary school. They've got all the white lines painted on over there, and because we have to walk across town to get there, the children feel like they're going on a trip. It gives the day more of a sense of occasion.'

Lizzie looked up briefly. She was too close to him for her to relax. It didn't matter how much time passed, Noah was as handsome as he was frustrating. She caught a waft of his aftershave; the same one he'd been wearing since they were at school together. She inhaled deeply and her stomach did something strange – a quiver or a little flip. She swallowed and attempted to regain her focus.

'The only things left on the list, then, are putting together a timetable for the day, contacting parents and staff with the details and gathering all the equipment that we'll need for the day, including medals etcetera.' At 'medals' he did air quotes to imply their fraudulent nature. They would either be home-made or plastic, she presumed.

They both looked up as Sophie came into the room.

'Sorry, don't mind me.' She was lifting and putting down piles of papers from one of the desks. 'I'm just looking for my resources for Monday.'

'Sophie, can I pick your brain for a moment?' Noah asked.

Sophie stopped and perched on the edge of the table. 'Of course. Ask away!'

'We were just discussing how to split up the jobs for sports day, and Lizzie suggested we divvy them up and go our separate

64

ways. I was thinking it might be easier to crack on with things together, though. What do you think? I'm just thinking in terms of Lizzie's training. What would be best for her?' He sat back in his chair and reached his hands behind his head.

He wasn't asking because he cared about her training. He was asking because he knew what Sophie's answer would be, and he wanted to win yet another disagreement. Lizzie chewed the inside of her mouth, the pain dulling some of the rage she felt brewing for Noah.

Sophie made a show of thinking through the two options, but, as predicted, agreed with Noah's suggestion. 'It's just better at this early stage to be guided by someone as you go through each step of the process. I guess just like I would take you through lesson planning step by step. It'll be good for you to have Noah by your side.'

At no point had Lizzie ever found it good for Noah to be *at her side*.

Not only had Sophie walked into Noah's trap, but she had also massaged his ego, and effectively given him permission to be in charge of the entire event, instead of them sharing the responsibility equally. What was already going to be an awkward few weeks was now going to be painful.

'If you think that's best,' Lizzie said quietly, ignoring Noah's gleeful smugness in her peripheral vision.

'I think so,' Sophie said, standing up again and giving the office one more look-over. 'If you see my purple folder, can you give me a shout?'

'Of course,' Lizzie said, nodding. 'No problem.'

Once Sophie had left the room, a slightly awkward silence descended.

'Are you all right?' Noah asked.

'I'm fine,' replied Lizzie. Her clipped tone was another Lizzieism Noah was most definitely used to. An expression crossed his perfectly put-together features – an expression that told Lizzie her attitude was annoying him. Well, good. It wasn't fair that he got to irritate her without something in return.

Noah cleared his throat. 'Why don't I send you the electronic version of the timetable from last year, and you can take a look at it over the next week? If you do it on Google Docs, I can keep checking in and making any suggestions, you know, just in case.'

'That sounds fine,' Lizzie said, completely lacklustre.

'Are you free to meet again on Thursday after school next week?'

Lizzie turned the page in her planner and was dismayed to see a gaping hole in the calendar on Thursday.

'Looks like it,' she said, pencilling in her meeting with Noah next week. 'Shall we meet here again?'

'Yes, perfect. Then once we've got the plan for the day itself sorted, we can communicate everything to staff and parents. Shall we talk through this briefly before you go off and go it alone?' he asked, sliding the timetable from last year in between them.

He shuffled his chair a little closer and Lizzie felt the charge from his proximity jump across to her. She shrank away. She needed to keep her mind clear and focused. She concentrated on remembering everything that had happened and how she'd felt once it was all over. That would be enough to keep the odd stirrings at the pit of her stomach at bay.

'Do you want to tell me what worked well then?' she said finally. 'And was there anything that at the time you thought you should change?' She focused all of her attention on the page between them.

'Well,' said Noah, leaning forward. She caught a waft of his scent again, waves of nostalgia floating over her. 'The general schedule for the event worked really well, but it was a massive error doing it in the morning. Teaching in the afternoon was a nightmare for everyone involved.'

'Mmm . . . I can imagine,' Lizzie said, chewing thoughtfully on her pen. 'Is there any way we could make lunch earlier that day? Then we could fit everything in during the afternoon session and parents can come and pick the children straight up from the secondary school.'

'I guess so. Good idea. I'll speak to Darren in the kitchen and see whether they can shift lunch slightly. That might just work.'

'Great,' Lizzie said. 'May I?' Her pen was poised above the paper copy of last year's plan.

Noah nodded. 'Go ahead.'

Lizzie scribbled some notes onto the sheet.

'Right, so shall we look at making a list of everything we need on the day?' Noah asked, reaching for his own notepad to write on.

'Actually,' Lizzie said, looking at her watch, 'I have to go. Sorry. Can we do the list next week?'

'Oh, really?' Noah looked genuinely disappointed. 'Of course.'

'Tom and I are going house hunting,' Lizzie said, gathering up her stuff from the table and putting it into her bag. 'We've got an appointment at 4.45 p.m.'

'You and Tom . . .' Noah narrowed his eyes slightly and rubbed a hand over his faintly stubbled chin.

Lizzie realised Noah had jumped to the wrong conclusion. He'd instantly assumed that Lizzie and Tom were some kind of item. She opened her mouth to correct him and then decided against it. She thought it was probably safer if Noah thought that about her. It meant that there would be no accidental blurring of the lines. While Noah continued to infuriate her daily, there was still something of a heat between them. She'd felt it that afternoon. And anything she could do to prevent fanning the fire was a good shout in Lizzie's book.

'Yes,' she said. 'Besides, we can't really make a list of what we need until the timetable is finalised. We'd be searching for things we didn't need and end up looking for stuff last minute that we decide we do need. It's just easier if we have a definitive list, don't you think?'

Noah nodded slowly, his mind clearly elsewhere. Lizzie smiled to herself at having made a sensible suggestion that even Noah couldn't argue with and stood up, put her chair under the table and walked towards the door.

'We'll need to discuss how we might use the fundraiser to scrape together a budget too,' Lizzie said, feeling like she was on a roll. She pulled the door open and stopped when Noah replied.

'I've sorted that. The PTA is going to run a stall for me selling wristbands, and any profits will come to us.'

Lizzie sighed, having thought she'd caught Noah out with a lack of plans for the fundraiser. But he'd already sorted it. Of course he had. Without another word, she turned to leave.

'Have a good weekend,' Noah called.

She could feel his eyes on her back, watching her leave.

'You too,' she said, without a second glance.

She was proud of how she'd kept it professional, but irritated by Noah winning every single round of the meeting. She'd have to pull something big out of the bag with her plans now to . . . what? Impress him? Why did she care so much about beating him? About winning?

'Ready?'

She jumped out of her thoughts when Tom rounded the corner and walked towards her down the corridor. All notions of Noah dissolved to nothing.

Lizzie nodded. 'So ready. Let's go.'

'What are you talking to yourself about?' he asked curiously, his gossip radar locked onto her.

'I didn't realise I was.'

'Have you just met with Noah?' Tom asked, guessing at Lizzie's anguish.

'Yes!' cried Lizzie, pulling a face. 'And I don't know why I care so much about getting one over on him. Our past is so long ago.'

'You've always been competitive,' Tom said. 'But there's something about Noah that's really got under your skin, isn't there?' His eyebrows wrinkled, as if trying to work out what that might be.

They both already knew the reason, though.

'I know. It's always been like that, I guess,' Lizzie said.

They pushed through the double doors of the foyer and went out into the June sunshine.

'Takeaway coffee?' Tom asked, linking arms with Lizzie.

'That's a good shout.'

Greg's was bustling with patrons, as always, but the queue wasn't too bad. Tom paid for the drinks and they walked side by side to their house viewing.

'Lizzie, I have to ask. Why do you care so much about getting one over on Noah? What are you not telling me?'

Lizzie shrugged. It wasn't that she needed to beat him at something. It was more that he'd managed to hurt her so much that she would do anything to protect herself from him doing anything to hurt her again. Somehow, that self-preservation had manifested itself in competition.

'It was a friendly rivalry that turned into a flirtation when we reached the sixth form. But then once we were together, after a while, it didn't seem quite so flirty any more. We were both far too competitive for it to work. That, and I didn't take too kindly to his cheating.' She tucked some stray hairs behind her ears, stopping them from blowing about in the warm breeze.

'What happened?' Tom asked as they crossed the green. He slurped his iced coffee up through the straw.

'I don't know, not really.' Lizzie pulled out her sunglasses and brushed her hair out of the way to put them on. 'Anyway, enough of all that. Let's talk about this choice of area,' she said, gesticulating wildly with her hand. 'I'm not sure I want to live here.'

They looked around at the houses on both sides of the street. They were tall and thin, but they didn't seem to extend far back either. The insides were doubtless poky. The gardens looked unkempt and there was a fridge-freezer on the corner waiting to be taken away by the council, except it looked like it had been there, waiting, for rather a long time. The road itself was full of potholes, earmarked with spray paint for repair, but again, the paint had faded in the sunshine, and Lizzie wondered how long the locals had been waiting for them to be fixed.

'Hmm . . .' Tom said thoughtfully in response to Lizzie's concern. 'Well, we're here now, so why don't we at least have a look at the house?'

'OK.' Lizzie's voice was laced with uncertainty. She wrinkled her nose up as if having caught an unpleasant smell.

As they neared the house with the 'To Let' sign up in the garden, a shiny black BMW rounded the corner and squealed to a halt next to them on the road. A man stepped out in a crisp white shirt and blue tie, and equally shiny shoes. His hair was well coiffed and his tan had a whiff of fake about it.

'Mr Langdon?' he said, holding out a hand for Tom.

'That's me. Call me Tom.' Tom smiled, took his outstretched hand and shook it. 'This is my friend Lizzie. We're looking for somewhere to share. As friends.'

Tom's last comment didn't go unnoticed.

'Nice to meet you, Lizzie. I'm Chris,' he said, flashing his brilliant white teeth at her in the process.

She caught a waft of his fancy but excessive aftershave. And noticed that Tom hadn't stopped grinning since Chris had stepped out of the car. She elbowed him in the ribs as they followed Chris up the garden path. Tom winced, and they shared a look which confirmed her suspicions. Tom was suffering from a case of lust at first sight.

The inside of the property did little to ease Lizzie's concerns about the place. In their current flat, the space was all open plan, and she liked it that way. Here, the house had been split into sections – teeny-tiny sections. The kitchen was long and thin, like a galley, and had little space for anything, least of all their wine fridge. The downstairs was split into two squarish rooms, with seventies wallpaper peeling off in the corners where the damp had finally won its battle. If you couldn't see the damp because of the tiny windows, you could smell it, hanging almost palpably in the air.

Despite Lizzie having made her mind up well before she'd even entered the property, they humoured Chris by venturing upstairs to look at the two bedrooms and bathroom. Besides, Tom was clearly enjoying spending time with Chris, whose smile lit up every room, even if it was dank and dark inside. And after several months of nothing on the dating front, Lizzie decided to let Tom enjoy his crush.

'And this is the bathroom,' Chris said, holding open the door and standing back so that Lizzie and Tom could get a better look.

It had been updated at least, but the toilet bowl was still scummy inside and the grout in between the tiles behind the sink and in the shower boasted months', even years' worth of mould and mildew.

Lizzie took one glance and turned around. Tom made more of a show of having a good look, probably just to appease Chris, but his face said it all.

'So what do you think?' Chris asked, all smiles, as he walked down the stairs with Lizzie and Tom in his wake.

'Erm.' Lizzie made an odd noise that neither confirmed nor denied her interest.

'I think I'd like to give it the weekend to think it over with Lizzie, if that's OK?' Tom said.

Lizzie's mouth dropped. He must really like him.

'No problem. Here's my card,' Chris said, passing it to Tom. Lizzie was almost sure a moment passed between them.

Tom looked down at the card. 'Thanks. And you have my number too,' he said.

'Hopefully I'll hear from you early next week then,' Chris said, flashing them his smile one last time.

Wait a minute. Were they still talking about property rental or had they lapsed into 'call me' territory? Lizzie stood quietly and let the scene unfold, suddenly finding a small tree by the garden fence fascinating.

'Bye.' Tom waved as Chris climbed into his BMW. And he drove off as quickly as he'd arrived.

'What did you think, honestly?' Lizzie asked once they were alone.

'Cute. Really cute. I think I'm in love,' Tom said, looking wistfully down the road in the direction Chris had left.

'I meant the house, Tom.' Lizzie gave him a playful push.

'Absolute dive. There is no way I will be living there.'

'Phew,' Lizzie said. 'I thought you might have let your love of Chris cloud your judgement.'

'No amount of love could cloud my judgement of this hideous place. I just didn't want to shut him down then and there. Otherwise, I might never have got to speak to him again,' he said triumphantly, twizzling Chris's card between his fingers with a cheeky grin.

How did he do it? Tom seemed to float from one romantic attachment to another without ever getting in too deep or getting hurt. Lizzie was envious. She'd had one serious relationship with Noah, followed by ten years of a few dates here and there. Either Noah had really got his claws into her, or she was really rather rubbish at this dating malarkey.

Chapter Seven

'How was the rest of your week?' Kirsty asked, as she, Lizzie and Tom carried their drinks from the bar out to the benches that were lined up along the river. It was the hottest weekend of the summer so far, and the place was heaving with people all out to catch a bit of sun and enjoy a Sunday roast or a pint of lager.

The pub itself was built out of yellow Cotswold stone. It was small and poky, but in a comforting way. What it lacked in square footage, it made up for in beer garden space. The building was next to the river and the beer garden extended along it until the trees and foliage became too thick for the landlord to place any more tables and benches. With the weather so pleasant, the place was packed with people from the town and folks who had moored their canal boats close by. Kayaks and paddleboards skated effortlessly up and down the still waters of the river.

Tom arranged the chairs around the table so that they were in a semicircle, all facing out to overlook the water. Geese were down by the river's edge, just far enough away for Lizzie to relax. There wasn't a trace of a breeze and the sun beat down relentlessly. Lizzie knew that they'd last about two minutes before they grabbed the parasol that lay on the floor in front of them and wrestled with it to find some shade.

'The rest of the week was surprisingly good,' Lizzie said, taking a sip of her lager shandy. 'I was knackered by the end of it, but it was fun. Sophie said she might get me in and teaching a bit here and there next week too.'

'Ooh, that's exciting,' Kirsty said, slipping her flip-flops off and sitting cross-legged on her chair.

'Sophie's class are lush, aren't they?' Tom said. 'Have you met Nigel properly yet? He's a right mischief.'

Lizzie nodded. 'Yes, we've met. He really is a rascal. He spent the whole of Friday morning break time following his mate around and putting sticky buds on him wherever he could without him noticing. He looked like a bush when he'd finished with him!'

Kirsty laughed. 'Do you remember Dad getting us with sticky buds when we'd go to the National Trust places back in the day?'

Lizzie smiled nostalgically and instinctively reached for her ring. 'It's one of my favourite childhood memories.'

The familiar sense of breathlessness came over her as her throat tightened in an attempt to stave off tears. It had been ten years since the fire and still the guilt of not being there to save them was as raw and painful as the day it had happened. The only good thing to come out of that horrible day was the closeness she'd forged with her sister. Until then, with a decade between them, they'd never been very sisterly, but the fire had brought them together. They'd had to grow close, to keep from falling apart.

Kirsty took a sip of her drink. 'So what do you think she'll have you teach?' she asked, breaking the silence.

'I'm praying for literacy and definitely not maths,' Lizzie

said with a roll of her eyes. 'I'd be happy doing one of the other subjects in the afternoon, though.'

'She might get you doing PE, with all your experience with the football team,' Tom said with a comic wiggle of his eyebrows.

'Ugh, I hope not.'

'How come?' Kirsty asked with faux innocence.

Tom waited for the seed he'd planted to blossom. Lizzie could tell he was still desperate to find out more about what had happened between her and Noah before. And despite knowing more than Tom, Kirsty was just as nosy – she'd be right there with him. Perhaps it was time to just share and give them what they wanted. Maybe it would shut them up. Perhaps it would make Lizzie feel better.

'I don't want to work with Noah any more than I already have to. We're already organising sports day. I don't really want to add anything else into the mix.'

Lizzie took another sip of her drink, then another, and then followed it with a large gulp.

'A few meetings after school and a couple of observations here and there are enough for me, thank you very much.' She placed her glass down heavily and folded her arms.

'The lady doth protest too much,' Tom said, unable to contain his curiosity. 'He can't have just broken up with you for no reason.'

Lizzie looked over to Kirsty for moral support, but she was looking out over the water and sipping her drink.

'Noah was my first love,' Lizzie said eventually. 'I genuinely thought we were going to be together for ever. And it wasn't in that lovey-dovey, high school sweetheart, first love kind of way. We really are . . . were' – she corrected herself – 'perfect for each other.'

'So what went wrong?' Tom asked.

'I found out that he was cheating on me.' She caught her

sister's eye briefly. 'Kirsty found out and told me.'

Kirsty looked down towards the river's edge and watched as the geese waddled about next to the reeds.

Tom shook his head. 'Sorry, Lizzie.'

'It was a long time ago.'

'Still, stuff like that hurts,' Tom said. 'And you, my love, are clearly still hurting.'

Lizzie nodded. 'I guess I am and I wish I weren't. I really loved him at the time and he broke my heart. I've not really passed more than a second or third date since. I just don't trust anyone and that's all his fault. I hate that I let him do that to me.'

Kirsty – coming out of her apparent trance – reached out a hand and rested it on Lizzie's arm. 'I'm sorry I wasn't there for you when it happened.'

'We had other things to deal with,' Lizzie said, thinking back to the horrors of that day. 'At least you had the decency to tell me about his Lothario ways. Without you, I'd never have known what he'd been getting up to.'

Kirsty half smiled and looked out over the water again.

'Is anyone else burning to a crisp?' Tom asked, leaping out of his seat and picking up the parasol.

He lifted it up and grappled with it until he'd managed to slot it into the hole in the table, with Lizzie steadying it while he wrestled to push the brolly part up and out.

'There.' Tom took a step back to admire his handiwork.

'So how do you feel about him now?' Kirsty asked, taking another sip of her drink. She had watched the umbrella drama unfold without lifting a finger, but now sat in its shade, fanning herself with the pub menu.

'I don't know,' Lizzie said noncommittally. And the truth was, she didn't really.

'Yes, you do.' Tom pointed an accusatory finger at her.

'Do you still like him?' Kirsty asked.

Lizzie pushed her sunglasses up and into her red hair now that they were sitting in the shade. 'There's just something about him. Every time I see him he takes me back to that time; he makes me feel seventeen again and all on edge and butterflies. But then I remember what happened that day and the butterflies all turn to stone. It makes me feel sick. I could never go back there. Too much happened.'

'And you can't see you guys salvaging anything? I mean, you've not dated anyone in for ever,' Tom said.

'Yes, thank you, Tom. I am aware of my current dating situation.'

The server came over to the table and set down their three roast dinners, placing cutlery wrapped up in napkins next to each of them. They all mumbled their thanks.

'But no,' continued Lizzie. 'Too much has happened and we're different people now. Besides, he's always been too competitive, and he infuriates me. So, I'll just get through sorting out this sports day thing and then keep as far away from him as possible.'

'Hi,' came a voice from behind them.

All three turned, forks poised and ready to deliver food to their mouths.

'Hi, Noah,' Lizzie said, wracking her brain for the last time she'd mentioned his name in their conversation, and whether it was obvious that they'd been talking about him.

'Hi,' he said again.

A moment passed as the four of them looked at each other without a word.

'Noah, you remember Kirsty, my sister.'

Noah nodded. 'Yes, Kirsty. Hi.' His eyes flickered towards her and then back to Lizzie.

'Hi, Noah,' said Kirsty, with a little wave. She looked away instantly and went back to her dinner.

An expression that Lizzie couldn't place flashed across Noah's face, and he seemed to press his lips together.

'And you know Tom from school.' Lizzie purposefully chose not to label their relationship, remembering that Noah had jumped to the wrong conclusion about him in their meeting on Friday and wanting to continue with the façade. It was safer while she was working through whatever feelings she was . . . feeling.

'Hi.' Tom continued to devour his roast dinner and gave very little attention to Noah, despite their previous conversation. Nothing came between Tom and his food.

'What are you doing here?' Lizzie asked. She had to fill the silence that would have otherwise continued and get some kind of conversation going.

The sun bounced off Noah's hair, which was pushed back with sunglasses in which Lizzie could see her own reflection. He looked different now he wasn't in his school PE kit. He was wearing board shorts and a tightish white T-shirt. It enhanced his muscular physique, highlighting how fit he was underneath his clothes. Lizzie swallowed and concentrated on her own reflection in his glasses.

'I was just dropping my nan off. She has lunch here every week with her friends, but it's too dangerous on the roads to get here by herself these days, so I drop her here whenever I can,' he explained.

'That's lovely,' Kirsty said, smiling.

Noah's eyes flicked once again to Kirsty, but only for the briefest of moments.

Lizzie could see Tom shooting her a sideways glance. She knew exactly what he was thinking. How could someone she'd painted such an awful picture of only seconds ago be lovely enough to give his nan a lift to the pub whenever he could?

'How did the house hunting go?' Noah asked, looking from Lizzie to Tom and back again.

'It was hideous,' Tom said. 'Absolute dive. So, we're back to the drawing board,' he added, putting a fork laden with every single aspect of his roast dinner into his mouth.

'I'm sorry,' Noah said, looking directly at Lizzie.

'Thanks. It's fine though. We'll find something.' She shrugged, despite not being entirely convinced by her own statement. It was just one of the things that had been niggling at her recently.

'Well, I have to rush,' he said.

Thank goodness, thought Lizzie.

'If I don't go now, it'll be time to come and pick Nan up again.'

Lizzie smiled. His kindness was killing her. Not to mention bringing some of those dead butterflies back to life.

'If you hear a commotion, that's probably her. Try to stop her from drinking any more vodkas,' he said, nodding towards the pub where a large gathering of older patrons were cheersing as their lunches arrived.

Lizzie smiled. 'Will do.' She lifted her own drink in a cheers.

'See you, Lizzie,' he said and turned to go, half walking and half jogging to his car.

'That's the horrible man you were just talking about?' Tom asked, incredulous. 'I mean, I thought maybe he was Jekyll at work and Hyde outside, but really Lizzie, Noah Hatton seems like a pretty lovely guy.' He shovelled in another forkful of food, mopping up his gravy by swirling his next one around the plate before eating it.

Looking at Kirsty, Lizzie could see that she was thinking the same thing. Her face was set in admiration for him.

'How was I supposed to know he does good deeds for the elderly?' Lizzie said. 'It doesn't change the past,' she added, huffing and folding her arms again.

'People change though,' Kirsty said.

'Not me,' Lizzie said stubbornly. 'And definitely not Noah Hatton,' she added, shovelling a forkful of beef and mashed potato into her mouth.

'I wish Steve would change,' Kirsty said, with a harrumph. She huffed and went back to her lunch.

'Still being difficult?' Lizzie asked.

Kirsty nodded. 'Yes. The only reason I've made it out today is because Steve's mum has taken the boys. I think he's at the game with his mates.'

'You put up with too much,' Lizzie said.

'What else can I do? The boys need a father figure.'

'Maybe not my place,' Tom said through glugs of his lager, 'but is Steve even really that much of a father figure?'

Lizzie looked from Tom to Kirsty, whose face was etched with agreement.

'He has a point,' Lizzie said, reaching across the space to squeeze Kirsty's hand.

'But what can I do?' Kirsty said, exasperated. 'We're a family. I wouldn't wish our relationship on anyone, but there's no way out of it. Besides, when we need him, Steve does always come through.' Kirsty went back to her dinner.

Lizzie and Tom shared a look, but neither took the comment any further. It was true that, sometimes, Steve played his role perfectly. But in Lizzie's experience, it was only when he was trying to put on a show for everyone else. It saddened Lizzie to think that Kirsty was still telling herself he was a good egg after all this time. It had been nearly twenty years since they'd got together, and Lizzie couldn't remember a time when she'd respected Steve or thought he was good for her sister. Even when she was just a child and they weren't that close. She went to ask another question, but changed her mind. The topic of Steve had a nasty habit of hijacking conversations.

'So, are you both free to join me at the school fundraiser next week?' Tom asked, changing the subject.

'I think so,' Lizzie said. 'Miss Davies mentioned it, so I should probably make the effort.'

'Probably not for me,' said Kirsty.

'Why not?' Tom said. 'There's food and drink and music . . .'

'I can't, sorry.' Kirsty looked somehow smaller in her seat. 'Steve and the boys will need me at home,' she added quietly.

Lizzie looked over at her sister, who was concentrating intently on her roast dinner and drink. Steve wouldn't need her at home. That was a lie. She was just worried about asking him if she could go out for the evening – as if she should have to. Lizzie was bothered by the look of fear that crossed Kirsty's face, and decided that there was a serious sister conversation there that needed to be had sooner rather than later.

Chapter Eight

As Lizzie came to, her alarm signalling the start of another busy week, she realised that she'd potentially be starting this week with third-degree burns. She pulled herself to the edge of the bed and looked at herself in the mirror. Her cheeks were bright red and so were her shoulders.

But she had slept – for once – so sunburn was definitely good for one thing. She didn't feel good about it, though.

'Are you as burnt as I am?' she called out to Tom.

A reply came in the form of a groan, which Lizzie took to mean yes. At least she wasn't in it on her own.

The anticipated coolness and enjoyment of a cold shower just led to further pain, and by the time she was out and drying herself, Lizzie felt like her whole body was throbbing. She would have to do something spectacular with her make-up and hope that her hair didn't clash with her new skin tone before school. And today was Monday too, which meant she would spend the last hour of her day with Noah in PE again.

Looking like a tomato. Not ideal.

Lizzie wrestled to sort out her hair and pulled it up into a ponytail before applying some foundation, which she hoped would remove a little of the redness from her cheeks. The result was passable. Disappointingly, Tom was nowhere to be seen, so for today, she'd have to be her own stylist.

'Are we walking?' she shouted out into the flat.

'Yep, yep,' came the flustered reply. 'I'll be ready in ten minutes.'

Lizzie took one last look at herself in the full-length mirror and went through to the kitchen to collect her lunch from the fridge.

'I made you one too,' she said, tossing a second Tupperware across the room to Tom as he came in. He was startled, but made the catch, avoiding a cascade of salad landing on the floor.

'Thanks.'

Tom's face was an even brighter shade of red than Lizzie's.

'Are you OK?' she asked, already certain of the answer.

'I've been better,' Tom said, shoving his lunch into his rucksack. 'My head's killing me. How much did I drink?' he asked, rubbing it.

'Not loads. I think it's the sunburn that's making you feel rotten. I feel just as bad and I only had a couple of shandies. Come on. Let's get going. It looks cooler out there today, so maybe a walk in the fresh air will do us some good.'

'I hope so,' Tom said, his characteristically bright demeanour slightly more shrivelled and decrepit than usual.

'Well, if not, here's some paracetamol.' Lizzie put a sheet of unopened tablets in his hand.

It was fresher outside than it had been the previous day, having rained during the night, and Lizzie enjoyed the cool breeze on her sun-damaged cheeks. The trees swayed slightly in the wind and fluffy clouds that hovered in the sky obscured the sun.

'See, it's nice,' Lizzie said, taking on the role of the responsible one for a change.

For their entire commute, all she got was a grunt or a shake of the head from Tom, who really had seen better days.

'Good luck today,' she said when they arrived at the school gates. She reached for his arm and gave it a friendly squeeze.

He winced.

'Ouch! You too,' he managed, with a weak smile.

She watched him trudge down the corridor, looking more like a bear on his way to hibernate for the winter, than a teaching assistant about to begin a new week of work.

The children arriving and saying good morning to both Sophie and Lizzie had become second nature to them now. Lizzie thought it may well be her favourite part of the day. It turned out Monday was even lovelier than the other mornings because they would regale her with little anecdotes from their weekends. One boy had been to a zoo and seen an elephant for the first time. Another little girl had celebrated her grandma's seventieth birthday. Audrey had spent Friday night at a friend's house for a sleepover.

'You came back then,' was Nigel's retort as he wandered in.

'Erm, yes?' Lizzie said.

'Well done,' he said.

How was he so much older than his eleven years? Lizzie and Sophie shared a look of disbelief and Sophie rolled her eyes.

A while later, as soon as the children had listened to Sophie explain their writing task for the day, she came over to where Lizzie was sitting.

'How do you feel about taking a bit of the literacy lesson later this week then?' she asked in a whisper as the children focused quietly on their writing.

Lizzie pulled a worried expression to give herself a moment to answer. This was a big deal.

'That sounds exciting,' she said eventually, terrified but genuinely thrilled that Sophie thought she might be ready. She was suddenly a bag of nervous energy.

'Have you got some time after school to talk it through?' Sophie asked.

Mondays were always a bit of a rush with football training at 7 p.m. Despite this, she said, 'Of course.' This was an important milestone, and she wanted to get it right and hopefully make a good impression.

'Great. Well, grab a hot drink when I let the children out after school and we can meet in the office,' Sophie said. 'It's better than sitting on these tiny chairs.'

Lizzie smiled knowingly.

Lunch was soon upon them, and the children quickly disappeared out of the classroom and off to the canteen or outside for a run around.

'Nice work during maths today,' Sophie said as she and Lizzie tidied away some of the sheets and pencils from the morning sessions.

'It worked really well. When I pretended I needed help, Benjamin could explain how to do the maths really clearly and Audrey, Sammy and Nigel checked it,' Lizzie said. 'The thing is, I was sort of genuinely asking them too. I'm finding some of the maths quite challenging. Any advice?' It embarrassed her to ask, but she knew it would be her nemesis until she did something about it.

'Yes,' Sophie said, wandering over to the cupboard and rifling around on one of the shelves. 'Try looking at this.' She passed Lizzie a dusty book.

Lizzie flicked through the pages to see problem after problem and lots of mathematical explanations. Her brow involuntarily furrowed at the amount of maths on display. It was too much.

'This book got me through my first year of teaching. Just borrow it and you'll be fine. We can leave the teaching of maths until later on in September too.'

'Thank you,' Lizzie said, genuinely grateful. 'That's really reassuring.'

'So, this afternoon,' Sophie said, 'we've got art first and they're finishing off their mosaics, so shall we set up quickly now for ten minutes and then get some lunch?'

'Sure,' said Lizzie, and they put out the pots of glue, the mosaic tiles and the children's work from the previous week.

Lizzie desperately tried to enjoy the art lesson that afternoon. The children's mosaics were impressive, and she loved how art sessions were a way of getting to know the children better as they talked and worked together. The classroom had a different atmosphere to the more formal learning setting of the mornings. The afternoons were the part of the day that Lizzie loved the most.

Except it was Monday, and she had the impending certainty of PE with Noah to deal with afterwards.

Predictably, art raced past and before she knew it, the children were packing away and getting changed for PE. Lizzie busied herself clearing up glue pots and spreaders.

'Are you happy to observe PE again today?' Sophie asked, dumping another table's glue pot and bits into the sink where Lizzie was cleaning them.

'Of course.' She wasn't going to let Noah Hatton get in the way of what she was really here for. Her teacher training was the most important thing right now and while Noah might have thrown her off on her first day, just knowing he'd be there that afternoon meant she was prepared for seeing him, which made things easier.

'I brought a kit to get changed into, though, this time. Taking part was tricky in my normal clothes last week.'

'Good idea. Do you want to go and get changed now?'

'Thanks.' Lizzie flicked the excess water off her hands and into the sink before drying them on a towel that looked like it had been there longer than the children in Year Six had been alive.

She took her bag from the cupboard and made her way down the corridor to the staff toilet, changing quickly into her football shirt, leggings and trainers.

Without consciously deciding to, Lizzie found herself redoing her ponytail and touching up her lip gloss. She rolled her eyes at herself in the mirror for even caring enough to consider reapplying make-up for Noah. Then she tried to convince herself that she normally retouched her make-up a few times a day; it just so happened that this time it was prior to seeing Noah again. Coincidentally.

Ugh, how was he messing with her like this? They'd barely spoken in school, and when they had, it had been awful. And yet here she was, caring what Noah thought of her and hating herself for touching up her make-up pre-emptively, even after all this time.

She raced back through the corridor, just in time to catch up with the warm-up.

'Nice of you to join us,' Noah said with a smirk as she slipped into the circle and joined in with the star jumps.

Lizzie felt her blood boil and went from caring about what Noah thought of her to not being able to care less. He was teasing her again and doing it on the sly because they were surrounded by children – the exact same reason Lizzie couldn't retaliate, and he knew it. She hated that. Why did he have to turn everything into some kind of one-upmanship?

Noah set the children racing off into a game of Stuck in the Mud and sidled up to Lizzie, who was sitting this one out to watch from the sidelines.

'You came prepared today then,' he said, looking her gym kit up and down.

Lizzie folded her arms, suddenly extremely self-conscious of both what she was wearing and of Noah's freely wandering eyes.

'I wanted to be fully prepared, just in case you wanted a rematch after last week,' she said, matching his mocking tone.

'Well, I won,' he said with a cocky tilt of the head. 'So, I guess if anyone wanted, or needed, a rematch, it'd be you.' He said it with a playful smile, but his words frustrated her.

Lizzie felt her temperature rise again. She took a deep breath.

'I just didn't want you to think it was a fluke win, which is, of course, what I believe it was.' Lizzie pointed dramatically at herself.

'Do you play for the Cranswell Ladies?' Noah asked, changing the subject and gesturing to Lizzie's football shirt.

She nodded. 'Yes, for the past five years.'

'You guys are doing really well in the cup tournament this year. Haven't you made it through to the final?'

'Yeah, we play in a few weeks,' Lizzie said, aware of how the tone of their conversation had changed and not quite sure how to shift gear.

Noah seemed to be impressed, and Lizzie liked it. She hated herself for that, too.

'That's great,' Noah said, with an appreciative nod.

His eyes locked with Lizzie's for a second longer than necessary and something funny happened to her insides – those butterflies were stirring again.

'Right, let's get this lot back in,' Noah said, clearing his throat and snapping back into teacher mode, making Lizzie jump. He blew his whistle, and the children ran back to their circle.

He began speaking once the class was assembled. 'Today, Year Six, we are going to play Capture the Flag.'

The room erupted into cheers and excited chatter.

'You're going to love this,' Audrey said to Lizzie, obviously noting the slightly confused look on her face.

'So, for those of you who don't know,' Noah said, pointedly looking in Lizzie's direction and causing the class to look around too and giggle, 'Capture the Flag is a game of teamwork, strategy and speed. We'll have two teams. The flags will begin in the end zone of the opposing team. Your job is to get across the pitch, take a flag and get it home before they tag you. If someone from the opposite team catches you, you must go to their prison and will only be released if someone from your team can get there to tag you. The winning team will be the team with the most flags at the end of the time, or the first team to get all their flags in their end zone, or to put the whole of the opposing team into prison. OK?'

The children were still chattering excitedly, but Lizzie was just plain confused. She was sure there was a logical game in there somewhere, but as with all games, it would probably only become clear once they started playing.

'Are you going to take part, Miss Morris?' Noah asked expectantly.

'I will, if you will,' she said, hoping on reflection that it came across as competitive rather than flirty. She cringed.

'We'll be the team captains, then. Let's choose our players.'

Lizzie wrestled with her competitive nature. She wanted to choose the most athletic and sporty students. But she also had a flashback to when she was at school herself and nobody ever chose her to be on their team, because she was the shortest and smoked too many cigarettes round the back of school at lunchtime.

On reflection, she went for a mix of the two. It made her feel like she was being morally sound, but also gave her a fighting chance at literally beating Noah at his own game, which right now, was of equal importance.

Lizzie's team put on their red bibs, the nostalgic scent of slightly fusty sports equipment hitting her like a punch. Noah's team had the yellow bibs. And with that, they were off.

After a few moments of play, Lizzie saw how it was working and that it was, to all intents and purposes, an extreme game of tag. At first, the children would lurch towards the flags in the end zones and then dodge back as a member of the other team went for them. It went on like this for a good few minutes. Somebody needed to make a break for it. That someone was Lizzie. She ran at the flags from the side, taking the opposite team, including Noah, by surprise. Reaching and grabbing a flag as she raced past, she ran as fast as she could to the opposite end of the hall, dodging and darting between the children as she did, until she reached their end zone, dropped the first flag there and celebrated like it was a touchdown in the Super Bowl.

Looking over at Noah, she could see he was frustrated, but impressed. He ran a hand through his hair and smiled across the hall at her, respect and irritation both etched across his beautiful features.

He blew his whistle.

'Team talk!' Noah shouted, and his group obediently gathered around him, huddling together to discuss their top-secret tactics now that Lizzie had broken their defence.

Lizzie beckoned her team over, too.

'That was awesome, Miss Morris!' Sammy said.

'We're winning!' said another little girl.

'At the moment we are, yes. But what we need to do now is surprise them. Put your hand up if you edged towards a flag and then jumped back because someone from the opposite team went for you.' Nearly everyone in the group raised their hand. 'Right, so what if we all did it at the same time, but committed and ran towards their end zone?'

'We'd all get put into prison,' one boy said sadly.

'But they wouldn't be able to get all of us,' said another.

'Spot on, Stan,' Lizzie said, pointing across the circle to Stan's surprise. 'Let's all go for the flags. Some of us will get them and be able to run for the end zone. Some of us will be caught, but then, Nigel, I've got an important job for you.'

'Yes, Miss!' he said, reporting for duty with a salute.

'Your job is to head over to the prison while all this is taking place, ready to release everyone who gets put there. Got it?'

'Got it, Miss.'

'Any questions?'

The children all shook their heads.

'Right, hands in,' she said, showing them what they needed to do. 'Let's goooooooooo team!' she said as they all raised their hands at the same time and ran off to their posts, clapping enthusiastically.

'Ready for this, Miss Morris?' Noah was practically gloating before he'd even done anything spectacular, presumably whatever he'd been talking about in his team huddle.

'I am, Mr Hatton. The question is, are you?' Lizzie could barely contain her excitement at being about to completely flatten Noah's team.

'Let's go,' he said, narrowing his eyes.

He blew the whistle and what transpired was absolute chaos.

Children ran everywhere, like tiny ants scrambling over the ground. Clearly, Lizzie and Noah had both had the same conversation with their teams. All the children ran for the flags and then aimed for each of the end zones, flying everywhere and dodging each other as they went. After ten minutes or so of flag stealing and prison breaking and absolute joy from the children, Noah blew the whistle.

The class came to a standstill. When he blew it again, they got into their circle. Lizzie joined them, breathing heavily and brushing her crazy hair back and out of her face. She could feel her sunburnt cheeks throbbing even more than they had been already with the added heat of the exercise. She hoped her foundation hadn't slipped with the exertion.

'Great job today, folks. Well done, everyone. I think after counting the flags, it's a draw!' Noah said, clapping his hands. Some of the children cheered and others groaned at the lack of a win.

'Hey, it's the taking part that counts, remember,' Lizzie said to the two children standing next to her. It was OK to lie about that, right?

'Shouldn't we do some sort of tie break?' Benjamin asked.

Other children nodded in agreement.

'Why don't you and Miss Morris do a climbing race?' Tilly said.

Lizzie shook her head and waved her hand to protest. 'No, no. I don't think so.' This was getting silly. They were in a lesson and should be focusing on the children. But then . . .

Noah raised an eyebrow and said, 'I'm game if you are.'

For goodness' sake. Lizzie could never refuse a challenge. She rolled her eyes, relented and went to stand over with Noah, who was on the crash mats next to the climbing frame.

'I knew you wouldn't be able to resist,' he said with a smile.

The lines were blurring between competition and flirtation. Lizzie's butterflies were reawakening and hitting their heads against the inside of her stomach simultaneously.

'I never could,' she said, unable to resist even the friendly banter.

He held her look again for that moment too long. She shouldn't have said that. Lizzie swallowed nervously – because of the challenge? Or because Noah made her nervous?

'So, everyone.' Noah turned to speak to the class only at the very last moment. 'Miss Morris and I will climb to the top of the climbing frame, go over the top and then climb back down again. The winner will be the first person to get both feet firmly on the floor. Tilly, Audrey, come and sit next to the climbing frame and watch the crash mats. Put your hands up as soon as you see both feet on the floor. OK?' The girls nodded and sat where he'd asked them to.

Lizzie redid her ponytail, scraping back her fringe so that she could properly see what she was doing. She tucked the front of her football shirt into her leggings too; she didn't want a repeat of Noah getting any unsolicited views again as she climbed.

'Benjamin. Will you count us in?' Noah asked.

Benjamin stood up. 'Ready?'

Lizzie and Noah looked at each other and nodded, poised to pounce on the climbing frame as soon as they could. Benjamin let the suspense hang for a few seconds, as though he'd indulged in one too many Saturday-night singing contests, before saying, 'Three, two, one, go!'

Lizzie lurched at the climbing frame, getting a firm footing on the third rung, and hoisted the rest of her body up. Out of the corner of her eye, she could see that Noah had made a good start, too. Both of them had similarly lean and athletic body types, so on paper, Lizzie couldn't pick a winner. Although she knew for definite that she wanted it far more than Noah did.

Below them, the children were jumping up and down and screaming, either for Miss Morris or Mr Hatton. The cheering spurred her on and Lizzie scrambled up the climbing frame, higher and higher, until she reached the top. She avoided looking down. This part had always terrified her, even as a child; that bit where your weight is balanced at the very top, but you've not really got anything to hold on to. For a split second, Lizzie wondered why they insisted on varnishing the wooden frames; surely that was just making them more slippery than they needed to be – especially once the varnish was mixed with the sweat of nerves and exertion.

In only a moment, Lizzie was over the top, but several rungs down, she could see Noah was ahead. There was no way she was going to let him win. Not this time. Using everything she had, Lizzie powered down the remaining rungs to land on the floor with a jump – at the exact moment that Noah did. Tilly and

Audrey jumped up to announce their person had won at the very same instant. There was absolutely nothing in it.

Lizzie and Noah shared a look as the children went wild.

'Rematch?' Lizzie said, raising an eyebrow.

'I think, actually, it might be time to go and get changed,' announced Sophie, who had appeared from nowhere at the back of the hall. Her arms were crossed over her chest and her eyebrows lowered as though annoyed at something. Her body language suggested she'd been there for a few minutes, perhaps watching the action unfold. Lizzie cringed. She'd let her competition with Noah take away from the children's lesson and Sophie was right to be annoyed. She felt instantly guilty and was sorry to think she'd let Sophie – and the children – down.

At the sound of Sophie's voice, the children instantly quietened down and got themselves into the line that would snake back to the classroom.

Lizzie felt like she'd been told off somehow, that icky feeling of nausea churning in her stomach. She didn't know why she suddenly felt sick, but whatever the reason was, it didn't feel good.

'Maybe next time,' Noah whispered into her ear as she passed him on the way out of the hall. His breath tickled her neck. He was so close. There was something about it that caused some of the butterflies in her stomach to hover slightly off the ground for the briefest of moments.

Lizzie was still thinking about the warmth of Noah's whisper on her neck as she waited in the office for Sophie to join her. She shivered involuntarily and used the break in her daydream to shake off the nostalgic feeling of lust for him. That's how they'd ended up together in the first place – a flirty friendship that had boiled over into something more. She couldn't fall into that trap again; even if Noah was interested – which she was fairly certain he wasn't.

'Hi, Lizzie.' Sophie came into the office and closed the door behind her.

'Hi.' Lizzie still felt as though she'd done something wrong and felt herself grow smaller.

'How was PE today?' Sophie asked, not hesitating to bring up the one thing Lizzie hoped she wouldn't.

'Great actually,' Lizzie said truthfully. She'd enjoyed the lesson itself this time. With the foresight of knowing Noah would be there, she hadn't had to contend with the element of surprise. It had felt good to run about and shake off the cobwebs. Plus, the children had really enjoyed it, which was the main thing.

'We played Capture the Flag. I can see how PE could help encourage other skills, like collaboration and strategy. The kids were great.'

'You're right,' she said, sitting on the opposite side of the round table. 'It's super important for the children's development. That's why we get the expert in.'

Lizzie nodded slightly to show her interest, while Sophie pulled some paper out of her purple folder.

'Speaking of Noah . . .'

Here we go, thought Lizzie.

'Do you two know each other? You know, outside of school?'

Technically, this was none of Sophie's business. So what if they did? But at the same time, she knew it hadn't looked good when Sophie had come into the hall earlier to find them racing; especially if she'd heard Lizzie's suggestion of a rematch following the disappointing draw. After all, she'd just said how important PE lessons were and there she was, using them as an opportunity to beat Noah at something instead of focusing on the children's learning.

'We went to school together,' explained Lizzie. It wasn't a lie. 'We've always had a bit of a friendly rivalry.' It didn't even scrape the surface of the vast sinkhole that was their shared past.

Sophie looked at Lizzie for a moment, her expression giving away that she knew full well that wasn't even the half of it. But Lizzie didn't offer her anything more. She desperately wanted to move on, and thankfully, Sophie didn't press her on it.

She saw Sophie's eyes narrow ever so slightly before she turned again to her folder.

Lizzie changed the subject. 'So, I'm excited about getting to teach something.'

'OK, well on Friday I was going to do some story planning with the children – using these.' Sophie lifted a set of red velvet bags from the table behind her, the kind a magician might use for their tricks. 'These are them,' she said, passing one to Lizzie. 'The idea is that the children take one thing out of each bag and put them together to plan their story.'

Lizzie rifled about in the bag, feeling each of the objects, and pulled out a Lego tree.

'Ah, so this is the location bag. If a child pulls out the tree, then their story would be set in a forest maybe, or a park.'

She took the tree and set it on the table before handing Lizzie the second bag. 'This is the character bag.'

Lizzie stuck her hand in and pulled out a Sylvanian Families rabbit dressed as a firefighter. She bristled ever so slightly at the occupation. What were the chances?

'So my character would be in the fire service and the action would take place in the park or forest.' Lizzie held the rabbit in her hand and picked up the tree again, holding them up and weighing up her options.

'Maybe. But your character could be a rabbit, a firefighter or both. They might even just be an authority figure. It's for the children to decide how far they take their interpretation.'

She held out the last bag to Lizzie. 'This last bag is the best one. This is the object bag. The children have to include this object in their story, which is often the catalyst for them to come up with their plot. Do you want to choose one?'

Lizzie stuck her hand in the final bag and pulled out a bean. 'A bean?' Her nose wrinkled involuntarily.

'Probably a magic bean,' Sophie said, as if they really existed. 'Can you start to see a narrative forming?'

'Yes, actually,' she said, as a story did in fact begin to come together in her mind. 'So, how should I go about teaching this to the children?'

'You'll need to explain how the story bags work and model it by doing something similar to what we just did. You'll probably want to do a couple of trial runs and think about the sorts of questions you might want to ask. For example, if they pulled out a Sylvanian Families figure like this one, you might ask them what sort of character this could be, which would prompt them to consider characteristics, employment, family, etcetera. It would be up to you to read the room and ask as many questions as required to ensure they all can go away and plan a story from the objects.'

It sounded to Lizzie like there were a few too many variables, but she liked the idea of the lesson itself. She could prepare for the unknown.

'OK, great,' she said, only a little uncertainty coming through her voice. 'So I can ask the children to come to the front and pick objects and maybe we could verbalise a story together by asking them questions.'

'Sounds perfect,' Sophie said. 'Why don't you write it up as a plan?' She pushed a lesson plan pro forma towards her. 'I can email you an electronic copy too, if you'd rather. And then I'll have a look over it on Thursday before Friday's lesson.'

'I'm actually really excited!' It was all finally coming together. For a fleeting moment, she smiled sadly at the thought of her mum and dad not being able to share in her success.

'Great. Right, I need to go and see Miss Davies. I'll see you tomorrow,' she said, packing away her bits and pieces.

'Yep. See you tomorrow, Sophie.' Lizzie gathered up her own belongings. 'And thanks for this.'

As Sophie left the office, Tom entered it.

'Are you ready?' he asked, picking up his bag from underneath the desk.

'Yep. We've just finished here.' Lizzie stood up and put her bag over her shoulder. It was far too warm to put her coat on as well, so she slung it over her bag.

'Come on, then.' Tom sounded keen to get out into the summer sun, despite his sunburn from yesterday begging to differ.

'Does it still hurt?' Lizzie asked, poking it playfully as they walked down the corridor.

'Ouch, yes!' He retaliated by poking her in the ribs.

'Bye, you two.'

Lizzie and Tom turned to see Noah standing in the corridor. It occurred to Lizzie that their playful banter might have come across as something more.

'See you tomorrow, Noah,' Tom said.

'Bye.' Lizzie raised her hand to wave and then linked arms with Tom before walking off down the corridor.

'I know what you're doing,' Tom said under his breath and through gritted teeth.

'I don't know what you mean.' Lizzie failed to hide her smile. 'But you know, you're an accomplice now, so I wouldn't say anything if I were you. You're in this as deep as I am.'

Tom used his free hand to mime locking his lips and throwing the key into a flower bed as they left the building.

'You are awful, Lizzie Morris,' he said as they began the walk home in the summer sunshine.

Chapter Nine

As soon as they arrived back at the flat, Lizzie changed out of her leggings and into her football shorts, and grabbed a quick snack before heading straight back out to football practice. Tom promised to have a proper dinner ready for her when she got home later that evening, but Lizzie didn't have high hopes. What Tom meant is that he'd possibly foot the bill for a takeaway and have it delivered before she got back, at best.

Lizzie gave her sister a squeeze after crossing the car park at the leisure centre.

'Hi Kirs.'

'Ouch! You look as burnt as I feel.'

Lizzie pushed her sunglasses to the top of her head to get a better look at her sister. It seemed Kirsty had found herself with the same fate as Tom and Lizzie that morning.

'I didn't realise it was that warm yesterday or that we were even in the sun. We had a parasol!'

'I know,' Kirsty said. 'I've learnt my lesson, though. This pain isn't worth an afternoon by the river with you two.'

'Charming!' Lizzie smiled. 'Come on, let's get inside.'

Lizzie took Kirsty's arm and they raced into the hall. For once, they weren't terribly late and began the warm-up at the same time as everyone else. Afterwards, they split into smaller groups to practise their skills. Lizzie and Kirsty were shooting from the penalty spot with four of the other girls.

'How was PE today?' Kirsty asked while they were waiting to take their turn against the keeper.

Lizzie couldn't help but smile at the memory. 'Good, thank you. Well, much better than last week, at least.'

'How so?' Kirsty asked, focusing her attention on Lizzie while the others took their turns.

'It helped that Noah wasn't a surprise this time. It meant I was prepared to get involved a bit more, and I got to actually work with the children, which was fun.' Lizzie rolled a football around on the floor idly with the ball of her foot.

'Lizzie, you know that I'm not asking about the teaching side of things. Did you speak to him?' Kirsty asked, a hint of excitement in her tone.

'A little. We drew in a climbing challenge,' Lizzie said, which of course was the most important thing to have come out of the lesson as far as she was concerned.

'Is the challenge a weekly thing now?' Kirsty rolled her eyes.

'I don't know. It shouldn't be really. I felt bad about it taking time away from the children.' She thought back to Sophie's arrival at the back of the hall and cringed. 'But I did better this week than last week . . .'

'Which, of course, is the key thing.' Kirsty laughed and shook her head before stepping forward to take her shot from the penalty spot. She aimed slightly left of the centre of the goal and hit the top post. 'Ugh,' she groaned.

Lizzie stepped up and took her turn, sending the ball one way and the goalkeeper the other. She turned, arms in the air. Victorious.

'He seems lovelier than you make him out to be, certainly by how he came across at the pub yesterday,' continued Kirsty, as they waited in line again for their next turn.

'That was out of character,' Lizzie said quickly. 'He's not normally like that. At least, I've never seen that side of him. Not since—'

'But he drives his nan to see her friends. That's lovely.'

'Kirsty.' Lizzie's tone warned her sister to move away from her line of questioning. 'Do you want to date him? You kinda sound like you do,' she joked, her hands on her hips.

'No. I just . . .' Kirsty flushed, which wasn't like her. 'It's just, he was doing something really lovely yesterday and you talk so negatively about him. Maybe he deserves a bit of slack?' She left the statement hanging as she went to take another shot at goal, just getting it past the keeper this time.

Was Kirsty right? Lizzie had spent so long hating Noah. Even during the years she'd not seen him. Even after all this time, he infuriated her with his competitive nature and the fact he seemed to be better than her at everything. Except scrambling over the climbing frame, of course. And Capture the Flag.

Lizzie wondered for a moment if it was true that if you were mean to someone, you liked them. She had assumed that was just a rumour about teenagers' conduct in school playgrounds – an old wives' tale. But perhaps it had been true for Lizzie and Noah during sixth form. Their friendly rivalry had blossomed into something more. But surely they had grown out of that sort of behaviour by now? Yes. Lizzie was certain that her negative feelings towards Noah were genuine. He'd hurt her in the past and she was holding a perfectly grown-up grudge.

Oh dear. Maybe Kirsty was right. Lizzie was always unkind to Noah, but he seemed different to the ogre she'd painted him out to be in her own memory. Was she being fair? But also, why did Kirsty care so much?

She stepped forward and smashed the ball into the back of the net without a moment's thought.

'Hit a nerve, did I?' Kirsty asked somewhat unkindly as Lizzie sloped back to the line. Kirsty raised an eyebrow in expectation of a response.

'I don't know,' came Lizzie's truthful answer. 'I think maybe I'm just confused because my past is suddenly muddying up my present. Perhaps I'm treating him unfairly, like he's still the Noah of old. Maybe he deserves better.'

'Do you still have feelings for him?'

Lizzie had expected Kirsty to move on but she continued with her inquisition. The question seemed to come from nowhere. They didn't talk about relationships. Lizzie never had anything interesting to say about her non-existent love life and they mostly stayed away from discussing Steve.

Kirsty was looking straight at her; Lizzie kept her eyes focused on the goal as the other girls from the team took their penalty shots.

'Definitely not,' Lizzie said, dribbling the ball to the back of the line to put some distance between herself and her sister. It felt like they'd got a little too close just then.

But even as she said it, Lizzie knew it wasn't true. Noah did something to her. He always had done. And it seemed he could still make her weak at the knees even ten years later. She would need to do something about that and shut it down fast. Her teacher training was important and she couldn't afford to let Noah get in the way of her doing a good job.

Coach Zoe blew the whistle and Lizzie and Kirsty ran over to the other side of the hall with the rest of the girls.

'Right. Good practice tonight, ladies,' Zoe said.

A few members of the team clapped, and one girl whooped. Lizzie hadn't even listened properly to what Coach Zoe had said; she just stared at the back of the head of the girl in front, lost in uncertain thoughts about Noah.

'I've picked my squad for the final. Here.' She handed out the fixtures sheet, which detailed who would play in the game.

Lizzie absent-mindedly took one and passed them on. It was only when Kirsty laid a hand on her shoulder and congratulated her, that she realised she'd made the team.

'Well done, sis,' Kirsty said.

A couple of the other girls congratulated her, too.

Lizzie looked down at the sheet of paper she held in a slightly trembling hand. She'd done it. She'd made the cut. She'd be playing in the final. She should have felt happy, elated even. This was huge and the culmination of years' worth of hard work. But Kirsty's comments about Noah had niggled at her and it was a feeling she now couldn't shake.

She turned around. 'Thanks,' she said weakly, as the group dissipated, a few more of the girls congratulating Lizzie as they left the building.

Kirsty put a supportive hand on her arm and Lizzie noticed a dark mark on her wrist. Lizzie held Kirsty's arm there for a second to get a better look before her sister pulled it quickly away, rolling her sleeve down at the same time.

'What was that?' Lizzie pulled Kirsty's arm back towards her and pushed her sleeve back up, despite her resistance.

Kirsty's forearm was circled with a band of blue.

'What happened?' Lizzie asked, letting go of Kirsty's arm. Her eyes were already glazed with tears at the realisation of what was happening in Kirsty's relationship.

Kirsty let her arm drop lifelessly to her side.

Lizzie felt sick, her heart suddenly beating out of kilter. 'What did he do to you?' She spoke through gritted teeth, fiercely protective of her sister.

Kirsty shook her head. 'Nothing. It's not what you think,' she said, her voice betraying her with uncertainty. 'One of the boys got a bit rough and tumble when we were playing yesterday. I'm fine. Really.'

'It looks awful, Kirs. Really painful.' Lizzie couldn't take her eyes away from the bruise, despite Kirsty's sleeve now covering it up again.

Kirsty shook her head. 'It's fine, really. Just fun and games.'

Never had anyone in the history of the world said such a sentence in such a melancholy tone. Kirsty's face was suddenly pale and Lizzie was sure hers matched as her blood ran cold at the scenarios running through her head.

'As long as you're sure,' Lizzie said, giving Kirsty the opportunity to share the truth that she feared. She didn't want to push her and knew that Kirsty was never forthcoming if forced.

There were still several players milling about in the hall. Kirsty looked around and took a step to one side before stepping back again. There was nowhere to run to or hide.

'Yep.' She nodded. Far too vigorously. 'I'm sure.'

They collected their things and afterwards, walked out to the car park in silence, Lizzie chewing on her lip as she thought about her sister, the cup final and Noah in an endless cycle of worry.

'Are you all right?' Kirsty asked as they reached the car park.

'Fine,' said Lizzie, coming back to reality. 'You?'

'I know that means you're not fine,' Kirsty said, calling her out immediately and ignoring her question.

'I am, really. It's just been a long day. Tom will have wine waiting for me at home, so I'll have a glass and then an early night.'

She spoke like a machine when her mind was really racing over what she had seen on Kirsty's arm. Why wasn't she telling her the truth? And now, somehow, Kirsty seemed to be worried about Lizzie. A competitive ex-boyfriend was nothing compared to the hundred hideous possibilities that were playing out in Lizzie's mind.

Kirsty said, 'As long as you're sure. I didn't mean to . . .'

'You didn't.' Lizzie put a friendly hand on her arm, more concerned about her sister than her feelings for Noah. 'Are you OK?'

'You made the team,' Kirsty said excitedly, ignoring Lizzie's question again and overcompensating with her enthusiasm for Lizzie's success.

'I know. I'm pleased, really I am,' Lizzie said, a sadness creeping in at the thought that maybe both of them were holding back truths from each other. It was upsetting to think that after all this time, they weren't able to be honest about their true feelings with each other.

Lizzie unlocked the car and threw her stuff into the passenger seat, defeated. 'See you next week.'

Kirsty pulled her in for a hug. 'See you next week, sis. I'll text you.'

Lizzie nodded and got into the car. She suddenly felt horrendously low. School had been great; she'd made herself look pretty good during the PE lesson in front of Noah; she'd planned her first lesson with Sophie; she'd even made the football team for the cup final, for crying out loud.

And yet some of the things Kirsty had said about Noah had really shaken her and, on top of that, she was worried about her sister too. You didn't get bruises that looked like fingerprints from rough and tumble with toddlers. She sat for a moment before turning on the ignition and driving home, hoping that Tom had dinner, wine and a sympathetic ear ready for when she walked through the door.

Chapter Ten

Thursday lunchtime disappeared while Lizzie put the finishing touches to her lesson plan for literacy on Friday. She had the office to herself, the radio blaring and she was enjoying a sandwich while she worked. It was fairly straightforward in terms of what she was actually going to do, but the lesson plan paperwork required things like identifying teaching standards and fine-tuning lesson objectives. Some of it she got, but some of it seemed like petty bureaucracy; Lizzie didn't really understand how it was helping her to become a better teacher. But with beginner's motivation on her side and the sun's light cascading in through the window, Lizzie was happy to do it.

'How are you getting on?' Tom asked, poking his head around the door and coming in with a cup of tea. 'Here you go.' He popped it down on the desk.

'Thanks.' Lizzie didn't take her eyes off the laptop. She finished typing her sentence with a flourish and looked up. 'It's going well,' she said, 'although I'm pretty sure this is going to be the most planned lesson there has ever been in the history of planned lessons.' She scrolled up and down the page for her twenty-minute session to demonstrate her point.

'You'll be great. You've got nothing to worry about.'

'I know.' Lizzie didn't realise she'd come across as though she was worrying about the lesson. In fact, she thought she was feeling fairly confident about the whole thing. Wasn't she?

'I've never been brave enough to go beyond the teaching assistant side of things,' Tom said, sitting down next to her.

'What do you mean, brave enough?' She took a sip of her tea.

Tom had done his trick of adding cooler water to it so that it was immediately drinkable.

'You know. The lesson bit's the easy bit. It's the standing up to speak in front of lots of people, even if they are children. And dealing with the behaviour. I've seen it. It's only really easy once you've been somewhere for a long time and established a bit of a reputation. Until then, it's like teaching zoo animals.'

Lizzie swallowed. 'Is that true?' She frowned.

Tom nodded.

'Do you think they're going to be mean to me?'

A flash of something crossed Tom's face and he immediately backtracked. 'Of course not. They love you,' he added, overcompensating with his enthusiasm.

'But you said—'

'I didn't mean . . . I just meant *I* wouldn't have the guts to teach. *You*, Lizzie, are going to make an excellent teacher. I just know it.' He stood up and kissed the top of her head. 'You'll be awesome. You've got this.'

Having unintentionally planted the seed of doubt, Tom picked up an unopened tub of glue sticks and left the office calling, 'Bye!'

'Um, thanks!' Lizzie called after him, her voice thick with sarcasm.

Lizzie hadn't even considered that the children might not do everything she asked them to. They always did everything Sophie told them to. But then, like Tom said, she'd been here for a long time and had spent the year so far whipping them into shape.

She looked at her beautiful, colour-coded lesson plan. Did any of it even matter if the children weren't on your side? How was she going to get them to listen and follow her instructions? What if they just chose not to? She made a silent plea to her mum, asking her to help her – or at least use whatever heavenly power she might have to make the children behave.

Suddenly, Lizzie felt very sick. She put down her cup of tea and threw her sandwich in the bin, printing out what she'd done regardless. Sophie wanted to have a look at the plan before the lesson took place. At least Lizzie could get that part right.

That afternoon, the lesson was all about Greece and the children were drawing maps on paper that they'd stained last week with tea bags to make them look old and scroll-like.

'Does anyone else need a black pen?' Lizzie asked as she went to get one for Benjamin. Nigel and Sammy said yes and Audrey put her hand up, too. Lizzie went over and gathered some from the pot on the windowsill.

'Here you go.' She placed them in the middle of the table. The children reached for them and each went over their pencil drawing of ancient Greece. Nigel finished quickly and began cutting into the edge of the paper to make it look even more historic.

'Have you ever been to Greece, Miss?' Audrey asked.

Lizzie nodded. 'Yes, actually.' She cast her mind back to the holiday she and her friends had taken to celebrate the end of Year

Twelve. Noah had been there. That's when they'd realised there was more to their friendship; or at least, it was when Lizzie had realised there were feelings there. It occurred to her that she'd never really asked Noah when his feelings for her had begun.

'Careful, Nigel,' Lizzie said, as his cutting became ever more flamboyant, and with that, dangerous.

'What was it like?' Audrey asked, her tongue poking out while she concentrated on drawing her map.

'Well, it was very warm when we were there. There were also lots of historical buildings to see,' she said – not that they'd seen many of them, but she could hardly tell a ten-year-old that Greece was great for sunbathing and clubbing.

'Nigel,' she said again, sterner this time as the scissors went a hair too close to Benjamin's earlobe.

'I think I'd like to go to Greece,' Audrey said, choosing a different colour to fill in the land mass on her map. 'But not nowadays Greece. I'd like to go to ancient Greece,' she said excitedly.

'You can't do that, stupid,' Nigel said unkindly.

'Nigel,' Lizzie said again.

Why was he being so difficult this afternoon?

'What would you do if you went to ancient Greece, Audrey?'

Audrey thought for a moment, looking around the room for inspiration. 'I think I'd go to a bear fight, but before the fight actually started, so that I could sneak in and set the bears free!'

Sophie sidled over to the table looking a little pale. 'I just need to pop out a minute,' she said. 'Are you OK to hold the fort here? I'll be two minutes, I promise.'

'Of course,' Lizzie said. Sophie left the classroom quickly, but before Lizzie had time to worry any more about her, there was a muffled scream from across the table.

'Arrrgh!'

Nigel flung the scissors he had been playing with to the ground as blood dripped from his mouth. From what Lizzie could see through the chaos, he'd managed to use the scissors to cut his lip. She jumped up to help to him, paper and pens flying everywhere.

'Are you OK?' she asked. She brushed his unruly hair back off his face and tried to see the wound, but the blood gushing from it prevented her from seeing it properly.

'What's going on?' Sophie said, rushing back into the room a moment later and over to Nigel.

'Nigel was using the scissors to cut into his map and he's somehow cut his lip,' Lizzie explained, concerned for Nigel, but also annoyed with him for not listening to her in the first place. Was this what happened when children misbehaved? Lizzie swallowed as Sophie stepped in and took control, an unwelcome feeling of guilt welling up in the pit of her stomach.

'Call Miss Davies,' Sophie said, instructing traumatised children out of the way. 'We'll need the big first aid kit.'

Lizzie ran to the front of the classroom and radioed Miss Davies, who responded instantly.

'Is everything OK?' she asked through the crackly speaker.

Lizzie, breathless from the adrenaline and racing across the classroom, said, 'Yes. Miss Lawson has asked if you can bring the big first aid kit over please.'

'Are you in Miss Lawson's room?'

'Mm-hmm.' Lizzie nodded even though Miss Davies couldn't see her, but she was afraid of what she might say if she spoke. Her throat grew tight as mild panic set in. Could she be told off for this? Or worse – lose her training place? She bit her bottom lip, worried about how Nigel was and about how much trouble she might be in for letting a child get injured.

'I'll be there now.' The radio clicked as the line was switched off from Miss Davies's end.

Why, of all the staff members, did Miss Davies have to be in charge of the big first aid kit? She would no doubt see Lizzie's ineptitude and fire her on the spot. This was all Tom's fault. He'd got Lizzie worrying, and she'd taken her eye off the ball.

On the other side of the classroom, Sophie was doing her best to attend to Nigel while white-faced children watched on in horror.

'Come on, everyone,' Lizzie said, seeing that having a huge audience was helping no one. 'Let's carry on with our story.'

Slowly, one by one, the children followed Lizzie over to the reading corner and settled down on the floor, only occasionally looking over towards Nigel, whom Sophie had now manoeuvred into the corner, where the children could hardly see him.

Lizzie picked up their class reader – *The Iron Giant* – and began to read, just as Miss Davies arrived to sort out Nigel. Lizzie's voice was shaky to begin with, threatening to crack with the emotion the ordeal had brought to the surface, but after a minute or so, she relaxed and the children stared up at her from the carpet with wide, engaged eyes. A few moments later and Nigel was removed from the room. Sophie gestured that she'd be two minutes and for Lizzie to read on.

Luckily, the children settled quickly and listened quietly. As the clock crept up to 3 p.m., with no sign of Sophie's return, Lizzie decided they'd better tidy up the classroom.

'Right, everyone,' she said, closing the book to a collective groan. 'We need to tidy up our mess from before as it's nearly home time, so can you please sort out your desks and stand quietly behind them once you've finished? Off you go.'

The children stood up dutifully and went about their task,

while Lizzie collected up the school's equipment. By the time Sophie reappeared at ten past three, the children were tidied up, packed away and ready to leave.

'Thanks,' Sophie said as they watched the children go to be picked up by their parents.

'No problem. It was kind of my fault it happened in the first place,' Lizzie murmured.

'It wasn't, Lizzie. Accidents happen. I heard you ask Nigel to stop playing with the scissors several times. There's only so much we can do. Besides, look at how you handled it. You made sure the rest of the class were calm and occupied, so me and Miss Davies could sort out Nigel.'

Guilt seemed so close to the surface of Lizzie's emotions that it often reared its head without warning – sometimes it was warranted, like the fire; other times it wasn't, and Lizzie consoled herself that perhaps today was one of those days.

Relenting slightly, but still a little guilt-ridden, Lizzie smiled, just a little. 'How is he?'

'Embarrassed and in pain. But he'll survive.'

'I'm sorry,' Lizzie said again.

'Don't be, it's fine.' She gave Lizzie's arm a friendly squeeze.

'And how are you? You didn't look so good earlier,' Lizzie said, hoping she wasn't overstepping the mark.

Sophie smiled. 'I'm fine. It had just got a little warm in here and I felt a little dizzy. All good.'

Lizzie was left alone as Sophie walked across the playground to speak with Nigel's mum. She felt awful. She knew it hadn't really been her fault, but it had sort of been on her watch. If she couldn't keep four children on a table under control, how was she ever going to look after an entire class full of them? Tomorrow's lesson was looming, and Lizzie was starting to panic.

It didn't help that, before she went home, she had another meeting planned with Noah to sort out the next steps for sports day. What she really wanted to do was have a proper evening in the flat and go over her plans for the next day.

'How was your day?' Noah asked as Lizzie entered the office and sat down.

'Up and down,' she said honestly.

'I heard about Nigel,' he said, pulling a comic face of pain.

'How did you . . . ?'

'News travels fast around here.' He smiled.

'Anyway, he's fine now. Thank goodness. Let's just focus on sports day.'

Noah looked as though he was going to say something further, but decided against it and went along with Lizzie's subject change.

'You seem a little flustered. Are you OK?' he asked.

'I'm fine,' she said, rifling through her folder of bits.

'I know you, Lizzie Morris. Fine means you're not fine,' he said, turning his body to face her.

The nostalgia of his comment sent an odd wave of warmth through her body. They used to fight about Lizzie refusing to talk about how she was feeling all the time. Lizzie being 'OK' had been a running joke and eventually one of the things that had turned a little sour towards the end of their relationship.

Why did everybody want to assess how 'fine' Lizzie was except for Lizzie? Kirsty had said the same thing at football practice the other day.

'It's just been a long day.'

She didn't really want to share anything with Noah. But after the afternoon she'd had, she couldn't help it. She needed to offload.

'There was the Nigel thing. And I've been trying to plan my first bit of teaching for tomorrow.'

'That's exciting,' he said.

It really wasn't. It was terrifying.

'Is it?' asked Lizzie. 'I'm feeling pretty nervous about it.' She played with a bit of flaky paint on the edge of the desk.

'There's nothing to worry about. They're just a group of ten-year-olds,' he said, rather unhelpfully.

It was exactly what she'd come to expect from him – and why she'd not wanted to tell him in the first place.

'I know,' she said, irritated that Noah was just palming it off as nothing to worry about. It was important to Lizzie. It had been important to her parents. She wanted it to go well.

'Have you brought the amended schedule for sports day with you?' he asked, changing the subject without a second thought.

God, he was maddening.

Lizzie nodded. She'd been working on it all week, along with her lesson planning, and she was pretty pleased with the result.

'Here you go.' She passed it to him, admittedly a little huffy. It flew off the edge of the table and floated to the floor.

Noah bent down to retrieve it and gave Lizzie a look she couldn't place before smoothing it out on the table. With the schedule colour-coded and broken down into event and year group, Lizzie knew she hadn't disappointed.

Noah read it thoughtfully, running a hand through his hair. Lizzie took the opportunity to look at him more closely. He was exactly as she remembered him from all those years ago. His broad muscular shoulders were slightly larger than before, filling out his football top, but it was his hair that she wanted to reach out and touch. It was long enough to have a mind of its own and she had loved the way it felt when she ran her fingers

118

through it, back when she was allowed to do such things. She was close enough to catch his aftershave again, the spicy, woody scent causing the very pit of her stomach to feel odd. Stop it, Lizzie. Noah Hatton is a rude, arrogant cheat, who doesn't know how to take anything seriously. You have to get over this.

Noah sat up straight, startling Lizzie, who had disappeared somewhere into the past.

'Are you OK?' he asked.

'Fine. I'm fine.' She tried to act as though she'd merely been sitting waiting for Noah to appraise her work, but knew her cheeks would have flushed the instant he looked up at her.

Noah raised an eyebrow, but didn't seem to notice anything out of the ordinary; he certainly didn't pursue it, at least. Lizzie's stomach lurched with lust and the adrenaline that came with having been caught thinking about him in all sorts of ways she shouldn't. She tried to focus on his infuriating qualities. She was sure he'd demonstrate at least one of them in the immediate future – that would help.

'This is great. I like how it's broken down. It's lovely that on the whole, competitors will also get the opportunity to watch most of the events, and the parent and teacher event at the end is an awesome idea. I hope you'll be getting involved,' he said, his voice laced with challenge.

'Try and stop me,' Lizzie said, not feeling quite as competitive as her voice sounded.

Noah smiled at her, holding her gaze for that moment too long again. Why did he always have to do that? His dark eyes were beautiful, almost black. They absorbed everything around them, including Lizzie. She tried to remember that she was finding him annoying.

Noah cleared his throat and pulled out his notebook. 'So let's make a list of what we need to do next.'

'Good idea.'

'So, the next couple of weeks will mostly be about admin, which is dull, but important. We need to write a list of all the things we need to organise or book, and all the people we need to contact so that they know about sports day going ahead.'

'All right. Shall I start?' Lizzie asked, wanting to show Noah that she could do it. Why his approval was so important, she didn't know. She only knew that it was. She guessed he'd be reporting back to Sophie and Miss Davies, and she wanted that report to be good. She wrote down all the things she thought they would need to do in terms of admin and contact.

Noah scooted round so that he could see what she was writing. His closeness didn't go unnoticed by Lizzie, who suddenly couldn't remember half of the things she had planned to write down.

'Don't forget to add emailing Sean so that he can put it all on social media. It's good to let the community know what we're up to,' Noah said, leaning his face in his hands, elbows on the desk.

Lizzie added social media to the list.

'And the sports field at the secondary school is already booked, right?'

'Yes,' said Noah. 'I already did that when we got the date agreed. I didn't want to plan lots of stuff to be told we couldn't go ahead there with the date.'

'Good point.'

'It's nothing. I normally book the field well in advance.' He sat back in his seat.

'OK. Have I missed anything?' Lizzie asked, putting the lid back on her pen. 'I've added our initials next to each thing so that we've each got certain jobs to do. I hope that's OK?'

'That's great.' Noah reached for the paper and read through

Lizzie's list. 'Perfect. Let me make a copy.' He walked over to the photocopier.

Lizzie put away her things. She was looking forward to getting home and relaxing tonight. She knew she wouldn't sleep with her first lesson tomorrow morning. Besides, she didn't particularly want to spend much more time in Noah's company. Things had felt strange that afternoon and she wanted the safety of being far away from him.

'Are you coming to the fundraiser tomorrow night?' Noah asked, pressing buttons on the machine to get it to copy.

Lizzie coughed. The question surprised her. Was he asking her to go? No, she thought. Be sensible. He's just making small talk. Was she going to the fundraiser tomorrow? He hadn't mentioned them going together or that he was even going himself . . . She should probably answer him before the silence went on for too much longer, she thought.

'I think Tom and I were planning on coming over for a bit,' she said, aiming for nonchalant, but finding herself having left a little too much of a pause between Noah's question and her answer.

'Oh,' said Noah.

Lizzie realised that she'd inadvertently mentioned Tom's name again. When she'd first done it last week, she'd enjoyed confusing him and leading him on. But now, somehow, things had changed. She didn't want Noah to think that she was with Tom. Or did she? The truth was, she was muddled, and she didn't really know herself any more.

'Will you be there?' she asked. She couldn't help herself.

'I'll be there,' he said, bringing the copies back over to the table and passing one to Lizzie. 'It'd be good to get a drink and catch up properly, you know.' He ran a hand through his hair.

For a moment, Lizzie thought he might look a little nervous. 'Yeah, it would.'

One of their moments hovered again, just for that beat too long. Something sparked between them. The fire of what they'd had previously wasn't just ash any more; there were embers and Lizzie didn't know what to do with that. Her mouth was suddenly dry and her body prickled all over. Her butterflies hopped as the hot ash burnt their feet.

'So, do you know what you're doing?' Noah asked, changing the subject and waving the sports day list. Thank God – otherwise Lizzie might have thought he was talking about something else.

'I think so. I guess I'll just make a start and give you a shout if I get lost on the way?'

'Sounds like a plan,' Noah said, suddenly very busy with paperwork and his rucksack.

'Great.' She didn't have the words any more, just an acute awareness of something shifting between them.

'We'll need to catch up again to see how things are going, but we don't need to worry too much now for a week or so,' Noah said.

Lizzie felt disappointed that this would be their last meeting at school for a while. At least they'd got a half-date planned for the fundraiser, hadn't they?

Noah said, 'If you can just start working through the list and then when we meet next, it'll just be to check through that we've done everything and to get the equipment together.'

Lizzie nodded. She liked it when he went all businesslike and efficient. It was safer that way.

'I'll see you tomorrow then,' she said, picking up her bag and heading to the door.

Noah stayed seated. 'See you tomorrow.' He smiled, looking

directly at her with those dark eyes.

Leaving the room, Lizzie went down the corridor to collect Tom for the walk home. She didn't really know what had just happened. All she knew was that something had changed between them. Sure, Noah still infuriated her every time she saw him. But she had seen something of the old Noah there today and her butterflies had definitely echoed that. She hoped it was just nostalgic lust and nothing more. She could sweep lust away under the carpet. If it was something more, that would be harder to deal with; and that was before she even had time to think about what was going on in Noah's head.

Now wasn't the time for all this silliness. She wasn't seventeen any more, and neither was he. She didn't have time to play silly games or deal with crushes. She was a teacher now, teaching her first lesson in the morning. She had a new house to find. She had a football match to play and win. Noah would have to wait – or better still, disappear. But somehow, Lizzie knew he wouldn't. He was under her skin now and there he would loiter until Lizzie worked out what to do about him.

Chapter Eleven

Through fear and confusion, Lizzie had shared a bottle of wine with Tom the previous night. And although she hadn't got blind drunk and wasn't waking up with a hangover, her body was still aware that she'd been drinking.

Noah was playing on her mind, like a fuzzy halo of worry floating around her genuine concern: her very first lesson. Why had she agreed to do it on a Friday, towards the end of term, when the children would be excitable? Lizzie rolled over and hid her head under the duvet. She just hoped that it wasn't windy out there too. She'd discovered quickly that inclement weather always riled the children.

'It's teaching day!' Tom sing-songed as he popped his head around the edge of the door. 'Tea and toast for the teacher,' he said, coming in and putting it on Lizzie's bedside table.

'Thanks,' Lizzie groaned, partially concealed by the duvet cover she wished she could take with her and hide behind all day.

'You don't look like someone excited about teaching their first lesson.' Tom furrowed his eyebrows in concern.

'No, Tom. I'm not,' Lizzie agreed, shuffling up a little more so that she could see Tom properly. 'This is the face of someone who is terrified to do just that.'

'You're going to be great. Come on,' he said, giving the duvet a playful push. 'Get up. Get showered. I'll pick you out a perfect first lesson outfit.'

'OK, OK.' Lizzie relented and walked over to the bathroom, the duvet still wrapped around her.

The journey to school was just what Lizzie needed. With every step, she grew in confidence, and Noah fizzled away into a minor shadow that occasionally floated in and out of her consciousness. The trees and flowers were out in full bloom. The day felt happy and Lizzie wouldn't have been surprised if the flowers had begun to sing like they were in a Disney film. She smiled.

Tom had picked out a pencil skirt and floaty top for her to wear that day. When she'd first come out of the bedroom in the outfit, he'd tutted, spun her around and instructed her to go back, tuck in the blouse and finish it with a belt. Paired with some kitten heels, she looked smart and professional.

She knew that part of the reason behind Tom's outfit choice was that he wanted to help her feel confident and capable, and it was doing just that. The fact that the day was so warm she could go without a coat or a cardigan improved her mood even further. It was summer, Lizzie was going to teach, and she was going to smash it. She hoped.

'You've got this,' Tom whispered as they said goodbye at the corridor junction.

Lizzie squeezed his hand. 'Thanks.'

She'd made it to the classroom even before Sophie, which was unheard of. Sophie was always at school in the early hours of the morning, setting up for lessons. Either she was poorly or stuck in traffic, or perhaps she genuinely trusted Lizzie not to mess this up? Lizzie let herself believe it for a second. But surely not.

She went about writing the date on the board and setting out the children's books, emptying and refilling each of the story bags, even though she'd done it twice the previous evening sat on the living room floor. Then she sat down, logged into the computer and set up the register.

'Wow,' Sophie said, coming into the room behind her.

Lizzie spun around on the desk chair. 'Morning, Sophie,' she said brightly, her vague hangover and general terror having made themselves scarce for the time being – probably something to do with the adrenaline that was rushing through her rather than them actually disappearing. Lizzie wasn't that lucky.

'Morning, Lizzie. You look super-ready to teach.' Sophie looked around the room at all of Lizzie's preparation with an expression of admiration on her face.

'On the surface, yes,' Lizzie said. 'I thought that if the room looked the part, then I might be able to trick the children into thinking the same thing!'

Sophie laughed. 'You're definitely ready. You're going to be excellent.'

'I hope so,' Lizzie said, her fingers crossed.

'Shall we let them in?'

Lizzie winced. 'OK.'

At the door, the children said good morning as always and came into the classroom, sitting in their allocated seats. The whole thing went by in a bit of a blur for Lizzie, who was running lines in her head. She'd pretty much written a script for herself for the whole lesson. There was no way this was how the professionals did it. It would be like writing and learning an entire play every day – totally impractical and definitely not sustainable. But it was her first go, so Lizzie cut herself some slack. If anything went wrong, she could turn to her script and everything would be OK.

'So today, Year Six, Miss Morris is going to be taking part of your literacy lesson.' Sophie stood at the front of the class to start with and introduced Lizzie as the teacher. 'You guys are really lucky and I know Miss Morris is looking forward to teaching you, so let's make sure you show her what you can do. Don't let me down,' she said pointedly, looking directly at Nigel, before walking over to where Lizzie had been observing from for the past few days – except somehow, she'd managed to locate a full-sized chair.

Sophie sat down and Lizzie took centre stage, their roles suddenly reversed. She felt like there was a spotlight on her. Her audience, thirty ten- and eleven-year-olds' faces, looked up at her expectantly.

'Thank you, Miss Lawson.' Lizzie looked around at the class.

For a moment, she knew what she wanted to say, but for some reason, it didn't want to come out. The pause went on longer than it should have done, and she hoped the children were none the wiser. Sophie would have clocked her anxiety – Lizzie was sure of it. A child coughed and it echoed out into the silence, prompting Lizzie to start talking.

'So today, we're going to be planning some stories.'

There was a general excited whisper around the room, as there usually was when Sophie announced what the lesson that day was going to cover.

'Now I know that for some of you, there will already be ideas zipping around your heads, but for others, writing a story probably sounds a bit scary. But don't worry. I've brought along something that will help you get started. Everybody come over and sit on the carpet,' she said and breathed a sigh of relief when they all dutifully stood up and gathered around her, sitting cross-legged on the floor.

Lizzie pulled the velvet story bags out from underneath the table – where she'd hidden them to ensure a big reveal – to a few gasps and oohs. It was exactly what she had been hoping for.

'These are my magic story bags. I'm going to be planning a story as well today, so I'm going to need your help. Shall we do one together?'

Several of the children nodded and Lizzie relaxed, seeing that all of them at least looked like they were engaged and listening.

'OK, well, let's see where our story is going to be set. Toby, can you pick something out of the bag?'

Toby leant forward and rummaged in the sack for an object. He was clearly having a good feel of them all before he picked out a flag on a cocktail stick.

'And what flag is that, Toby?' Lizzie asked.

'Greece,' he said.

Lizzie knew he was certain because ancient Greece was their topic that term, and they'd learnt a little bit about modern-day Greece too in their geography lessons.

'Excellent,' Lizzie said, only momentarily flustered by the mention of Greece again. Last time she'd talked about it in the classroom she'd tried to push thoughts of her and Noah getting together on a Greek island holiday out of her head. She didn't need Noah to pop into her thoughts at this exact moment. The lesson was too important to her. She took a deep breath and pushed the image in her mind away.

'Now,' she began, picking up a second bag.

Instantly, thirty hands shot up, wanting to pick something from the bag.

'This bag will give us a character or characters. Lyndsey, would you like to pick something?'

Lyndsey was sitting further back, so stepped carefully between the other children sitting on the floor in front of her and reached into the bag. She didn't have a feel of all the objects like Toby had. She simply picked whatever she came into contact with first, spontaneous. Lizzie liked her style.

Pulling her hand out of the bag, Lyndsey looked down at the object. It was a little model of Mickey and Minnie Mouse.

'Wonderful choice,' Lizzie said. 'Now, we're not going to have Mickey and Minnie in the story themselves, but what could they represent? Do they give us any ideas about the types of characters we could use?'

'Mice?' said a little voice from the centre of the carpet.

'Yes,' Lizzie said. 'Mice would be an interesting idea.'

'What about best friends?' Benjamin asked.

'I think they are best friends, so we could have mice characters, or humans who are best friends, OK.'

'Don't they fall in love?' Audrey asked quietly.

Lizzie was thrown for a moment at the mention of the L-word. Why were the story bags teasing her? Greece? Love? She just hoped the object in the final bag wouldn't tease her further. Dammit, she needed to concentrate.

'Maybe, Audrey,' she said, recovering. 'They can fall in love in your story if you'd like them to. Now the last bag.'

She moved on quickly. She wasn't going to let Noah ruin this. It was going too well. She picked the bag up off the floor and the sea of hands rose again.

'This bag is a bag full of objects. The object you choose must appear somewhere in your story. Nigel, would you like to choose one?'

Nigel had been quiet, mostly because his lip was swollen and bruised and talking was painful. Lizzie still felt awful about it, but she guessed the silver lining was that he couldn't talk over her. She wondered how he might behave if his mischievousness hadn't been impaired, and then decided that it was probably best if she just enjoyed it while it lasted.

Nigel nodded and leant over another child to rummage about in the bag. He pulled out a small footballing trophy. Phew. At least this would divert the story away from anything that might have happened in real life.

'Excellent. Thank you, Nigel,' Lizzie said, placing all three objects on the table by the whiteboard. 'These are our three ideas. They're only ideas, so you can interpret them however you want to. Greece, for example, could be modern-day Greece; it could be ancient Greece; it could be a journey to Greece; maybe your character is Greek. It's up to you.'

'I'm going to give you this planning sheet,' she said, holding up her example. 'You'll need to write the three objects in this space here and then plan your story using the arc here as a guide. There are sections to fill in for each part of the story.' Lizzie ran her finger along the arc on the page. She looked around to try and gauge their understanding. 'Josh, what must you do first?'

Josh looked surprised, but Lizzie was pleased when he said, 'We have to write down those objects in the boxes at the top.'

'Fab. And Freddie. Where do you need to plan your story?'

'On the arc on the sheet,' he said, pointing towards Lizzie's example.

'Fantastic. So if you've already got ideas, you can use our

three objects. If you're struggling, or you want something a bit different, I'll come round with the story bags. Just put your hand up if you need any extra help and me or Miss Lawson will come around and answer your questions. Back to your tables, folks.'

The class stood up in unison and wandered back to their seats. Through the sea of movement and excited chatter, Lizzie could see Sophie's face. Lizzie pulled an expression that asked silently if that had been OK. Sophie smiled and nodded, and Lizzie exhaled a breath she hadn't realised she'd been holding.

At break time, Lizzie hotfooted it to the staffroom for a celebratory cup of tea.

'How did it go?' Tom asked, running up to her and squeezing her arm.

The jolt caused Lizzie to pour boiling water onto the work surface. She tutted and realigned the kettle to pour some into her own cup, and then into one for Tom too – before answering, leaving him waiting in suspense.

'Really good,' she said, breaking into a grin she just couldn't keep concealed.

'Yeah?'

'Yeah.' She nodded. 'I'm so pleased.'

'Well, that was the first hurdle. Every lesson after this one will get easier and easier. I'm so proud of you!'

Tom pulled her in for a hug as the door creaked open and Noah walked in.

Lizzie pushed him away, much to Tom's disgust and intrigue. His face said she'd be answering questions later, whether she liked it or not.

'Hi,' Noah said, crossing the staffroom and refilling his water bottle at the sink.

'Hi,' Lizzie said. She looked down at her mug of tea and picked at a chip in the china, then moved to one side as Noah reached over to the biscuit tin. She shuffled awkwardly, her feet getting in the way of one other.

'Sorry,' she said, as their arms brushed. Something jumped between them and Lizzie distracted herself by drinking her tea, too embarrassed to notice Noah's reaction.

Tom watched on, clearly assessing the situation, apparently too preoccupied with the inner workings of his mind to focus on etiquette and say hi himself.

'How did the lesson go?' Noah asked.

He'd remembered. After brushing it off as unimportant yesterday, he'd actually remembered.

'Really well, actually,' Lizzie said, suddenly bashful. She felt her cheeks warming and knew instinctively that they'd be blushing pink.

'I told you it would be fine.'

He winked at her. Then, after eating his biscuit in a couple of bites, he reached for an apple from the counter and threw it up into the air, catching it and leaving the room again as suddenly as he'd entered.

Lizzie watched him go and was only brought back to the moment with Tom's squeaky and incredulous voice demanding to know what had just happened.

'Your guess is as good as mine,' Lizzie said enigmatically.

'Well,' Tom said. 'I'd like to hear your guess, because your loathing of Noah seems to have changed dramatically. I want to know when and I want to know why.' He listed his demands on his fingers.

'You'll have to wait until later.' Lizzie topped up her tea with cold water and gulped down half of it before leaving the room.

She could picture Tom's expression of disbelief and enjoyed tormenting him. He'd get over it. They could catch up properly later that evening at the fundraiser. There would be fewer ears lurking and besides, she felt like she really needed to talk it through and thirty seconds in the staffroom wasn't going to cut it any more. Without her realising, things had gone way past that.

The rest of the day was joyous. Lizzie was riding on a wave of success and she oozed confidence because of how well her lesson had gone. She moved around the classroom, getting to know more of the students better, and they all treated her as though she was an expert, a real-life teacher. They even listened to her when she had to intervene with behaviour issues. Thankfully, her fear of bad behaviour was disappearing fast. She reached for her mum's ring, twisting it around her finger, and smiled to herself, feeling the warmth of satisfaction run through her body. Friday had been a good day.

Chapter Twelve

'I brought celebratory Prosecco!'

Tom opened the fridge and took the bottle out, waving it in the air as part of the big reveal. Lizzie was sitting on the sofa painting her toenails.

'Ooh,' she said excitedly, half clapping her hands while trying not to spill nail varnish anywhere. 'Yum.'

'Shall I pour you a glass?'

'Yes, please.' She went back to focusing on painting her toenails in a bright shade of hot pink.

Tom popped the bottle and filled two glasses, placing one on the coffee table in front of Lizzie. She instantly snatched it up and raised it towards Tom.

'Cheers,' she said.

'Here's to the next super champion teacher.' Tom clinked her glass with his.

Lizzie pushed the towel that was wrapped around her hair back to balance on her head and finished painting her last toenail.

She carefully put the lid back on the nail varnish and pushed it as far away on the coffee table as she could, to avoid the kind of accident Lizzie knew she was likely to cause.

'Don't take too long now, Lizzie. I want to get going. They've got music on all night and there's a band I'd like to catch at eight.'

'OK, OK.' She checked her fingernails were dry by waving them back and forth and giving them a cursory blow, despite having painted them at least twenty minutes ago. 'I'll go and get ready.'

It was a balmy June evening, and it felt later in the summer than it actually was. It had been warm all day, so Lizzie was veering towards wearing a long, floaty skirt and top. Then she could wear her flip-flops and avoid squishing the nail varnish she'd just applied. She realised after having gone through each hanger in her wardrobe twice that she was overthinking things a little bit. It was only now, as she paused to consider her options, that she realised why.

Noah.

He was going to be there later. It would be the first time they'd seen each other outside of a professional school environment for ten years, and the reality was that some of the feelings she'd worked so hard to bury were resurfacing. She didn't know what it meant and didn't really want to think about it. But deep down, she knew, whether or not something happened in the future, she wanted to look good at the fundraiser because a tiny part of her wanted to impress Noah.

She rolled her eyes at her feminist failure and downed her Prosecco, padding through to the kitchen to refill her glass.

'Please tell me you've at least chosen an outfit,' Tom said.

Lizzie looked down at herself. She was still wearing her dressing gown, her towel still balanced on her head.

'Yes, yes,' she said, waving a hand. 'I'll be thirty minutes, tops.'

'I'm timing you.'

Lizzie swanned out of the room and back to her bedroom to get dressed.

After drying and straightening her unruly hair, she slipped into her chosen outfit – a long blue skirt, a white, beachy embroidered top and elegant flip-flops.

'You look great,' Tom said, downing his drink and slipping his own flip-flops on. 'Let's go.'

It was the perfect weather for an outdoor fundraiser like Cranswell Fest. The day had been hot and while the evening had cooled the air slightly, it was still pleasantly warm. The committee had erected a stage in the school field and fairy lights were strung everywhere. They were wrapped around the trees and along the front of the stage. And around the field there were glass jars shining brightly like they were filled with glow-worms.

Some of the PTA were running a hog roast and BBQ next to the bar, and a few local craftspeople had set up stalls around the edge of the field. Noah's sports day fundraising stand was over by the beer tent, which meant it was getting a lot of footfall, and Lizzie hoped they could raise some money for the day. The fundraiser was already busy, with people gathering in groups, sitting on the bales of hay that had been brought in as 'furniture', and there were children running around everywhere.

'Right, food and drink first,' Tom said, getting out his wallet. 'Then, we find a hay bale and we talk about what is going on with you.'

Ordinarily, Lizzie would protest, but she was hungry and the two glasses of Prosecco she'd had before she left were making her feel a little giggly. Plus, she genuinely wanted to talk about Noah with Tom, if only to muddle through her own feelings and try to work out what on earth was going on.

'Fine,' she said. 'I'll get the food, you get the drinks.'

Minutes later, they reconvened on a hay bale near to the stage, with pork baps and apple sauce, and halves of cider. They ate silently for a moment.

'So, spill,' Tom said, wiping apple sauce from the corner of his mouth with a napkin. 'What's going on? You were dead set against Noah last weekend, even though he'd taken his nan out to see her friends.'

Lizzie laughed. 'I know.'

'So what's changed?'

'I didn't realise I still felt anything for him until both you and Kirsty mentioned it. I've spent so long hating him that anything I felt years ago had completely disappeared. Or at least I thought it had.' She took a sip of her cider and then balanced it carefully on the uneven floor again. 'I don't know. I suppose there was always going to be something there. I didn't stop loving him. He cheated on me, remember. We ended because of something he did, not because I wanted it to. Or because I was over him.'

Tom had listened intently. 'I thought I was going to get gossip,' he said, disappointed, 'but there are actual feelings here, aren't there?'

Lizzie nodded. 'I think there might be,' she said, taking another bite of her roll.

'What are you going to do?'

'Nothing. He broke my heart; that hasn't changed. And besides, I've got my teacher training to worry about and that's much more important right now. I can't let a relationship' – she paused and stumbled over the words, quickly correcting herself – 'or odd feelings jeopardise that.'

They sat in a companionable silence for a moment or two, finishing their food. Lizzie screwed up the cardboard tray her roll had come in and offered to take Tom's too, dashing to the bin to dispose of it.

'Anyway. Let's not talk about it any more,' Lizzie said, pushing her hair back from her face and tucking some of it behind her ear. 'It makes me feel funny. Let's talk about Chris instead.'

Tom's cheeks instantly coloured, and he looked down at the ground.

'Thomas,' she said, fake admonishment lacing her voice. 'Tell me more.'

'He's got another place to show us on Monday if you're free?' he said, diverting the conversation for a moment.

'I am.' Lizzie took another swig of her drink.

'Great,' Tom said, suddenly lost for words.

'I've never seen you speechless.' She gave him a playful push. 'What's going on? You really like him, don't you?'

'Nothing's going on, not really,' Tom said, looking anywhere but at Lizzie. 'We've been texting, partly to sort out the house viewing, I suppose. But it just feels like maybe there's something more than that in the messages. It's hard to tell.'

Lizzie smiled. 'That's exciting. I guess we'll see on Monday. We'll have to come up with a secret word or something you can say to get rid of me if things are going well.' She wiggled her eyebrows playfully.

Tom laughed before Noah silenced him by walking up to them both.

'Hi.'

Lizzie looked up. By now the sun was setting and all she could really see was his silhouette, surrounded by fairy lights and the lights from the stage. It was unmistakably him, though. She would recognise him anywhere.

Tom made his lame excuses and absented himself, leaving Noah to take his place on the hay bale.

'Can I get you a drink?' Noah nodded towards Lizzie's empty glass.

Her head said it was probably a bad idea to carry on drinking; she'd be reaching that dangerous point which, if overstepped, could potentially lead to terrible things. On the other hand, Noah was offering to buy her a drink, which meant they would have a conversation for at least as long as it took them both to drink it. She wanted to say yes. Besides, it would give them something to do while they relaxed into the conversation. *For God's sake, Lizzie. It's just a drink. Stop overanalysing it.* She realised she'd not replied for a moment too long and Noah was still waiting for a response.

'Thank you,' Lizzie said eventually. 'I'll come with you.'

They both stood. Lizzie smoothed down her skirt and brushed the tufts of hay off it and onto the floor before they walked side by side over to the beer tent.

Across the field, she spotted Sophie and a couple of her teacher friends. Sophie smiled and gave a little wave. Lizzie smiled back and mouthed, 'Hi.'

She felt Noah glancing to the side, watching her. Finally, as if the brief encounter had given him permission to ask, he said, 'So, you had a good day then?'

'I did.' Lizzie could barely keep the smile from creeping across her face. 'The lesson went really well. I'm so relieved.'

'I'm glad,' he said, appearing to hesitate before adding, 'it's good to see you smile.'

Lizzie felt her cheeks flush. They shared a smile as a member of the bar team moved in front of them and asked for their order.

Noah cleared his throat and seemed to tear his eyes away from hers so as not to miss his opportunity. 'Two pints of cider, please.'

He'd done well to get in there amongst the throng of people who seemed to have forgotten how to queue.

They stood quietly, leaning on the bar as they waited for their drinks. Lizzie struggled to ignore the fact that squashing up between two crowds of people to get served meant their bodies were in contact. Both their shoulders and legs were touching. Neither of them moved; they couldn't have even if they wanted to, but Lizzie knew she didn't want to either. The heat she felt wherever Noah was touching her was intense. Despite her three drinks and counting, her mouth was suddenly dry.

'Here.' Noah passed Lizzie her cider, and she gulped down a good measure to cool herself down before they reversed out of the tent and looked for somewhere to sit.

'Shall we go back over there?' Lizzie asked, pointing out their original hay bale, still free.

'Let's go somewhere where we can talk properly.' He looked around the field for such a place.

Lizzie's heart was racing, and she downed half of her cider before they'd even found a place to sit.

Noah took them over to a bench in a little clearing at the very edge of the field, just before the school grounds petered out into a section of woodland. It was where the children did Forest School on a Friday morning sometimes. Their little pots and pans hung on the boughs of trees, ready to make mud pies or be used as drums.

'It's mad that we've run into each other again after all these years,' Noah said, brushing the bench off for Lizzie to sit down. He always had been a gentleman.

'It was a surprise. You can definitely say that,' Lizzie said, sipping her cider. The edges of her focus were becoming a little hazy. This would definitely need to be her last drink.

'What have you been up to, you know, since university?' He asked the question innocently, but all it did for Lizzie was remind her how things had changed for the worse between them while she was there.

'I stayed on to do a master's and then travelled for a bit. I worked at a library for a while. I didn't really know what to do, to be honest. After the fire . . .'

Lizzie's face grew warm, and she stumbled for the next word.

'I mean, I struggled to know what to do afterwards. But teaching's what Mum and Dad always wanted me to do. I hope they'd be proud.' She knew that the alcohol or perhaps the nervous energy was making her talk without pausing for breath.

'I heard about what happened with the fire,' Noah said. He reached out his hand to touch Lizzie's and then appeared to think better of it, running it over his slight stubble and through his hair instead. 'I'm sorry I wasn't there for you. If I'd known, I would never have—'

'It wasn't your job to be there at that point.' Lizzie struggled to keep the bitterness from her voice. 'I just wish I'd not been so distracted by the break-up at the time.' She waved her hand in the space between them and then, looking down to the ground, added, 'I should have been there. I could have saved them.'

Noah narrowed his eyes and tilted his head. He put a hand on Lizzie's arm. 'You know none of it was your fault, right? Even if you had been there, you couldn't have changed things.'

It wasn't the first time someone had said it to her, but she would never believe it. If she'd not turned her phone off and been wandering the streets aimlessly – heartbroken – then perhaps she might have travelled home from university that weekend, or even been able to answer the phone. She would never know if they'd called her for help. Her stomach cramped with the pain of the memory. She wiped a tear away with the back of her hand.

'You never gave me the chance to know whether me being there could have saved them or not.' She bit her bottom lip, hearing the harshness of her accusation. Then added, 'Sorry.'

Noah shook his head, a tiny gesture to tell her it was OK to be upset. But it wasn't. The ball of anger she'd been hiding – the anger at Noah for hurting her, breaking up with her after accusing her of seeing other people, making her shut herself off from the world on the one evening the world stopped turning because of her absence – began to unfurl. She remembered why she hated him. Not just the cheating or the break-up itself, but the hurt he'd caused at what turned out to be the lowest point of her entire life. It might have been her fault that she'd turned her phone off, never knowing if there had been a final panicked call from her parents, but it was Noah's actions that had made her do it in the first place. But she didn't think she had the fight in her to confront Noah tonight – if ever.

'It was hard, but I'm OK,' she lied. 'It's brought me and Kirsty closer together like I never thought we'd be, so something good has come out of it all. Although obviously I wish they were still here.'

Lizzie wiped the corner of her eye again, where another tear threatened to betray her. She took another large swig of her drink.

'What have you been doing over the last ten years?' she asked, changing the subject, looking for a way to end the conversation and to get away from him. Noah, the past. It was all too much to take. Lizzie felt a little nauseous and didn't know whether it was

Noah, nostalgia or the cider bubbling away in her stomach that was making her feel that way.

'I finished working soon after you left for university, and did sports and nutrition at college before getting this gig like a sort of apprenticeship. I've been doing it ever since. I might train to teach properly at some point; but for now, it's my dream job.'

Noah had walked away from them and lived his dream life, getting the job he wanted, probably meeting a nice girl. Lizzie rubbed her head, an ache forming where she'd been grinding her teeth.

'It certainly suits you. I mean, it's exactly what I could imagine you doing.' Internally, she rolled her eyes at the pitiful small talk she couldn't seem to move away from. The bench was beginning to feel a little wobbly.

She realised then that perhaps this was the moment to ask the questions she had spent a decade wanting answers to. Perhaps she could clear up what had happened. Yes, the alcohol rushing around Lizzie's system definitely thought that was a good idea.

'What happened to us?' she said after a moment. Her head was definitely not expecting that to be the next thing to come out of her mouth. But there it was. The question was out there, hovering between them.

'I don't know.' Noah took a swig of his own drink and looked suitably awkward.

Lizzie swore she saw a hint of a blush on his cheek.

After a while, he said, 'We were young, I guess.'

Lizzie finished the rest of her cider and attempted to place it on the uneven floor. 'And foolish?' asked the drink.

'Huh?' Noah said, his brow furrowed.

'You know, young and foolish,' explained Lizzie, 'the saying.' In her own head it made perfect sense, but the tiny sober part of her could see this was unintelligible and going horribly south.

'I don't know what you mean.' Noah's voice was tinged with irritation.

'Yes you do, Noah,' she said, standing up, a little wobbly on her feet. 'You cheated on me. Are you blaming your youth for that? Or was I just not good enough for you?'

Noah stood too, his arms reaching out to steady Lizzie. 'I didn't . . . I don't know what . . . I didn't cheat on you, Lizzie. You broke up with me. Or it was mutual or . . .' Noah tailed off uncertainly.

'I'm just not worth sticking around for, is that it? You left me, just like that.' She clicked her fingers in front of his face and they made a satisfying snap. 'You left me, just like they did. And if you hadn't, I might've saved them. We might have all been OK.' Lizzie swayed, reaching out for a tree to steady herself. The drink had affected her suddenly.

Noah was understandably confused. Her flailing arms batted away his attempts to steady her.

'I don't know what you're saying.' His brows lowered, and he craned his neck down to look in her eyes, as if that would clear up any misunderstanding that her slurred words couldn't.

'You're worse, though. You had a choice. You chose to leave.' Lizzie swung around and with what dignity she had left – which at this point was minimal – she stormed off through the trees back out to the festival.

She saw Tom across the field and waved, racing towards him. Behind her, Noah called her name, but she put her head down and walked on, ignoring him.

'Come on, Tom, I need another drink.' She grabbed his arm on her way past and dragged him over to the beer tent.

'I'm not sure you do,' Tom said, attempting to slow her down.

'I really do. I've never needed one more.' Lizzie shuffled her way through to the front of the bar, and ordered two more ciders and a couple of shots. 'Here,' she said, passing one to Tom and knocking hers back in an instant.

'Woah, Lizzie, careful. Are you sure you've not had enough?' he asked.

Lizzie shook her head dramatically and swiped Tom's shot from his hand. 'If you don't want it, I'll have it.' Downing it, she grabbed Tom by the hand and led him away from the bar. 'Come on. I want to dance.'

Chapter Thirteen

As expected, Lizzie woke up with a headache and fuzzy vision. She wasn't hungover; she was still drunk. Her bladder was full to burst. She lay for a while, her vision cloudy and not yet clearing, trying to work out whether her bladder could power through until she absolutely had to get up – and if possible, until the morning. She knew it couldn't, but she wasn't in the mood for rising. She wasn't sure if she could realistically make it to the toilet and back without being sick. Her stomach gave a lurch and her ears were ringing, beeping shrilly and steadily like the beat of a song.

With a groan, she rolled over and slid out of bed. Brushing her hair back from her face, she rubbed her eyes and wondered why they wouldn't clear and why her ears were still ringing so. She stumbled clumsily to the door, where suddenly, her vision came into focus and she realised it was blurred because of the smoke hovering threateningly in her room. The screaming beeps were the relentless call of the smoke alarm.

'What the . . .'

'Lizzie! Lizzie!' came a muffled cry from the other side of the door.

'Tom?' Lizzie looked around for something to protect her hand from the door handle. Her sober self jumped to the forefront of her consciousness and was mindful that it could be hot. She reached for a hoodie, slung earlier on the floor, and pulled the door open a crack. She didn't know what was waiting for her on the other side. In her nightmares, she never got to the door and escaped from the building. She heaved, but nothing came up.

'Come on, Lizzie!' Tom screamed above the noise of the smoke alarm. He was in the corridor, in his boxers, with a T-shirt held tightly over his mouth.

'What's going on?' Lizzie asked, still slow to come round. Her head thumped and her stomach lurched again with nausea.

'There's a fire in the kitchen. We need to get out now.'

Tom's serious tone was enough to snap Lizzie into action. She pulled the hoodie she'd used to open the door over her head and slid her feet into her slippers, grabbing her phone to call the fire brigade as she left. Together, they hurried down the stairs and out of the building, Tom smashing the fire alarm on the way out to alert the neighbours.

By the time they got downstairs, a couple from one of the other flats was sitting on the wall outside and with the noise of the building's fire alarm, neighbours began coming down to the car park in various stages of undress to see what on earth was going on.

Lizzie dialled 999 and relayed what she thought was happening, along with their address. Then she slouched on the wall, pulling her hoodie down over her knees, while other people congregated in front of the building.

It was dark out still and stars twinkled in the clear sky. The warm evening had made way for a pleasantly cool night. Flashes of the fundraiser jumped in and out of Lizzie's consciousness, fuelling her nausea further. And every time she blinked, the image of her recurring dreams came sharply into focus. An image she'd pictured a thousand times – one that she imagined her parents had witnessed in their final moments. She hiccupped and struggled to catch her breath despite now being outside in the open air.

Tom sat down next to her and put an arm around her shoulders. 'Are you OK?' he asked, barely audible above the surrounding chaos.

In the distance, the sound of a fire engine hummed on the breeze.

'Not really, no.' A warm tear streaked down Lizzie's face. She wiped it away with the sleeve of her hoodie, hoping that Tom hadn't noticed.

It was too real – hell – it was real. Despite walking only momentarily through the smoke to get out of the flat, Lizzie's throat felt sore, with a fresh wave of discomfort – bordering on pain – every time she breathed or swallowed. Was this how they had felt just before . . . ? She hoped they'd remained asleep. Then, feeling her resolve seriously falter and losing control of her bottom lip, Lizzie pushed the thought out of her mind and tried to think about something else – simultaneously ignoring the chaos around her and attempting to swallow back the impending tears.

She ran her tongue around the inside of her mouth. It felt like fur, the sugar in whatever she had been drinking coating her teeth. She could almost feel it eroding them away. Despite her efforts, she found it difficult to focus on anything, her senses still struggling against the effects of the alcohol. She wondered how long it had been since they'd got home. How had they got home, now she came to think about it?

A neighbour let out a screech and Lizzie looked up in time to see the glass from their kitchen window shatter into pieces and cascade down onto the pavement. Several onlookers stepped back away from the danger.

The scent of thick, toxic smoke laced the air, stifling when Lizzie breathed it in. She didn't know whether it was the fumes or the panic that prevented her from getting proper lungfuls of air. She swallowed painfully and hunched over, her head in her hands, and closed her eyes.

It was the dream she'd had so many times since the fire. She'd not been there. She'd been away at university, heartbroken and not answering her phone. But the same scene would have surrounded her parents: perhaps waking in the night to impenetrable smoke and panicked screams. Perhaps aware of the searing white heat of the flames as they licked the bottom of the door. Had they even realised it was happening? Again, she closed her eyes and attempted to push the image from her mind, but it was seared on the inside of her eyelids like a bright light.

Perhaps there had been no screams, no chaos or panic. Had her parents already perished in the fire by then? Were they in their beds, sleeping and unconscious of the surrounding peril? Were they gasping for their final breaths before the toxic smoke suffocated them and carried them away?

Tears streamed down her face. She didn't know when she'd begun to cry but she felt sure that she'd never stop. The pit of her stomach felt heavy, twisted somehow, and her heart tightened with the guilt she felt for having not been there. The tears came faster – the kind of tears that grip your whole body and leave you struggling for breath.

Tom held her tighter and suggested they go for a walk. But Lizzie told him she wanted to stay. She felt strangely close to her parents, here, in the same situation in which they'd died.

The confusion around them seemed to both hurry into a blur, and continue in slow motion. At some point, the fire brigade must have arrived and raced past them into the building. From their kitchen window, water now dripped down, and the smoke had changed colour from that of an alive fire to that of a fire extinguished. The sun was just appearing above the horizon.

Tom was talking to one of the firefighters.

'Do you know what happened?' Lizzie heard him ask.

'Electrical fault,' he said, taking off his helmet and holding it by his side. He peeled off his gloves, too.

'A fault?' Lizzie asked, suddenly tuning into the conversation.

'Yes, some faulty wiring from the hob we suspect.' He wiped the sweat from his dirty brow.

'God.' Lizzie crumpled back down to the wall again.

'Not a thing anyone could do, I'm afraid. It was a ticking time bomb waiting to happen.'

'So it was no one's fault?' Tom asked.

'Nope. It's good you caught it when you did. There's not much damage, except for the broken window, and the place is fairly habitable. It might be worth finding somewhere to stay tonight, but once the window's boarded up, it should be fine.'

'Thanks,' Tom said.

'Yes,' Lizzie said. 'Thank you.' She hugged her arms around her body.

'I have to go,' the firefighter said, nodding towards the truck, where the other firefighters were waiting to head back to the station. 'We'll be in touch.'

He left, and Tom sat back down next to Lizzie.

By now, people had begun to return to their properties, where it was safe to do so. Lizzie and Tom needed to find somewhere else to stay, the firefighter had said. At least for the rest of the night.

'It's not your fault, Lizzie,' Tom said, brushing her hair back from her face. 'And it wasn't your fault the last time, either. I hope you know that,' he said, fully understanding her sorrow like only a best friend could.

'Shall we go?' she asked, ignoring his support. She stood – a little unsteady on her legs – and began to walk.

'OK,' he said. 'I'll text Mum. I'm sure it'll be fine to use the house. They're in Spain until next weekend. I'll just need to pop back in and get my key.'

Tom quickly ran upstairs to get a few things. Lizzie continued to walk slowly away from the building. Suddenly alone and overwhelmed by the events of the evening, she hung her head over the wall and threw up into a bush.

Chapter Fourteen

Throwing up was the last thing Lizzie remembered when she woke up the next morning on Tom's mum's sofa. Well, it was the last thing she remembered for certain, anyway. There was the focused memory of the aftermath of the fire and hazy memories of waking up to smoke, conversations with Noah, an argument? Lizzie pulled the duvet over her head. This was the lowest place she'd been for a long time.

'Morning,' Tom said, crawling onto the sofa with Lizzie and draping an arm over her. 'I thought you could probably do with a hug.'

'I really could.' She groaned, her stomach lurching with the effort of speech.

'Can you remember much about last night?'

Lizzie shook her head. 'Not really. I remember getting to the fundraiser and I remember being outside and everything that happened after the fire. There's a whole heap of stuff in the middle that I can't remember anything about.'

'Do you want to know what happened?' Tom asked.

'Yes,' said Lizzie, struggling to sit up with both of them on the narrow sofa. 'Actually, no. It's bad enough we set fire to the flat. I can't bear to hear what happened at the fundraiser.'

'No one's to blame for the fire, remember – faulty electrics, the firefighter said.'

Lizzie ignored his point, not wanting to think too much about the fire. 'Anyway, I've got loads of work to do today, so I'm going to have to get over this hangover quickly. I'm going to wander to the shop for one of those ready-made bacon sandwiches and a Berocca. Do you want anything?'

'There's no way you can be this chipper after last night.' Tom snuggled further down into the duvet.

Lizzie put her finger to her lips. 'Shhh. I said I didn't want to know what happened.'

'I know,' Tom said. 'But as a friend and as someone who witnessed just how drunk you were last night, I feel duty-bound to let you know that you are more likely to be still drunk than to have escaped hangover free. I'd make the most of it, cause when it hits, it's going to suck.'

'Thank you for the advice, Thomas.' Lizzie wriggled off the sofa and pulled on her jeans and a jumper. Her stomach lurched again. She was kidding herself and she knew it, but her philosophy was that if you pretended you weren't hungover, then you wouldn't be. She wondered whether, in fact, if she pretended a lot of things hadn't happened last night, then they hadn't.

A fleeting image of memories merged from the previous evening and from the fires of her nightmares slid into her mind, but she pushed them away again. Last night might have made Lizzie confront some things, but she wasn't ready to deal with that particular guilt head-on just yet.

She pulled on her jacket and left Tom on the sofa. Outside, the sun was already high in the cloudless sky. Birds sat on the green until they were disturbed by the two children who were running their dad ragged across the grass. The town centre was already full of life and Lizzie had very nearly missed it by dying in bed all day.

Having purchased the necessary hangover provisions, despite her throbbing head and extremely questionable gag reflex, Lizzie headed back towards the house, hoping to sit down and tackle the sports day to-do list before her hangover kicked in properly. She'd need to go back to the flat and collect some proper clothes and her school bag at some point, though. Perhaps it would be best to get it out of the way, assess the damage even. She didn't relish the thought of sleeping on Tom's parents' sofa for a second night.

At the flat, things weren't as bad as she expected they would be. Most of the damage was on the kitchen wall and the dramatic window smashing seemed the worst of it. With a bit of air and a board for the window, the flat would be habitable, just as the firefighter had said.

The alcohol and the drama and the raw imaginings the fire had dredged up must have worked together to create something much more terrifying than it needed to be. Lizzie didn't like that it had forced her to think about her parents. And she couldn't shake the feeling that both fires and their consequences had been her fault somehow, despite what the firefighter had said about faulty electrics. She took a deep breath and tried to relax her shoulders. It would probably be OK.

She would probably be OK.

There was nothing she could do now, so she just needed to relax and stop blaming herself for everything.

A wave of nausea washed over her; not physical nausea, just

the type caused by morning-after shame. As she distracted herself from thoughts of the fire, it occurred to her that a lot of parents and other colleagues had been at the fundraiser last night. And Noah. She hoped she hadn't done anything too ridiculous.

Lizzie's phone vibrated in her pocket. She pulled it out and swiped it open to see a text: *Is everything OK? The flat doesn't look too good . . . Xx.* The sender was someone she'd saved in her contacts as 'Noooh'. Ironic. There could be only one person and as she thought it, the memory of a second conversation she'd previously forgotten from later in the evening flashed into her mind. Was this message from . . . ? Surely not. Please no.

Lizzie shook her head as the memory of shouting at Noah came racing back to her. And then they'd spoken again, apparently. She had a vague recollection of having their phones out and maybe swapping numbers. She hoped she hadn't asked for his. He'd held her hand or held her up? Oh no. This was bad. And he had no idea of the drama that had unfolded thereafter. Or maybe he did . . . ?

She looked down at her phone again and reread the message. It sounded suspiciously like he might be outside. She sidled closer to the window and saw him standing in the car park, a hand shielding his eyes as he looked up, directly at her. He waved.

'Hi,' Lizzie called.

'Are you OK?' He sounded genuinely concerned.

Lizzie nodded. 'Hang on. I'll come down.'

Noah was sitting on the wall when she got down to the car park. He looked up from his phone, squinting in the sunshine. 'What happened?'

Lizzie sighed. 'Small fire. The firefighter said something about an electrical fault.'

Noah stood, concern throwing him into action. 'Are you all

right? That must have been horrible.'

'I'm fine. It was a bit of a shock and a bit too close to home given everything that happened . . .' Lizzie sat down on the wall and Noah joined her.

'Oh, Lizzie. I'd not even thought about . . .' He tailed off and shuffled closer to her to put an arm around her shoulder. 'That must have been . . .'

Lizzie wasn't surprised he couldn't think of the words. She didn't know what they should be either. Noah's arm around her didn't help the clarity of her mind.

'It's OK. I'm safe. Tom's safe.'

Noah let his arm drop and rested it on the wall. 'I'm glad Tom is OK too. I'm glad you both are.'

He looked across the car park, his eyes narrow and his thoughts suddenly elsewhere. Lizzie could feel the change in his demeanour. He really believed that she and Tom were something to each other.

Lizzie opened her mouth to correct him, but before she could say anything, he stood up and brushed down his trousers.

'I just wanted to check that you were OK after last night. You were pretty out of it. I let Tom take you home because he was so persistent, but he was also very drunk. I guess I just wanted to make sure you'd got back safely. I'm sorry about the fire.'

'Me too.' Lizzie stood and Noah took further steps away from her. 'I mean . . . I'm sorry about a lot of things.' She hoped that would cover all of her potential faux pas from the previous evening.

Noah ignored her apology. 'Let me know if there's anything I can do to help, if there's anything you need.' He began to walk across the car park towards the street.

'Will do,' Lizzie said quietly. She felt the conversation and the potential of the moment slipping away and as it did, her true hangover crept closer. She swallowed nauseously.

He turned briefly. 'See you on Monday, Lizzie.'

She raised a hand to wave and said nothing. She'd always written off hangover days as if she were a different person. She'd re-enter the human race once she felt like herself again in the morning. She'd have to wait until Monday to make sure that everything was all right between them after the night at the fundraiser.

After a criminally strong coffee and a lukewarm bacon sandwich, she sat down at the little desk in her bedroom, where there was a window and significantly less damp and smoke damage than in the kitchen, and got down to sending emails and drafting letters to various people and parents. By lunchtime, she felt like she'd been dragged through some kind of assault course by her ankles and went back to bed. Her room was far away from the kitchen and with the window open for a little fresh air, it was perfectly habitable.

'Hangover kicked in?' Tom asked, appearing around her door a few hours later.

'God yeah,' Lizzie said, closing her eyes and falling asleep.

Chapter Fifteen

Lizzie spent Sunday worrying and recovering. Tom filled her in on her terrible dancing and outrageous flirting with Noah. He told her that Noah had offered them a lift home but that he'd said no through fear that Lizzie would do something stupid once they'd got back to the flat – which explained Noah's visit. He also told her she had instigated the number swap, just in case she needed help with planning for sports day but she knew very well that drunk Lizzie would not have been very sly about her true motives at all.

Predictably, she had the same familiar nightmare again, and every time she closed her eyes – even for just a second – she could see the smoke and sense the chaos. Each time she would break out into a sweat and feel her heart rate climb. Coupled with her body trying to rid itself of the alcohol toxins and her mind dealing with the shame, it made for a hideous Sunday. She felt sick with worry and struggled to focus on anything except old repeats of *Friends*.

The hangover lasted well into Sunday evening. It was only

when the Corrie theme tune came on that she realised she felt normal again.

Tom was making dinner; well, he was putting oven chips and chicken dippers into the oven. Lizzie had curled up on the sofa with a large glass of water. She swiped open her phone and reread Noah's message, frustrated at how the conversation outside the flat yesterday afternoon had panned out. It annoyed her that he'd walked away. Somehow, it felt like she'd done something wrong, but her head was such a mess, she didn't know which of them was in the right and the wrong any more.

She had thought an early night was what she needed, but it was a night of fitful sleep, that same old nightmare. By 4 a.m., Lizzie was up and drinking coffee while sitting on the windowsill, once again looking out over the green. Once she'd calmed down from her terrifyingly vivid dreams, all that remained was the cringe factor and guilt of Friday night, which hadn't quite left her yet. Today, she was going to have to face the music – and Noah. Her stomach churned. If only PE were the first lesson of the day instead of the last. Lizzie knew it would be a long old slog. Familiar with the odd hangover though, she also knew that time would heal the ickiness, and whatever happened, everything would be fine in a few weeks' time. She ignored the part of her that screamed about how long a few weeks were, and finished her coffee just as Tom surfaced from his room.

'You've been up a while?' He came and sat next to her and put an arm around her shoulder.

'A little while.'

'Oh, Lizzie.'

'The nightmares have been back big time recently and Friday night didn't help. And I've got the shame about everything. I just couldn't sleep.'

159

'It will all be fine.'

He brushed her hair back, like she was a child, and they sat like that for a while before Lizzie noticed the time.

'We need to get going,' she said, hopping down from the windowsill and putting her lunch in her bag.

'Give me twenty minutes.'

Despite Lizzie's growing confidence at school, especially since her teaching had gone so well on Friday, she felt timid all day. She was slightly embarrassed and recognised that at any moment she could come face to face with someone who had seen her drunk, or dancing, or fighting with Noah. What if someone had witnessed the fire? If Sophie had been party to anything, Lizzie was thankful to her for not bringing it up.

'So the lesson on Friday went really well,' Sophie said as they did their rounds on duty at lunchtime.

'I was pleased with it.' Lizzie took a swig from her water bottle.

'We'll need to do official feedback at our mentor meeting later this week, but I didn't want you to be worrying about it until then. I was really impressed.'

'Thanks. It felt really good,' Lizzie said, struggling to wipe the smile off her face. It was nice to have something to smile about after the weekend.

'Do you think you'd be ready to embrace some maths next week?' Sophie stopped and turned to judge Lizzie's reaction.

'Based only on the fact that I'm going to have to teach it eventually, I guess I could give it a go,' she said, definitely lacking in the confidence she was showing on the outside.

'Great, I'll pencil you in for next Thursday for the group task. The plan is on the computer in the shared area, so you'll just need to have a look at it and decide how you'd like to go about delivering it. We're carrying on with our work on percentages, so nothing new to learn, just consolidation of the skills we've been working on. Want to put something together by yourself and then we can talk about it before the lesson?'

'Sure.' Lizzie knew she sounded uncertain. She appreciated Sophie trusting her to work on it independently, but that also added another layer of terror to the scenario. 'I'll come up with a plan and get it written before the end of the week,' she said, mentally adding it to her to-do list, which was growing exponentially by the day.

Clearly sensing that Lizzie suddenly seemed overwhelmed, Sophie suggested she take the art lesson as planning time, so that she could go and get some of her work done.

'You can take part in PE while I do my planning. How does that sound?'

'Great,' Lizzie said – a lie. 'Thanks.'

'Can I be cheeky and head in for a quick breather? This heat is making me feel funny.' Now that Sophie said it, Lizzie did notice that she looked a bit red in the face.

'Of course, no problem. I'll carry on lapping the building,' Lizzie said.

Sophie sighed. 'Thank you. I owe you one,' she added as she took herself off to the classroom.

Lizzie thought that time to work would be good for her, that she'd be able to get some of the minor jobs ticked off her sports day list and the rest of her to-do list. All it really did, though, was give her the time to worry more about the impending PE lesson with Noah. The only saving grace was that if she was worrying about Noah, she wasn't thinking about the fire and the reminders it had brought with it.

Five minutes before PE was due to start, Lizzie got changed into her gym kit and this time felt no shame in redoing her hair and touching up her make-up. She looked OK. She no longer had the bags under her eyes and the horrible skin of a person who had drunk too much in the last couple of days, thankfully. It would be fine.

Much like her habit at football practice, Lizzie rocked up to the PE lesson just as the warm-up was coming to a close.

'Sorry,' she mouthed, trying not to disturb the children as she slipped into the circle.

Noah didn't react, instead continuing with his spiel to the children. Lizzie tried not to read too much into it.

'So today, guys, we're going to do some football exercises before we go into mini five-a-side games. And we're really lucky, because we have Miss Morris here to help us, who is a proper football player.'

'In real life?' Audrey asked, her face full of wonder.

'In real life,' confirmed Noah with a smile, first at Audrey and then at Lizzie.

There were gasps from the other children and heads turned towards Lizzie.

She smiled self-consciously. 'I just play a little on a Monday night,' she said, brushing off Noah's compliment.

'Actually, Miss Morris is being modest.' He smiled across the room at her again. 'She's going to be in the final of a tournament. It's the first time Cranswell Ladies have made it to the final in five years and it's been twenty years since they won,' he announced to more gasps from the children. 'So you'll need to listen very carefully to everything that she tells you. She's the expert. Right, here's the first exercise. You'll need to be in groups of three.'

Noah explained the exercise and Lizzie listened carefully, so that when the children split up into their groups, she could go over and help those who were struggling or had questions.

After the children had practised their dribbling and shooting, Noah organised them into three five-a-side games. With only twenty-eight in the class, Lizzie and Noah joined two of the teams, but played in separate games, thank God. There was no risk of competition between the two of them.

When it reached three o'clock and Sophie came in to collect the children, Lizzie finally relaxed. She'd made it through the day and it hadn't been as hideous as her midnight brain had assumed it would be.

'Miss Morris,' Noah called as she was about to leave the hall behind the snaking children. 'I found this in the office. I thought it might be yours.' He pulled Lizzie's football trophy from his pocket and passed it to her, their hands brushing slightly in the exchange. 'Actually, I knew it was yours. I remember the day you won it playing the school down the road.'

Lizzie swallowed. She couldn't look him in the eye after everything that had happened at the weekend. 'It must have fallen out of one of the storytelling bags last week. Thank you,' she said, turning to leave.

'Wait,' Noah said, taking a couple more steps to catch her up again. 'I heard you made the team for the ladies' cup final.'

Lizzie nodded, having barely even registered it with everything else that had been going on. 'Yeah, we play a week Saturday.'

Noah looked awkward. Maybe he was embarrassed about Friday night too. Had she embarrassed him? Or was he still upset at how their conversation had ended when he'd appeared at the flat? She got that icky feeling again; the shame was coming.

'I just wondered whether you fancied doing a bit of extra training before the big day,' he said, his eyes bright. He smiled.

'Extra training?' she asked, surprised.

'You'd be doing me a favour. I've been doing a bit of personal training recently and I'm trying to build up a bit of a portfolio by doing a few free gigs. It would really help me out,' he explained. 'In exchange for a testimonial maybe?'

'Um, sure, I guess.' She didn't know what to say and the surprise of his suggestion had thrown her. There was nothing to say but yes.

'How about Friday after school? We can use the field before we go home.'

Lizzie hesitated. Was this a good idea? Almost certainly not – but, eventually, with no other response to hand, she said, 'Sounds good.'

'Well, you've got my number,' he said, a knowing smile spread across his face.

It was now or never. Lizzie had to bring up the weekend, otherwise it would go unspoken for ever, she'd never be able to look Noah in the eye again and she'd drown in the embarrassment.

'About Friday night,' she began, and swallowed nervously. 'I'm pretty sure I was more drunk than I planned on being.' She looked at the ground and back up at Noah's dark eyes. 'Rumour has it you dealt with the brunt of it. I just wanted to say sorry.'

'Nothing to be sorry about, Lizzie,' he said. 'Cranswell Fest is notorious for being an absolute drunken mess by the end of the night. You just peaked a little earlier than some. Don't worry about it.' He winked.

'Well, thanks for being nice about it.' Lizzie smiled, feeling the relief of her weekend of worry washing over her and away.

'See, I can be nice.' He flashed her a grin.

'OK, I deserved that,' she said, the memory of their conversation flooding back.

'It might be OK, but I'm definitely going to be throwing

some of these in whenever I get the opportunity, just to make you squirm.' He poked her playfully in the arm. 'Is everything all right back at the flat?'

Lizzie nodded. 'Yes. It smells a bit smoky and there's a bit of the kitchen out of use, but we're back in and it'll all be fine. Tom and I are moving in a week or so anyway. I can't believe there was another fire.' Lizzie's eyes glazed over as visions of her familiar nightmare flashed into her mind. She sniffed, conscious that there might be tears on the way, and then came back to the room when Noah spoke.

He said, 'I'm glad everything's OK.'

'I'd better get back to the children. They'll be nearly changed and ready for home time.'

'Lizzie,' he began, but Lizzie began to walk away. 'Lizzie!'

She turned back to his raised voice.

'You've not done anything wrong,' he said.

Lizzie wasn't sure what Noah was talking about any more. There was so much between them, over the weekend, in her life, that he could be referring to.

'Thanks, Noah,' she said, smiling. She turned to leave. 'I'll see you on Friday.' She waved without turning around and felt him watch her go. She liked that he seemed to be on her side, despite not really fully understanding what was going on between them. She was so glad that they were speaking, and that she hadn't broken their relationship completely by being a drunken mess. It was nice to have some hope there, even if Lizzie wasn't sure what she was hoping for just yet.

Chapter Sixteen

'House viewing, house viewing, house viewing,' Tom said, coming up behind Lizzie in the corridor later that day and clapping his hands.

'I wonder why you could be so excited about a house viewing.' Lizzie tapped her finger dramatically on her chin in thought, at the same time relieved that they were moving so they didn't have to deal with the fire damage and arrange for the insurance company to come and patch up the kitchen. In an odd way, it was good timing for Landlord Stanley to be kicking them out.

'Come on, get your stuff. Let's go!' Tom darted into the staffroom to pick up his things, while Lizzie popped into the classroom to get hers.

Kirsty had warned Lizzie that a sunny day could make the outside of a house more beautiful than it really was. 'It's important to imagine it in the rain,' she'd said. But when they arrived outside the house, it was stunning and Lizzie felt sure that it would be just as beautiful in the winter as in the summer.

The flat they were here to see was in a newly converted Victorian house on the other side of town. It was a tall building with four flats built into its four storeys, including the cellar, which had also been remodelled and refurbished into a flat. The front door was painted black with a beautiful stained-glass window that sparkled where the sun hit it. Lizzie was already in love with it.

'What time is Chris meeting us?' Lizzie asked.

'Any time now.' Tom was jittery and hopping from one leg to another.

'It's rush hour, so it's busy. He'll be here in a minute. Keep nice and calm, won't you?' Lizzie joked.

Even as Lizzie finished speaking, Chris's black BMW raced round the corner and parked up in front of the building.

'Hi, Tom, Lizzie,' Chris said, shaking their hands and flashing his bright smile.

'Hi, Chris. Nice to see you again,' Lizzie said.

Tom was suddenly speechless. Lizzie widened her eyes to prompt him.

'Nice to see you again, Chris,' he said finally, his voice almost a whisper.

Chris smiled at him and then swallowed and looked down at the ground shyly. 'Shall we go in and have a look round?' He reached for an enormous bunch of keys from his car seat, then shut the door and led the way up the garden path.

'Great,' Lizzie said in an attempt to keep some form of conversation going.

She followed Chris and dragged Tom behind her, glaring at him.

Chris took them in through the beautiful stained-glass door and up the stairs to the top-floor flat. Inside, it was bright and airy – so very different to the house they'd seen before. Because it was in the space right at the very top of the building, the flat had sloping ceilings and roof windows in all the rooms. The living space was open plan and both of the bedrooms were en suite. It was perfect.

'So what do you think?' Chris asked once he'd given them the tour.

They gathered in the living space, a long kitchen area running across one side of the large square room. Lizzie peered through one of the three roof windows. It looked out over the top of town. She could see the school building from up here.

'It's lovely,' Tom said, gazing around in awe of the place. 'How much is it, though?'

Lizzie had been thinking the same thing. Surely somewhere as gorgeous as this couldn't be within their price range.

'£900 a month,' Chris said, looking down nervously at his clipboard. 'I know it's a little bit more than the one we saw the other day, but you clearly didn't like that one, so I wanted to show you what you could get for £150 more a month. I've also managed to knock the landlord down by fifty quid.' He winked at Lizzie and then put the end of his pen between his teeth and locked eyes with Tom. 'Do you want to go away and think about it? You can always call me in a few days' time.'

Tom blushed and found the view from one of the roof windows to be fascinating.

Lizzie was already working out how she could afford it. This place was too good to miss. But if they thought about it overnight, it would give Tom another chance for him to contact Chris, which was clearly what they both wanted. The sexual tension in the room was palpable.

'Shall we think about it tonight and then Tom can get in touch with you tomorrow morning, Chris?'

Tom shared a look of appreciation with Lizzie across the room.

'Sounds great,' Chris said. 'I'll speak to you tomorrow then.' He looked at Tom and held his gaze for a moment longer than necessary. Lizzie smiled to herself, pleased at her not so subtle matchmaking.

'Unless you're showing anyone else around today. You're not, are you?' Lizzie asked. She desperately didn't want to go back to the fire-damaged flat for long – she wanted to be as far away from the memory of the fire as possible. Besides, Stanley, the landlord, was still evicting them in order to sell the place. They needed to find somewhere to live – and fast.

'Nope. That's something estate agents say to get you to decide more quickly,' said Chris with his winning smile.

'I thought it probably was. Worth an ask, though. Come on, let's go,' she said to Tom, who had been speechless for an increasingly awkward amount of time. She led the way out of the flat and down the stairs. Tom followed her begrudgingly and Chris locked the door behind them before leaving the building too.

'Well, it was nice to see you again,' he said, offering his hand. Lizzie shook it.

'And you,' Tom said, taking his hand. 'I mean, this place is great. Thanks for showing it to us.'

'No problem,' Chris said, dazzling them with his teeth once more. He was still holding Tom's hand and only dropped it when he said, 'I'll speak to you tomorrow. See you.'

'Bye.' Tom offered a little wave as Chris drove off. He held the hand Chris had touched in his other hand and looked down at it, as if savouring the contact.

'You guys,' Lizzie joked, fluttering her eyelids.

'Stop it,' Tom said, pushing her playfully. 'I could say the same about you and Noah.'

'We're going to get that flat, aren't we?' she said, partly to ignore his comment and partly because she was desperate for him to say yes.

'Yes, definitely. It was perfect.'

'Good. I was worried you might not have been looking at it properly and ogling Chris instead.' Lizzie laughed.

'I have some morals,' Tom said, folding his arms in a huff. 'I'm mostly excited that it's got a kitchen with no fire damage,' he added, deadpan.

'Too soon, Thomas,' Lizzie said. 'Too soon.'

Tom laughed. 'Sorry.'

He sounded genuine, knowing the guilt Lizzie felt about fires in general.

She said, 'Come on, fancy a quick drink?'

'Sure.' And Tom followed her.

'It'll have to be super quick, though. I need to get to football practice.'

The pub across the road was small and villagey. It would be nice to live opposite somewhere so quaint. Inside, it was decorated in a fairly modern style. There weren't any of those strange bronze things hanging off the walls and the whole place was painted in magnolia, so it felt bright and airy, unlike some of the darker pubs they could choose to frequent around the town. They bought their drinks and went to sit down.

'So how was school after, you know?' Tom raised an eyebrow as they shuffled into a booth.

'Better than I thought it'd be,' Lizzie said, sipping her ice-cold lemonade. 'I was worried that everyone would be whispering about me in the corridors and that Noah wouldn't be talking to me at all. But actually he was very nice about it – said that everyone got drunk every year at the fundraiser, that it was notorious, just that I peaked sooner than everyone else did.'

'The man's got a point.' Tom put his drink down and rested back in the seat. 'Are you ever going to tell me what happened between you two?' he asked after a moment.

'What do you mean?' Lizzie asked, buying time.

'You know, back in the day, when you were at school, when you left for uni. What's the story? I mean, only if you want to tell it.'

'Do you really want to know?' Lizzie said, scrunching up her face.

'I really, really do,' Tom said, sitting forward and resting his chin in his hands.

Lizzie took a deep breath. 'Noah was my first kiss. We were ten and sitting behind the sports club on the day Cranswell Ladies last won the cup.' She looked up at Tom and then went back to running her finger through the condensation on her glass. 'But I imagine that's not the bit of the story you're after.'

Tom shook his head.

Lizzie took another sip of her drink and put it down to get comfy before she started her story properly.

'When we were seventeen, we were in the same circle of friends. We always had been, but we'd grown closer over the summer following our AS Levels. We went on a group holiday to Greece where we sort of hooked up, and when we got back, Noah asked if I wanted to be his girlfriend. I had thought it would just be a holiday romance or whatever, but I was excited when he wanted it to carry on at home.'

'Go on,' Tom said. He smiled encouragingly.

'So, it all went well for a year or so. We had the normal spats and we've always been super competitive with each other.'

'You surprise me,' Tom said dryly.

Lizzie smiled. 'I know. After we'd finished at sixth form, I went off to university and Noah stayed here. And then . . .'

'And then . . . ?'

Lizzie swallowed. 'And then he cheated on me.'

Tom frowned. 'What happened? How did you find out?' He shifted in his seat to sit cross-legged.

'Kirsty told me. She said she'd seen him with several girls in the pubs around town. Once she'd said it, I couldn't trust him any more.'

'Did you just take her word for it?' asked Tom, frowning again.

'Of course I did, she's my sister. I mean, look at him – he's gorgeous. He's always had a million girls throwing themselves at him. I couldn't believe my luck when he actually wanted to be with me. And when he cheated? I couldn't believe my stupidity for not expecting it sooner.'

'That sucks, Lizzie,' Tom said, reaching over and giving her arm a squeeze. 'How did you react?'

'He tried to deny it, but after one horrible argument over the phone, we broke up. I just stood aside, I guess. And then we never had a chance to talk about it again. You see, the day we broke up was the day of the fire too.' Lizzie's throat grew suddenly tight and she swallowed uncomfortably before she spoke again. 'I turned my phone off after we argued and wallowed in my own self-pity. And while I was being selfish, my parents died.' She choked on the last word.

Tom went to speak but instead shuffled closer to her and pulled her in for a hug, squeezing her tightly.

'It was his fault or my fault or something like that. I should've been there.'

'They might not have even tried to call you,' Tom reasoned.

Lizzie knew he was speaking sense. But that didn't stop the horrible feeling in the pit of her stomach telling her she could have done something more. Noah's actions had prevented her from doing anything or even knowing if she could have helped.

'I know,' she said eventually. 'And you'd have thought that several years of therapy would have taken that feeling away, but it hasn't.'

'I'm so sorry, Lizzie.'

She pulled away from him and sat up before taking a long sip of her drink, then cleared her throat.

She said, 'Well, you know. It's all such a long time ago now. The Noah thing is all water under the bridge.'

'Did you have friends at uni who got you through it? I assume with Jäger Bombs?' Tom asked, presumably sensing the serious part of the conversation was over.

'Yeah, it was fine, I guess,' she said, fiddling with the corner of the beer mat. 'He broke my heart though, Tom. And he broke my trust. I feel like he ruined my ability to get close to someone like that. I worry that if I do, something awful like the fire could happen again. I know it sounds crazy.' She laughed, embarrassed by what she was saying, but keen to lighten the mood.

'It doesn't sound crazy. It makes perfect sense.'

'I've not trusted anyone since.'

'Not trusted anyone or not been with anyone?' Tom asked, sensing the subtext.

Lizzie pulled a face.

'Are you telling me you've not had sex for a decade?' he asked, incredulous. And loudly.

Lizzie shook her head. 'But I'd rather you didn't share that with the rest of the pub, thank you.' She looked around, blushing.

'Oh God. Lizzie, I'm so sorry,' he said, shaking his head sadly as if she'd suffered a further terrible injustice.

'Tom! It's just not felt right with anyone else since then. Besides, I don't think I've made it through to a third date with anyone to even get that far.'

'Lizzie, Lizzie, Lizzie,' he said dramatically. 'We have got to get you back out there. And you have to stop measuring every single man against Noah. Not everyone will treat you like he did and more importantly, no one will ever measure up to your first love.'

'Don't I deserve that though?'

'Of course. But it's not realistic,' Tom said quickly.

'Great,' she said sarcastically, and looked at her watch. 'Look, I have to get back to get ready for practice. Are you coming?'

'I'm not going to sit here drinking alone, am I?' he said, downing the last of his pint.

'It wouldn't be the first time.'

'Fair point.'

'Two training sessions to go until the big game,' Coach Zoe said as the girls warmed up later that evening. 'So we need to make this time count.'

She walked around as if to assess them.

'So after warm-up, I want the squad down this end and everyone else up here. We're going to play a full match and you guys,' she indicated the end to which she was about to send the cup final squad, 'are going to need to show me that I picked the right people. I've still got a week and a half to change my mind, remember.'

Lizzie had finally realised that making the squad was not only important, but pretty impressive. She was definitely not going to mess this up.

By half-time, she'd scored one goal and assisted another. It was going well.

'Drink?' Kirsty asked, passing her a plastic cup of water.

'Thanks.' Lizzie drained it, thirsty from the exertion.

'How was your day?'

'Better than expected,' Lizzie said, refilling her cup and downing another.

'How come?' Kirsty leant against the wall and stretched out her leg.

'To cut a long story short, I got extremely drunk on Friday night at a school thing and thought today would be horribly embarrassing. Luckily, it wasn't as bad as I thought it was going to be. Plus, I think Tom and I have found a flat to rent.' She didn't mention the fire. It was bad enough that she was having to deal with the memories of her parents resurfacing. She didn't want Kirsty to have to deal with it as well. She had enough to deal with.

'That's great news,' Kirsty said, moving on to stretch out her other leg. 'I wondered what was happening on Friday. You sent a bit of an odd message.'

'Sorry,' Lizzie said, grimacing. 'What did it say?'

'Can't remember now. Something about Noah and it being

like having to put out a fire. I don't know.'

'Ugh!' Lizzie rolled her eyes, suddenly feeling sick. 'Sorry,' she said again.

'Have you finally given up on that, then?' she asked.

'Given up on what?'

'Noah.'

'I don't know,' Lizzie said, folding her arms and leaning back against the wall. 'It's not a priority at the moment. I guess I'll just see what happens.'

Kirsty nodded, and smiled what Lizzie assumed was a smile of understanding.

'How are things at home, anyway?' Lizzie asked. Her eyes flickered over to Kirsty's wrist. She'd noticed at the start of training she was wearing another long-sleeved top – despite the fact she was exercising in the height of summer – and seemed to obsessively pull both sleeves down over her hands.

Kirsty looked down at her hands for a moment and then back towards Lizzie.

'Fine.'

'Really fine?'

They looked at each other as though in a stand-off. Kirsty clearly knew what Lizzie was getting at and Lizzie knew she knew, but neither wanted to say the words.

'Not now, Lizzie,' Kirsty said quietly. 'Please not now.'

Lizzie could swear she saw the sheen of a tear in her eye.

'All right, Kirs. But soon.'

Kirsty nodded.

'And you need to promise me that you're safe. Please promise me that.' Lizzie pleaded with her eyes.

'I am. I promise.' She smiled a sad smile.

Lizzie took her hand and squeezed it. 'I'm here, Kirs.'

Kirsty nodded and wiped a single tear on the sleeve of her top.

'Let's get back on it, ladies,' came Zoe's cry over the general bustle of half-time. 'Let's go, let's go,' she said, clapping her hands.

'Come on,' Kirsty said, bringing them back to practice.

Lizzie watched Kirsty run to her end of the pitch. Lizzie ran to the opposite end, determined to round off practice with an impressive second half but somewhat distracted by her worry for her sister. She took a deep breath and tried to refocus.

Coach Zoe blew the whistle to signal the start of the second half and Lizzie was off, receiving the ball straight away and moving down the pitch, passing it between herself and her teammates until they were close to the goal. One of the players from the opposition raced in to tackle her, missing by a centimetre thanks to Lizzie's quick thinking, before another ran at her to attempt the same. Lizzie jumped over her leg to line up the ball, shoot and score. In seconds, she was surrounded by her team congratulating her. Across the pitch, Coach Zoe was looking on with respect. Lizzie had definitely booked her place in the cup final game. But she struggled to celebrate, her mind on her sister, hoping that everything was really OK.

As they walked over to their cars, Lizzie decided she couldn't wait any longer. She had a hundred questions on the tip of her tongue and she was wrestling to keep her thoughts to herself.

'Look, Kirsty,' she said, reaching for Kirsty's arm to stop her walking ahead. 'I need to know, are things really OK?'

'Of course. I'd tell you if they weren't.' She took another step.

'You don't have to be the mother hen all the time, you know?'

Kirsty stopped. She didn't turn, but Lizzie knew she was listening. Kirsty took a breath and her shoulders sagged.

'It's OK to not be OK, to be vulnerable, to ask for help – even if it is from your younger sister. I guess . . . I guess I just want you to know that I'm here for you.'

Kirsty turned and wiped a tear from her cheek.

'I think I want to leave him.' She sniffed. 'But I don't know how.' And then her silent tears turned into great shakes of her body as she fell into Lizzie's arms.

'Oh, Kirs.' Lizzie stroked her hair as her sister cried onto her shoulder.

'What am I going to do, Lizzie?' her muffled voice came from Lizzie's shoulder.

'I don't know, but we'll figure something out. You can stay on mine and Tom's sofa, even bring the boys. If you decide that's what you want to do. I'm here.'

Chapter Seventeen

The week was busy, and despite worrying about Kirsty all day every day, Lizzie was getting into the swing of things and enjoying getting up and going to school every day. For now, Kirsty had decided to stay put with Steve and the boys, but Lizzie had made sure that Kirsty knew the offer of sanctuary at hers and Tom's was still there.

Despite her concern, Lizzie found herself to be in a good place. Every morning she was up before Tom and raring to go. She picked out her own outfits and twice, she'd made Tom a cooked breakfast before he'd even risen. She was finally making up for all the times he had done it for her. She'd not thought about the fire for a few days either, the horrors nestling back into her subconscious somewhere – for a little while, at least.

At school, things were going well too. Lizzie had got her head around the maths curriculum and had already planned her lesson ready for next week. At their mentor meeting, Sophie had said she thought it was great, and they'd role-played a couple of the tricky bits and made a few tweaks so that it was perfect – or at least as perfect as it could be at the planning stage. There was no way to know whether it would go well, or whether the children would behave as expected. Lizzie was learning quickly that flexibility was super important in teaching.

By 3 p.m. on Friday, Lizzie was ready for the weekend – and her training session with Noah. The thought of it meant she'd been on edge all day, the kind of feeling you get the night before Christmas combined with the night before an important exam bubbling away in her stomach. It was an excited yet terrified kind of anxiety and the clock had moved ridiculously slowly all afternoon, just to add to the tension.

After waving the children off home at the school gate, Lizzie went to the staffroom and changed into her gym kit before coming out and bumping into Tom.

'Excited?' he asked with raised eyebrows.

'Shhh,' said Lizzie, a finger to her lips. She looked around to check they were by themselves.

'I'm joking,' he said, filling the kettle up.

'I know, but someone might hear you.'

'You're really hung up on him, aren't you?' Tom leant back against the counter to relish in his torment.

'I haven't got time for this, Thomas,' Lizzie said, only half serious.

'I'm sorry, I'm sorry.' He held his hands up in defence.

'I have to go.' She checked her hair using the reflection in the window.

'Have fun,' Tom said, his voice full of teasing.

'I will.' She left the staffroom to make her way out onto the school field, where Noah was already waiting.

'Hi,' he said as she jogged over.

'Hi.'

'Thanks for doing this.' He untied an enormous bag of footballs and allowed several to roll out onto the grass.

'Well, no pressure, but I'm hoping this is going to give me the edge so that we can win next Saturday.'

'Well, it's helping with my portfolio too, so thanks,' he said, smiling. He reached down to line up the balls next to a series of cones that he'd already laid out on the field. 'Right, I thought we'd do dribbling, passing, tackling and shooting. Possibly in that order, possibly not. Sound good?'

'Sounds exhausting after a week of school,' Lizzie said, feeling positively lethargic. She stifled a well-timed yawn.

'You've got this. Let's warm up.' He didn't give her a chance to respond and set off in a run around the field. 'Come on, Lizzie,' he shouted, when he noticed she hadn't followed him.

With a groan, Lizzie set off too. They ran twice round the field and then headed back to where they'd stretched.

'So, we're going to spend ten minutes on this first exercise,' Noah said, gesturing towards the cones laid out on the field. 'Take the ball, run it through the course of cones, take it round the end one and then bring it back again. OK?'

Lizzie watched intently as Noah demonstrated the exercise. With the June heat growing, he already had a slight sheen on his skin from the warmth of the sun. Lizzie watched the power in his strong legs as he ran, dodging this way and that to direct the ball where he wanted to take it.

Noah returned to the starting point and ran a hand through his hair to push it off his face.

'OK?' He picked up the ball and passed it to her.

'OK.'

Dropping the ball to the floor, Lizzie copied what Noah had

shown her, all the while desperately concentrating on not falling down or making a fool of herself in some other way.

'Good job. Now, let's pick up the speed,' Noah shouted from where he stood to the side, watching and assessing.

Lizzie upped her speed and took ten balls back and forth along the course Noah had set. The heat was sweltering, and she knew she probably looked a state. Afterwards, she bent over to catch her breath.

'That was excellent.' Noah placed a hand on her lower back.

'Thanks.' She was exhausted, but tingled at his lingering touch. It did nothing to slow her breathing down.

'Ready for shooting?'

Lizzie held up a finger to tell him to wait and reached for her water bottle. She took a swig and threw it to the floor.

'You're a slave driver, Mr Hatton,' Lizzie said, composing herself for the next exercise.

'You'll thank me.' He smiled with something more than your average smile.

His flirting made Lizzie blush. Extra football practice was turning out to be fun.

Noah said, 'Let's run across to the goal line and pass to each other as we go. We can move on to the tackling exercise I've got lined up after we've done that once or twice.'

'OK.' Lizzie was looking forward to this. Passing, shooting and tackling were all much more her thing than dribbling for any length of time. She liked to pass and get rid of the ball; it gave her the opportunity to find a more convenient space.

'So how long did your hangover last?' Noah asked. He grinned as he passed the ball to her and began to run.

'Long enough.' Lizzie blushed further, kicking the ball back to Noah.

'It's fine, Lizzie. It was cute.'

Cue more blushing, and only partly because she was embarrassed this time. She swallowed and took her eyes away from Noah to concentrate on the ball.

'It's a good job Tom was there to look after you,' he said, returning the ball.

'I know. I'm lucky. He said you almost drove me home, so thank you.'

'No problem. I was worried about you, to be honest.'

'Sorry,' said Lizzie, kicking the ball back to Noah.

'And I feel awful for having not been there now I know what happened afterwards,' he added.

'You couldn't have done anything. The fire happened a long time after you would have been there, even if you had taken us home.' As she said it, she realised that it was the kind of advice that perhaps she should have been listening to herself all this time.

'I guess so.' Noah's breathing came less easily as they sped across the field. 'You and Tom have any luck with the house hunting?' he asked, after a moment.

'Yes, I think we've found a place. Tom's been speaking to the estate agent. Hopefully, we'll be moving on Monday. It was empty, so things have been able to move fast. Good job really, after what happened on Friday night.'

'Still in town, I hope? . . . I mean, you've not got far to move?' He corrected himself self-consciously.

'Just the other side of the green. One of the Victorian town houses. We've got one of the top-floor flat conversions. It's gorgeous. I can't wait.'

Noah slowed to a halt by the goal. 'Congratulations.'

Lizzie reached for her water bottle and took another swig.

'Thanks. It was such a relief after getting the eviction notice out of nowhere.'

'You were evicted? I didn't know. I'm sorry,' Noah said.

'It's OK. Well, it is now everything's sorted. The guy who owns our flat wants to sell, so we need to be out. It's the risk you run with renting, I suppose.' She shrugged. 'Do you live in town?' – a natural way for the conversation to go, but it also gave Lizzie the opportunity to feed her curiosity.

'With Mum actually.'

'Oh?' Lizzie's interest piqued.

'I broke up with someone at the beginning of last year. A long-term relationship,' he added, a little awkwardly.

He avoided eye contact with Lizzie, and she was glad. She couldn't trust her face not to react to what he was saying.

'And Mum's been ill, so it seemed like a good idea to move in and take care of her for a while.'

'I'm so sorry, Noah.' Lizzie lifted her hand to comfort him, then changed her mind.

'It's fine. I mean, it's not, but it's OK at the moment. And living at home is fine. In fact, it's quite nice to be back and to be able to spend time with Mum.'

'Yes, I bet it is,' Lizzie said, her mind wandering to her own parents and how she would never be able to do this with them. What she'd give to spend some time with her own mum and dad.

'Lizzie . . . sorry . . . I didn't mean to . . .' Noah flustered over his words, running a hand through his hair again.

'OK, so we're both sorry.' Lizzie smiled.

'Yes. We are,' Noah said, suddenly serious.

Lizzie wasn't sure what it was they were apologising for any more.

'Tackling?' Noah changed the subject, snapping back into training mode.

Lizzie was glad. 'Tackling.' She nodded, relieved that they were moving away from whatever territory that had been. Tackling was far safer.

Noah picked up the ball and threw it to Lizzie. 'We're going to go full speed, so you'll need to start at the halfway line and I'll go from here.' He indicated the goal line.

'Oh, so I have to do the running? Are you trying to wear me out so I don't win the tackle?' she asked, jogging slowly to the halfway line.

'You're the one who's training,' he shouted after her.

When she got to the halfway line, Lizzie turned around to see Noah, smaller in the distance. He was poised, prepared to run, the whistle between his teeth, ready to blow it and set them both to running.

'Ready?' he shouted through his gritted teeth.

'Ready,' Lizzie called back.

Noah blew the whistle and let it fall, racing out of the blocks straight away. A couple of seconds later, Lizzie set off too, the wind rushing through her hair. It felt good to really stretch her legs and speed across the pitch.

Noah was heading straight for her. Was she supposed to get involved in a head-on tackle? Or was it acceptable to dart around him and shoot? In a split second, Lizzie took the choice she'd take in a real-life match and decided on the latter, veering to one side and forcing Noah to change direction.

'Cheeky,' he shouted as he closed the gap between them.

Lizzie laughed, suddenly carefree. She felt like a child must when they just ran for the fun of it, no purpose or pressure. She raced, listening to her feet smacking on the hard ground beneath her, until she felt her ankle give way and stumbled to the floor, Noah flying over the top of her and landing nearby.

'Ugh.' Lizzie spat out the grass that had forced its way into her mouth as she'd landed and rolled over onto her back, laughing. Her ankle smarted, but she didn't care. She turned to see Noah's whereabouts. He, too, was on his back, holding his stomach and laughing.

'Are you OK?' he asked, rolling onto his side and towards Lizzie, using his elbow to prop up his head.

'I'm fine.' Lizzie brushed her hair back from her face and looked up into the blue sky, a little afraid to look directly at Noah at such close proximity. She could feel his breath on her cheek. 'Are you?'

'Yes. No thanks to you! If you hadn't changed direction and headed straight to the goal like you were supposed to, we'd be fine!'

'I would never have done that in real life,' she protested.

'It was a practice!'

Lizzie giggled. 'Sorry.'

'You're covered in mud.'

Lizzie brushed her face to try and remove it. 'Where?'

'Here,' he said, and brushed a hand over her cheek to remove the dirt.

He was so close, Lizzie could feel the faintness of his breath on her neck. His dark eyes revealed nothing, even at this proximity – pools of endless black. He pulled his hand back and Lizzie touched her cheek where it had been; the warmth remaining. It was the first time he'd touched her like that in ten years, but it felt so familiar. Like home.

For a moment, they locked eyes with one another. Lizzie didn't like the thought of breaking the spell. She wanted to lie like this with Noah for ever; although maybe in a bed, or on a beach instead. She was acutely aware that if either of them moved, it would be so easy to kiss. She swallowed.

Noah cleared his throat. 'Come on, let's try again.' He put a stop to the moment and jumped up, reaching out a hand to help Lizzie up too. 'Is your ankle all right?'

Lizzie took his hand and pulled herself up. 'It's fine. Let's go.' She dribbled the ball back to the halfway line and turned to see Noah again in the distance. She wasn't sure whether what had just happened was all in her mind or whether they'd really just had a moment. Either way, it felt nice, and the butterflies in her stomach ahhh-ed collectively.

Chapter Eighteen

The more she thought about it, the more Lizzie worried that what had happened at their Friday football training was going to be awkward after all. As time passed after her and Noah's 'moment', Lizzie began to overanalyse what had happened and thought that maybe she was just reading too much into it. After all, Noah had jumped up and carried on their training session without so much as a backward glance. Maybe he'd felt awkward and had wanted to run away. Either way, the deliciousness of the memory was beginning to fade and turn into something more akin to anxiety.

By the time art came around on Monday afternoon, Lizzie had worked herself up into a frenzy.

'Miss, can you help me draw my goddess's hand?' Audrey asked.

Lizzie drifted back to the room, her worries becoming a faint haze in her mind, and looked down at Audrey's drawing. They were drawing black and orange mythology pictures of ancient Greek pottery. Audrey's goddess had a hand that looked like an anvil. Come to think of it, her picture was coming across much more Medusa than Aphrodite.

'I think you need to reconsider the perspective,' Lizzie said carefully. She didn't want to hurt Audrey's feelings. 'Is my hand the size of my head?' she held it up for comparison.

Audrey shook her head, and Nigel guffawed. Lizzie looked at him, his lip still swollen and sore from the incident with the scissors. She shot him a look that told him to be kind, and he went back to his own work. Audrey was already redrawing her hand, and it was looking much better.

Sophie came over and crouched down near Lizzie's seat. 'Are you OK to observe PE again today? I think from next week you can probably use the time for planning, but one more lesson might be useful so you can see how the curriculum builds over a term. You can use it as one of your write-ups for this week.'

'Sure.' Lizzie was surprised to feel a little deflated that the afternoon's lesson might be her and Noah's last for a while. It was OK; she'd gone ten years without seeing him – and for a legitimate reason, she reminded herself. Taking away their weekly PE lesson wouldn't affect her at all. If anything, it might make her less anxious before coming into school every Monday, and perhaps she could enjoy the odd art lesson for a change instead of letting the children down while her mind was elsewhere.

As always, Lizzie changed into her sports kit and met the children in the hall for the warm-up; except today, they were doing the main part of the lesson outside on the field in the sunshine.

'Right, one lap for everyone before we start,' Noah said, blowing his whistle. 'You too, Miss Morris,' he added, gesturing for them to go.

Lizzie headed off, put to shame by some of the lankier Year Six boys, who raced around the field. She finished somewhere at the back of the pack, having slowed down to encourage some of the more athletically challenged children – at least, that's what she was telling herself.

'Well done, guys!' Noah gave them a round of applause as they returned to the start. When they'd settled down to listen, he said, 'Today, we're going to do a mini Olympics.'

Lizzie glanced around the field, where she saw that Noah had set up a range of equipment. There was a standing long jump measured out, a pile of quoits to replicate some of the throwing events, and the ladder to mimic a mini hurdle event, among others.

'You'll need to get into your normal PE groups and move over to one of the events,' he said, and they followed his instructions, with only minimal chaos.

He walked over to Lizzie as they organised themselves.

'We'll be keeping a record of who gets what. I thought it might be best not to be in direct competition with each other.' He smiled.

Lizzie returned his smile and felt her face warm. So he cared about beating her, too. At least it wasn't just Lizzie who had a competitive streak – it turned out Noah wanted to win just as much. And he was right, of course – it was safer this way.

'Good idea.' Lizzie took the clipboard from him and traipsed over to the throwing area. She organised the children into a single-file line, and a student reluctant to take part volunteered to take the measurements to get out of doing the activity itself.

'Right, let's go then. Toby, you're up,' she said, and he came forward to stand along the start line. As he lifted the quoit, Lizzie could see he was visualising an epic throw. Unfortunately, he didn't visualise it quite hard enough, and it landed disappointingly at Lizzie's feet. As children do, those who were queuing behind thought this was hilarious. Lizzie attempted to shush them so Toby wouldn't lose his confidence. Their laughs and comments dissolved into faint mumblings. Toby trudged to the back of the line, scuffing his feet in the long grass, but Lizzie managed to catch his eye and gave him an encouraging smile.

'Next up,' Lizzie said and one of the girls came forward, throwing the quoit a decent enough middle distance.

'Good job, Sarah!' Lizzie wrote her distance down underneath where she had scrawled an X for Toby. Leading the little group, Lizzie started to enjoy herself. She was in charge and sort of teaching PE; it was another experience that made her realise she loved doing this, and her confidence grew.

It wasn't hideous either, of course, that while she coordinated her throwing event, now and then she could steal a glance in Noah's direction. And sometimes he was looking back. She didn't know if she was imagining it, or if they really had thawed a little. Maybe she had just started to forget the past, with him suddenly turning up in her present almost like a new man. Maybe she'd forgiven him for cheating all those years ago. But even as she thought it, she decided that she definitely hadn't. It was like that single act and what had happened afterwards with her parents had built up a barrier between them – so that no matter how cute he looked in his shorts, or how kind he was to his mum and his nan, Lizzie would never quite be able to get past it.

'So, do you want to meet this week to sort out the final sports day details?' Noah asked as they walked side by side, following the children in to get changed.

'I can't tonight, house stuff. But I could do Thursday? We could spend some time getting the stuff we need out of the store cupboard too then,' Lizzie suggested.

'Sounds good. So, did you get the flat you wanted in the end?'

'Yep!' Lizzie did a little skip. She was beyond excited about it. At first she'd been sad to have to move, but this new place was such a little gem, she was quite pleased that the whole horrible situation had happened in the first place – and it wasn't even a little bit fire damaged, which was a bonus. 'We're moving tonight.'

'Wow, that's really quick. I bet you and Tom are really excited.'

'You know Tom and I aren't together, right?' Lizzie said after a moment. She didn't know why she'd felt compelled to clear it up – maybe because she'd spent so much time giving off the illusion that they were house hunting together as a couple; maybe something had changed that meant she wanted Noah to know the truth; maybe she was falling . . . *No. Stop it. It's just good to be an honest and truthful person, right?*

'You aren't?' Noah turned to look at her, sounding genuinely surprised.

'Nope. I'm not with anyone at the moment,' she added, even though he hadn't asked. Her butterflies were screaming at her to stop talking. She was being far too obvious, but she couldn't stop herself. 'Tom and I have been flatmates for a few years now,' she added, hoping to take the heat off what she had said before.

Noah smiled, and his shoulders seemed to visibly relax. 'You do seem to get on really well. He's a top lad.'

Lizzie, in all her years of knowing Tom, had never heard him called a 'top lad'. She giggled. 'Well, I'd better get going. You'll be shocked to hear I've not yet finished packing.'

'Why doesn't that surprise me?' said Noah with a roll of his eyes.

'Be nice!' she joked, and elbowed him playfully. For a brief second, their hands seemed to entwine of their own accord and a spark shot through her body. 'I'll see you on Thursday then?'

'After school in the office?' Noah looked similarly thrown by the conversation and contact.

'Sounds great. See you then.' Lizzie broke into a jog to get back to the classroom in time, to help the children get changed and ready for pick-up.

Chapter Nineteen

'Right, come on you,' Kirsty said, taking a pile of Lizzie's clothes out of the wardrobe and dumping them on the bed. 'You've left it too late for a sort-out, so I guess we're just taking everything.'

'You would guess right,' Lizzie said, picking up the same pile and transferring it unfolded into a box labelled 'clothes'. It was box number five and they hadn't even broken the back of the clothes mountain that Lizzie had accumulated during her time in the flat.

Kirsty picked up a slinky red dress and held it up against her, an eyebrow raised. 'Really?'

'Erm, thank you very much.' Lizzie snatched it from her. 'This is my Jessica Rabbit dress and I love it. I may not fit into it, but I'm entirely sure future Lizzie will!' She scrunched it up and added it to the box.

Kirsty shook her head disapprovingly.

Tom kept popping up periodically to move the boxes down

to the van as Lizzie and Kirsty packed. Football training was in two hours, so the plan was to dump things in the van and worry about sorting it all out later, at the other end.

Lizzie rifled through the bag of jewellery and trinkets that were on the bed. She pulled out a necklace and held it up. It had a little pearl hanging from the bottom. She removed the other bits of jewellery that were caught in it.

'We haven't got time for . . .' Kirsty began, frustrated at Lizzie's lack of a sense of urgency. 'Is that Mum's?' She spoke quietly, having noticed what Lizzie was untangling. She sat down on the edge of the bed.

'I think so. There are a couple of bits in here that were hers.' Lizzie looped the necklace over her head and held the pearly adornment tightly in her hand.

'And you just keep them in there, with all of your other junk?' Incredulity spread across Kirsty's face.

'All right, Kirs. There's no need to be rude. It's safe, isn't it?' she said, running her finger over the pearl and back again. 'And I wear her ring all the time,' she added holding out her hand to admire the simple silver band. 'The rest of it was all a bit too showy for me.' Lizzie shrugged.

'It's safe, I guess, but shouldn't you keep it somewhere precious?' Kirsty folded another dress and dumped it in the box.

'I kept it, that's precious enough for me,' Lizzie said. 'You know me, I've never been the person who keeps things for sentimentality. That's just not my style.'

'I know, but they're Mum's . . .'

'Do you want them?' Lizzie asked, irritation creeping into her voice.

'No, I just . . .'

'Well, then.'

They slipped into a slightly awkward silence while Lizzie sorted through the rest of her jewellery and hair bits and pieces, before dumping them into the open box. She was acutely aware that something had shifted between them.

'Sorry,' Kirsty said, her shoulders slumping. 'It's just sometimes I . . .' She paused, her voice audibly choked.

'I know,' Lizzie said, joining her sister on the bed. 'But fighting with each other won't bring them back.'

'You're right.' Despite her agreement, Kirsty's voice remained annoyed. She was clearly relenting for an easy life.

It irritated Lizzie that Kirsty never really resolved arguments, not with her sister . . . not with her husband . . . Although, now she thought about it, that was exactly how Lizzie dealt with her own disagreements – especially with Noah. Perhaps it was a family trait.

Lizzie and Kirsty had only grown close since their parents had died, and since Lizzie had started teaching, she sensed the gap widening between them again. It was like it had been before, as if they had nothing interesting to say to each other any more. And when they did, it lapsed into semi-bickering.

It was true that for Lizzie, life seemed to be all about school, school, school at the moment – with a sprinkle of Noah for good measure. As a lawyer in an unhappy marriage, Kirsty just couldn't relate to anything her sister was saying.

Lizzie found her eyes wandering to Kirsty's arm, where she'd noticed the bruise before. With the fire and everything that was happening, she'd pushed it to the back of her mind – probably because she didn't really want to confront what it might mean. Even when she had attempted to address the subject, Kirsty had mostly pushed back. Lizzie worried that if they continued in this rough patch, she might never understand what was going on. She reminded herself that Kirsty had promised her she was safe. She wondered whether she should ask her again, just to be sure.

As if noticing Lizzie's glance, Kirsty pulled her sleeves down and fiddled with the lid of the box. Lizzie decided the conversation would keep, but certainly not for long.

'Shall we take these down to the van?' Lizzie said, looking around her now nearly empty room. It was bare except for the classic rogue hair grip and general fluff that had collected underneath her furniture.

'Yes. I think we're good to go,' Kirsty said. 'And just in time. I'm going to head back and get changed for practice. What's your plan?'

'Me and Tom will go over to the new place, unpack the boxes from the van and then I'll head over to the sports centre. Tom has promised he'll put my bed together, which is all I really need until tomorrow. We'll do the rest as and when we need it.'

Kirsty looked horrified. It was another example of how different they were.

'OK. Let's get these downstairs then,' Kirsty said, having clearly decided not to question Lizzie and Tom's plan. She lifted the box, shifting it in her grip to make sure it was safe to carry down the stairs to the van.

Once she'd left, Lizzie looked around her room. It had been good to her, this room. She'd had a lovely few years in this flat. But she couldn't help looking forward to getting to the new place. It felt like it symbolised the future for her, one that felt full of promise. Excited, Lizzie smiled to herself, put at least five tote bags onto her shoulder in one go and wedged them in by lifting the last box. She took it down to the van, where Tom was waiting.

'Is that everything?' he asked, a thin layer of sweat beading on his forehead. He wiped it with his arm.

'Think so.' Lizzie passed him the box and threw the tote bags into the van herself. 'I just need to do one last check and run the hoover round before we go.'

The new place was just as beautiful as she remembered. Tom got all flustered when he saw Chris was waiting outside to hand deliver the keys. The sexual tension between them was clear to see, but there was a sweetness too, a kindness that Lizzie couldn't help but smile at as Chris handed over the keys and left them to it.

Once they were in, Lizzie breathed a sigh of relief. The gorgeous June sunlight flooded in through the roof windows, which had been left open to let in the air. It was clean, spacious and empty – a perfect blank canvas for Lizzie and Tom to put their mark on.

'It's so big up here,' Lizzie said, spinning around in awe to take it all in.

'It won't be in a minute, once all your crap is in here,' Tom said, puffing his way into the room with the first of the boxes.

'Hang on. I'll give you a hand.' Lizzie followed him downstairs, and they began the laborious task of collecting everything from the van and bringing it up to the flat. It was the first and only time that Lizzie begrudged the fact that the flat was up on the third floor of the converted town house.

Within an hour they were done, or at least everything they owned was in the building, vaguely in the right zone or room.

'I'm really sorry, but I've got to get going,' Lizzie said,

looking at her watch and realising the time. 'Are you all right from here?'

'I'll be fine.' He didn't look fine. Tom's face was bright red and dripping with sweat. Lizzie was pretty sure that he hadn't exerted himself like this for a really long time.

By the time Lizzie arrived at training, she, too, was looking a little worse for wear. Rushing across town combined with the warmth of the evening's weather meant that she felt and looked rough.

She raced into the room just as warm-up was kicking off. Kirsty was already there.

'Hi,' Kirsty said. 'Everything go all right at the other end?'

'Yeah, fine,' Lizzie said, breaking into a jog next to her sister. 'Tom's setting us up so we can survive until the weekend.'

'He's handy to have around, that one,' said Kirsty.

They paused to do star jumps and burpees.

'He certainly is.' Lizzie ran again.

'Are you sure he's gay?' Kirsty asked.

'Why, are you interested?'

'No, I meant for you, silly. I've got Steve,' Kirsty said with a roll of her eyes. But in those eyes, there was a look of sadness.

'I'm not interested, no.' Lizzie laughed. 'I'm still trying to get my head around whatever this thing with Noah is.' She said it before she could stop herself.

'What?' Kirsty sounded confused and, to be honest, a little irritated.

'Well, I mean . . . I don't know . . . there's something there, isn't there?' Lizzie felt suddenly flustered. Perhaps she shouldn't have shared anything with her sister.

'I thought you were past all this, not interested any more.

199

The longer you hang onto him, the longer it'll be before either of you move on. It's not fair on you. And it's not fair on Noah, keeping him hanging like that.'

Lizzie felt like she'd been told off by a teacher. She frowned, her emotions an odd cocktail of rage and embarrassment.

'I'm not hanging onto him,' Lizzie said eventually, hurt. 'But he's back in my life and I need to explore things. It's an opportunity for me to get closure if nothing else.'

Kirsty didn't answer. Instead, she shook her head and let out a kind of snort. Before either of them could speak again, Coach Zoe called them in and sorted them into groups to go into their training exercises.

Lizzie and Kirsty walked over to their group, who were practising set pieces for free kicks. Coach Zoe was there too.

'This one's important, ladies,' she said. 'We might need this on Saturday and we need to be good.' She spoke with the pride of a military leader, thumping a fist into the palm of her other hand. The first set of girls got going under Zoe's watchful eye, the coach pacing up and down as if they were on inspection parade.

'I think you're probably better off without Noah,' Kirsty said while they waited, leaning against the wall.

'What? Why? Where's that come from?' Lizzie turned to read her sister's expression. She felt a little hurt, but couldn't pinpoint why.

'Lizzie, take it from me, your older and far more worldly-wise sister. Noah cheated on you. Once a cheater, always a cheater. I just think you're entering a situation where you're going to get hurt.' There was a snap to her voice that told Lizzie she meant every single word.

'Wow! Don't hold back, Kirs!' Lizzie looked down at her

feet for a moment, but couldn't leave it. 'The thing is, there's something there between us and I think . . .' She tailed off for a second before building up the courage to say it. 'I think I might be falling for him again.'

'What?' exclaimed Kirsty.

Lizzie had thought their conversations over the past couple of weeks might have given Kirsty a clue that this was where her heart was heading, but she looked genuinely shocked.

'You can't be!' she cried.

'Why not?' Lizzie was becoming frustrated with Kirsty's reactions. She'd thought her sister might be excited or curious – supportive even – but she just seemed angry somehow.

'Because,' she said, sighing with exasperation, 'he cheated on you. How many times do you need to hear that, Lizzie?'

'It was ten years ago.'

'And don't forget his actions were the reason you weren't able to be there for Mum and Dad.'

Lizzie was speechless. Kirsty had spent every minute since the fire telling Lizzie it hadn't been her fault, and now she was using the exact opposite argument to put her off Noah.

'Low blow, Kirs,' Lizzie said quietly.

Kirsty narrowed her eyes and seemed unrepentant.

Coach Zoe blew her whistle for the two groups to swap places. Lizzie lined up to take her shot, still smarting from their row.

Between her and the goal, Kirsty formed part of the defence. She was still looking pretty peeved as she stood there waiting for Lizzie to make her move.

Coach Zoe blew her whistle, and Lizzie assessed her options. To her left, one of their teammates, Leanne, waited to assist; to her right, she had a clear shot of the goal. That would be the obvious choice though, and the defence knew it. In an instant, she was racing to the left, waiting for Leanne to find a space to receive the ball.

She kicked the ball off the line and began moving towards her, before, out of nowhere, Lizzie felt an enormous weight beat her down from the right and floor her. She let out a scream as her body made contact with the concrete floor, one bone at a time. There was a collective gasp from onlookers as Lizzie gave herself and her body a moment to recover from the tackle. The concrete floor of the gymnasium was far harder than the school field, where she'd been floored by Noah. It was cool on her face and her arms and legs. It took her a moment to realise she'd been tackled from the side.

Jumping up a moment later, Lizzie looked around, still a little startled. And she was surprised to see that Kirsty was rubbing her arm, clearly the instigator of the tackle. What was she thinking? Had she really annoyed her that much this afternoon? Lizzie thought back through everything that had happened since the end of the school day. They'd rowed about Mum's jewellery, sure, and she'd been a little spiky in the last couple of minutes when they'd spoken about Noah, but what had she actually done? Was her relationship with Noah the problem here? No – she shelved that idea as quickly as it had jumped into her head. Kirsty must have argued with Steve before leaving the house and was still reeling from it, taking it out on Lizzie.

'What the hell, Kirsty?' Lizzie said, rubbing the knee she'd landed on.

'Sorry,' Kirsty mumbled; although quite clearly, she wasn't, accompanying her apology with a shrug.

They glared at each other for a moment before Coach Zoe shouted, 'Let's switch it up,' and everyone moved to another exercise.

Lizzie watched them go and Kirsty moved off, too.

'Sorry,' Kirsty said again.

'What is going on with you that you are that angry with me?' Lizzie snapped, looking pointedly down at Kirsty's arm. She knew it wasn't the right time to bring it up – they were both far too irritated – but there had to be something going on that was making Kirsty react like this.

Kirsty played with the sleeve of her football top and looked down for a moment.

'Nothing's going on with me,' she said. 'I'm just worried about what's going on with you. And Noah,' she added. 'You need to ignore whatever's been going on with you both, otherwise neither of you will ever move on.'

'Nothing. Nothing is going on with us. And you seem to be more worried about him than you are me. *I'm* your sister!'

Lizzie sloped off to take a swig from her water bottle before joining another group who were practising their shooting. After the tackle and the accusations, Lizzie had had enough.

'And then she just sort of tackled me,' Lizzie explained when she finally got back to the new flat.

Tom had created a 'living room' out of upturned boxes, and had a pizza delivery ready for Lizzie's return. They sat cross-legged on the floor, on towels that Tom had laid out like rugs. It was homely in an odd, flea-market kind of way.

'Wasn't that what you were practising?' Tom asked, tilting his head to catch the pizza that had flopped over in his mouth.

'Not really. We were doing a free kick set piece. I guess tackling is sometimes involved, but if that had been on a pitch, in an actual game, she'd have been sent off. There was no need for it.'

'She seemed a bit moody earlier. Maybe she's having a bad time of it with Steve at the moment?'

'She's always having a bad time with Steve,' Lizzie said. Her mind slipped to the bruise again. 'That's the other thing . . .' She was on the fence about broaching the subject with Tom.

'What?'

'I think maybe they're fighting.'

'We know that they're fighting,' Tom said, matter-of-fact.

'No, I mean, like really fighting. Physical fighting. I thought I saw some bruises the other day at practice and since then, Kirsty's been really strange about covering up her arms. She even mentioned that she might leave him. I never thought she would, but she was pretty convincing the other day.'

'You think Steve is getting violent?' Tom asked, his pizza flopping back into the box.

Lizzie nodded. 'I'm worried he might be. And I don't know what to do. I'd have thought Kirsty could either hold her own, or walk away from something like that. But now I'm not so sure.'

'You have to talk to her again,' Tom said. 'Even if it's for your own peace of mind. You'd hate yourself if anything terrible happened.'

'I've broached it with her, but she told me it wasn't the time. You're right, though. I need to try again.'

Lizzie nodded and made a sound in agreement, reaching for another slice of pizza. She knew Tom was right. Kirsty might have behaved oddly that evening – and she'd get to why in time. But she worried about her sister. Kirsty maintained that on occasion, her and Steve's relationship was a good one, and they had a lovely life with their three boys – but from time to time Steve simply wasn't a very nice person, and Lizzie wondered whether Kirsty was staying with him because she loved him, or for the boys' sake. She really hoped it was the former, but the more time that passed, the more convinced Lizzie became that things were seriously wrong with the relationship. She resolved to bring it up with her next time they met.

Chapter Twenty

Tom couldn't calm Lizzie on the walk to school that Thursday. It was the day of the maths lesson – a real test. Maths certainly wasn't Lizzie's strong point and even the planning had taken an absolute age.

'It will be fine,' Tom said.

It was the hundredth time he'd tried to console her. Lizzie nibbled the inside of her lip and tried to convince herself he was right.

'Remember, these kids are ten and eleven. They won't know if what you're saying is true or not; and if you realise you've made a mistake, you can just back-pedal and correct yourself later on.'

'I don't think you're giving these children enough credit,' Lizzie said, taking her sunglasses from her head and putting them on to block out the June sunshine.

It was a gorgeous day, and July was just around the corner. It felt like they were walking along the coast in the Mediterranean, just the slight wisp of a breeze in the air.

'Besides, Sophie will be observing me too and I don't want to look like an idiot.'

'You'll be fine.' It was as if he were a toy doll who only said two or three key phrases if you pulled the string on his back.

'Are you OK?' asked Lizzie. 'You seem a little preoccupied.'

'Mmm, fine.' A smile played at the corner of his lips.

'Tom, what is it?' she said, elbowing him playfully.

'Nothing.' He shook his head and pressed his lips firmly together, the edges still slightly upturned in a half smile.

'Thomas.' Lizzie stopped and reached for his arm to stop him too. 'What are you not telling me?'

'So, promise not to get too excited?' A huge smile spread across his face.

'Well, not now, no! Tell me, tell me, tell me!'

He started walking again, looking straight ahead. 'I've got a date with Chris on Saturday night!' He followed it with an excited squeak.

'Yay!' Lizzie clapped her hands together. 'You kept that quiet.'

'Well, we've been talking and texting, and we finally agreed to meet up when we spoke last night, so we're going for drinks on Saturday.'

'I'm so pleased, Tom. That's great news.'

'I know!' Tom squeaked again and Lizzie squeezed his arm.

By the time break arrived, Lizzie was in the swing of things, and the lesson she was about to teach didn't seem quite so daunting any more, thank God.

Sophie left her to set up. She put the tasks up on the board and set out the resources each student would need on the tables. Looking around, she felt the room looked exciting, and Lizzie hoped the children would come in feeling enthusiastic.

She raced to the staffroom to make a swift cup of tea and hurried back to greet everyone at the door. Once settled, she began.

'So today we're going to have a go at a maths challenge,' she said, clasping her hands to feign the enthusiasm she hoped the children would join her in. There were a couple of 'ooh's as if a mediocre firework display had gone off.

OK, plough on, thought Lizzie.

'I'm going to set you up in groups and each table will work on a different task. It will be a competition, so you will try to solve each of the maths problems as quickly as you can in your groups.'

There were some more 'ooh's and a ripple of excitement in a couple of places. In other pockets of the classroom, there were blank faces and one boy was already building a tower out of the cubes. Lizzie swallowed. Even as she tried to explain herself, she could hear the ideas growing muddled between her brain and her mouth.

'Right. Here's the first thing you need to do.' She carried on regardless, remembering Tom's advice to be confident, however terrified she might be feeling inside. 'Everyone needs to find the table with their name on it. That will be where you start. You've got thirty seconds. Go!'

Children leapt up and scurried around, trying to find where they needed to go. Across the room, through the chaos, Lizzie spotted Sophie's expression. It was the face of someone who was slightly concerned about where the lesson was going. Lizzie resolved to continue. She looked around at the children. They were everywhere, and only a third of them had made it to their designated tables. She was sure it would be fine. Wouldn't it?

'Three, two, one,' Lizzie said, her hand in the air. She'd seen Sophie do it before to get the class's attention, so she knew it worked. And it sort of did, although there were some stragglers who took a few more moments to be quiet and listen this time. Lizzie put it down to the excitement of an active maths lesson in unfamiliar groups. She'd put some thought into who each child should work with, so it wasn't random, but they didn't know that, and she could see how it might get some of them riled up.

'OK. Your first problem is on the upside-down sheet on your table. In a second—Shhh, Benjamin.' She paused and brought her finger to her lips, waiting for him to stop whispering to Toby before carrying on. 'One person will need to turn it over and read out the instructions. Then, in your group, you need to come up with the answer to the question and write it on your group's answer sheet. When you're done, pop your hand up and I'll record your time. Remember, this is a maths challenge. It's a competition. So there's a prize for the winner.'

This got Lizzie a little more enthusiasm, and the children settled quickly into silence, waiting for Lizzie to say go. Underneath the silence, there was already some wrestling over sheets and resources. Lizzie hoped they were just excited and raring to get started.

'Go!' she said.

And then the chaos really began. Children tussled over the plastic cubes and counters. The volume escalated from a near-silence to a cacophony of excitability and arguments. Lizzie watched it unfold and waited to see if it would calm down. But it didn't. Then the children's hands started to shoot up.

'Miss, what does this mean?'

'Miss Morris, James won't let me use the bricks.'

'Miss! Miss! Sarah's reading the instructions out in a stupid voice.'

'Listen in!' Lizzie screamed, losing her cool. She could feel the back of her neck breaking out into a sweat. 'Three, two, one.' And the noise died down. Eventually. It took much longer than Lizzie had anticipated and inside, she was panicking. This lesson looked nothing like Sophie's. Where had she gone wrong?

'OK. Let's take a step back and focus on one problem at a time. Audrey, can you read out your maths problem please?' She clicked the computer mouse to make sure that the corresponding problem and diagram were also being projected onto the board.

Audrey dutifully read out the question and Lizzie modelled it on the board, talking them through the steps they needed to solve the problem.

'Right. You've got four minutes. Everybody now needs to have a go at this problem here.' She put a similar one on the board and pointed to it. 'The first team to get the correct answer, with the correct working, gets five points.'

Instantly, the children started trying to work out the answer and Sophie, sitting in the corner of the room making copious notes, looked relieved by Lizzie's U-turn. She hoped that she'd done something right at last. Goodness knew it felt better than the chaos that had ensued only minutes before.

The classroom looked like the Tasmanian Devil had ripped through it once the children had left at the end of the lesson. Lizzie slumped down at the desk and put her head in her hands.

'Are you OK?' Sophie asked, coming to sit next to her.

'I think so. Are you?' Lizzie joked, as if they'd both been through some kind of horrific ordeal together. Lizzie certainly felt like she had.

'You did fine,' Sophie said, placing her observation notes down on the desk.

Lizzie tried really hard not to look at them. 'Really? Were you in the same lesson as I was?'

'All right,' Sophie said. 'There were a few things that didn't go quite right to begin with, but you were flexible with your plan and made it right in the end. It was absolutely the right thing to do to stop the lesson, model the problem solving and help them all to understand the maths. Looking at your learning objectives, they got there. They just took a slightly different route to the one that you had planned.'

'I suppose so.' Lizzie still wasn't convinced. She was warm, flustered and sweating. Did teachers go through this every day?

'We can talk more about it at your mentor meeting. The bottom line is, you didn't quite set up the lesson properly at the outset, but you solved it by adapting your lesson plan as you went. They all went away being able to do something that they couldn't do at the start of the lesson, which is the key thing, right?'

'Maybe,' Lizzie said, still unsure.

'Well, you don't have to believe me, but it's true. Maybe you should come back and have another go tomorrow at a similar activity, and see if you can adapt it so that it works a little more like you imagined it?'

'Really? You'd let me do that?' Lizzie asked. 'I guess I could plan something. Will you need to see the plan before tomorrow?' She was worried about turning something around that quickly.

'No. I trust you. You do the maths lesson tomorrow and see how it goes. I'll be about after school if you want to run anything past me.' She picked up her paperwork and stood, ready to leave. 'I know you're disappointed in that lesson, Lizzie, but you don't need to be. The best way to get over that first hurdle is to get back in the saddle and try again. It'll be good for you.'

Lizzie pulled a face to show that she wasn't sure she agreed with Sophie's assessment.

'You probably need a break.' Sophie moved towards the door. 'Have your lunch and chalk it up to experience. It was better than you think it was. But a big part of teaching is going away and reflecting on what happened in the classroom, so that you can come back and make it better next time.'

That sounded like the kind of advice she could do with in more than one area of her life.

Despite Sophie's praise, Lizzie was pretty sure that she was just being kind. She certainly didn't feel like she'd learnt anything, or that the children had either. In fact, she felt pretty deflated, and her self-pity ruined the afternoon. The rest of the school day was uneventful and disappeared under a cloud of disappointment – for Lizzie, anyway.

By the end of the day, Lizzie had almost forgotten that she'd agreed to meet Noah for their final sports day planning meeting. She hadn't had any time to get worked up or worry. And she hadn't visited the staff toilet to fix her hair, which had grown bigger and frizzier and more dishevelled as her day had gone horribly downhill.

'Are you all right?' Noah asked, as Lizzie appeared around the hall door. They had agreed to meet at the store cupboard, so that they could organise all the equipment they would need for sports day next week.

Lizzie pushed her mad hair back off her face, suddenly self-conscious.

'I'm fine.' She carefully stepped over the debris of what Noah had already cleared out from the cupboard.

Noah stopped what he was doing and focused his attention on Lizzie. '"Fine" is always a brush-off with you.' He pushed a bag of netballs back onto the shelf as they threatened to tumble down. 'Besides, you don't look fine.'

Lizzie relented. 'OK. You're right.' She folded her arms defensively. 'I've had a shocker of a day. I taught my first maths lesson and predictably, it was appalling.'

'I'm sure it wasn't,' Noah said, taking a step further out of the cupboard.

'It really was.' She'd always had a nasty habit of becoming self-deprecating when already feeling low – and she was certainly feeling low after the day she'd had. 'The children didn't understand what I asked them to do, and I basically had to throw my lesson plan – that had taken hours to write, I might add – out the window. It was a complete nightmare.' She perched on the edge of the pile of gym mats.

'Lizzie, I'm sure it was much better than you think it was. And with teaching, it's always one of those things. Kids are unpredictable and sometimes things go horribly wrong, even for the best of teachers.'

He placed a hand on her shoulder and Lizzie smiled, acutely aware of his touch.

'I'm fine, really.' She shook the moment away and attempted to refocus on the task at hand. Although she struggled to shake off the feeling of ickiness that the day had brought upon her.

'As long as you're sure.' Noah turned his touch into something friendlier by giving Lizzie's shoulder a couple of pats.

His change in gear didn't go unnoticed by Lizzie.

'Let's take your mind off it by sorting out this cupboard,' he said with mock cheer.

'Ugh.' Lizzie peeled herself off the mats and peered into the cupboard. It was no Narnia.

Noah pointed to a large A3 sheet of paper full of things they might need. 'I made a list of what we need here. We just need to find each one and tick it off. I brought some tubs over there, where we can put everything to keep it separate ready for next week.'

'Great.'

The cupboard was long and thin and smelt of decades-old PE. It was a mixture of decaying rubber and unwashed gym kit – powerful enough to take Lizzie's breath away as she made her way inside.

'How do you work in these conditions?' She pushed the bibs that hung off the wall back, so that she could get to the centre of the cupboard – the optimum position to gather things.

'Actually, we could start with bibs,' Noah said, ignoring her comment.

Lizzie rolled her eyes. 'How many do we need and what colours?' She turned and counted them.

'Don't mind which colours,' Noah said, scanning the list. 'But we need four different colours and four of each.'

Lizzie rifled through them and counted out what they needed.

'Actually,' Noah said, as she passed them towards him, 'could we go with red instead of the white? I think it's more obvious against the yellow when the kids are out on the field.'

Lizzie held her tongue, but tutted involuntarily at his change of mind, taking the bibs back and attempting to rehang them before picking out the ones Noah had suggested. As she picked out the red he had indicated, the whole lot slipped off the tiny hook and cascaded to the floor. Lizzie groaned.

'Why is this cupboard so messy?' she grumbled.

'It's not. It's fine.' Noah climbed over all the things on the floor to get in and help her.

'It isn't, Noah. Look at it.' She held out her hands emphatically. 'You can't get to anything. When you do, it falls all over the place. It stinks.'

Lizzie was mildly aware that she was taking her crappy day out on Noah, but she couldn't help it. And she didn't stop herself.

'Calm down, Lizzie. You've only got to spend about twenty minutes in here and then you won't ever have to be in here again.' He picked bibs up off the floor, choosing some to keep and putting others back onto the hooks.

'Don't tell me to calm down, Noah,' Lizzie said, doing the same.

He should have left it there, but he didn't. 'Well, stop getting so stressed about something that's not at all important.'

'Noah.' Lizzie's voice had become strained and squeaky, but she had no control over it. 'I've had a hideous day . . .'

'I know, but there's no need to take it out on me.'

'And I . . . ugh. Never mind.'

As if she were looking down on the pair of them, Lizzie could see them a decade ago, rowing about who would drive to see whom, or why Noah's flat was so untidy.

'What's going on, you two?' Miss Davies, the headteacher, popped her head round the door, looking completely out of place in her tailored business suit and bright red lipstick.

'Um, nothing,' Lizzie said, her cheeks warming. She picked up another bib and passed it to Noah, who took it off her and added to the pile.

'We just had an accident with some of the equipment,' Noah explained, clamouring over everything on the floor to get out of the cupboard.

'OK. Well, try to keep it down, will you? There's an after-school club going on next door and they can hear you in there,' she said, before turning and walking away.

Lizzie was mortified. Her face instantly flushed again, her pink skin clashing with her red hair.

'Oh my God,' she said. 'That's so embarrassing.' She delved further into the cupboard as if to hide from her embarrassment.

'It's just Flo,' Noah said. 'No harm done.'

'For you, maybe. I'm trying to make a good impression here.'

'It's fine,' Noah said again, irritatingly blasé.

Lizzie passed him the rest of the bibs, ignoring her frustration, which, if Noah carried on as he was, would never dissipate.

'Right, next up is the tape measure and stopwatches. If I remember rightly, they are in a green tub somewhere near the back.' Noah pointed a finger, which covered at least half of the cupboard. Helpful.

Lizzie rolled her eyes and carefully stepped further into the space, trying desperately to ignore the fact that probably half of the UK's spider population lived somewhere in the depths of the storage cupboard. She located the tub on the top shelf, stepped up tentatively onto a cardboard box to hoist herself up, reached for it, and crawled back out to pass it to Noah.

'I'm getting the silent treatment, am I?' Noah said.

Lizzie said nothing.

'Great. Mature as ever, Lizzie.'

Lizzie said nothing, simply raised her eyebrows and shrugged.

'Fine. We need that box of quoits and beanbags,' he said, pointing towards a clear storage tub close to the entrance.

Lizzie picked it up and added it to their accumulating pile of equipment, turning to hide the frustrated tears that she was worried would escape in front of Noah.

'Look, Lizzie.' Noah reached for her arm as she turned to scramble back into the cupboard.

She stopped and turned to face him.

'I'm fed up with fighting. All we've ever done is fight and compete and it's boring. I just want us to be friends. Can we at least try to do that?'

Just 'friends' was a sucker punch to Lizzie's gut, but at the same time, his attempt at a reconciliation felt like a step forward, perhaps with potential and promise.

Lizzie relented like a moody teenager. 'Fine.'

'I hate it when you say fine.'

'I thought we weren't going to fight any more.' Lizzie swiped the list off him and scanned it for the next item to locate.

'Fine,' he said.

Lizzie smiled. 'Fine.'

Chapter Twenty-One

Thursday night was a night of fitful sleep. But for once, instead of dreaming about the fire, Lizzie had nightmares about maths. She lay there for a long time, running the lesson repeatedly in her head. Sometimes it was a rehash of the lesson that had gone wrong and other times it was a mental rehearsal for the lesson she would teach on Friday. Even when she finally closed her eyes, numbers and maths problems floated in front of her eyes.

She was nervous, worried about the maths problems themselves, terrified of the children's behaviour. But at the same time, she knew she had to do this. And if she at least pretended that she knew what she was doing, then everything would be OK, right?

During break time, she set the classroom out in a similar fashion to the day before. Each table was a different maths station and was littered with resources – plastic cubes, counters, beads. But this time, she'd thought carefully about how to address the beginning of the lesson, including how she'd model what was going to happen. She'd also edited the instructions at each station to make them more straightforward and had reconsidered the groups. Other little things, like making more copies of the resources, would hopefully resolve some of the arguments about who was going to read what.

Forty minutes in and so far, it was working. Lizzie stood in the middle of the classroom with a stopwatch that she'd stolen from the sports day haul.

'Go!'

It was the third challenge of five and so far, all the children were engaged and seemed to know what was going on. She'd seen a lot of what she thought was correct maths, and had only had to encourage a couple of them to get involved – and even then it was only because of the group size rather than their behaviour.

As always, Sophie was there, scribbling copious notes, but she didn't look as pained as she had done the previous day. Lizzie looked over and she did a little thumbs up, mouthing 'yay!', which allowed Lizzie to relax and enjoy how the lesson was going.

'Thank you, Miss,' Nigel said on his way out of the classroom at lunchtime.

'Thanks, Miss Morris,' said another student.

And once the classroom was empty except for Lizzie and Sophie, Lizzie felt a sense of calm and pride, rather than the icky feeling in the pit of her stomach she'd had to contend with yesterday.

'See?' Sophie walked over to her with her notes.

Lizzie nodded and allowed herself to smile.

'That was great. You changed all the bits you needed to change, but still got them to do what you wanted them to. Well done. You should be really proud of that.'

'Thanks.' Lizzie moved between the tables to collect the children's work and tidy up the mess they'd created. It was a good mess though – the kind of mess that suggested they'd had fun while they were learning.

'How did it go?' Tom asked, entering the staffroom later to find Lizzie eating her sandwich at lunchtime.

'Great,' she said through a mouthful of bread and ham. 'Exactly as I dreamt it would be.'

'Yay!' Tom slumped down next to her on one of the staffroom chairs. 'Did they behave?'

'Yeah, they did. I guess it's because they had something to do and knew how to do it, so they didn't get off track and find other ways of keeping themselves entertained.'

Tom tucked into a bag of crisps. 'I'm so pleased for you, Lizzie. Nice one.'

'The lesson went well, did it?' Noah asked, sweeping into the room while they spoke. He went to the counter and grabbed an apple.

'Yes thanks,' she said, waiting for the *I told you so*.

'Told you so,' he said predictably, taking a bite of his apple and leaving the room as quickly as he had entered it.

Noah never disappointed. Except when he did.

Lizzie turned back to Tom. 'So, are you excited about your date tomorrow night?'

'Don't bring up Chris just to try and get out of talking about that one.' Tom waved a finger at where Noah had just been.

'I didn't,' Lizzie said, drinking some of her water before biting into her own apple. 'I'm genuinely interested in your date tomorrow night.'

'Lizzie . . .'

'What?' she said innocently.

Tom stared at her, wide-eyed and serious.

'There's nothing going on. We spend all of our time fighting or making up. He's impossible.'

'But you still like him?' Tom pressed her.

Lizzie took another bite of apple. 'Yes, but I don't think it's wise to go back to the past.' She wasn't quite sure whom she was trying to convince.

'You sound like your sister. The Lizzie I know isn't sensible and measured. The Lizzie I know is carefree and spontaneous. That Lizzie would go for it.'

'Stop talking about me in the third person. It's freaking me out,' she said, attempting a diversion, any diversion. 'And don't compare me to Kirsty. I love her, but I am most definitely not her.'

'Well, we'll see,' Tom said, taking a satisfied bite out of his sandwich. 'Have you spoken to her yet?' His tone grew serious. 'You know, about . . .' He let the statement hang between them.

Guiltily, Lizzie looked down at her feet. They ached from her choice of heeled shoe.

'Not yet. I text her every day to check in, but I'm going to bring it up properly after the football match tomorrow. She asked me to wait, and I have, but I think it's time. We're going for brunch and it'll just be the two of us, so I'll be able to talk to her properly.'

Tom squeezed Lizzie's knee supportively. 'It'll be OK.'

Lizzie glanced at him briefly. 'I really hope it will be.'

Chapter Twenty-Two

Saturday was cup final day. It had finally arrived. The birds were just beginning to chirp when Lizzie first opened her eyes and realised what day it was and what was happening. And for once, she'd had a peaceful night's sleep and slept right through to her alarm. Today was important, and she was ready to win.

Jumping out of bed, she headed for the shower to wake herself properly. Who was she kidding? Even though it was an exciting day, it would still take a mildly cold shower and a cup of tea to get her ready for any kind of social interaction.

After showering, she pulled on her football kit – freshly washed and pressed for once – and padded out into the kitchen to make breakfast. She was just heating some porridge in the microwave when Tom walked in and flopped face down on the sofa in his dressing gown.

'Morning,' Lizzie said, taking the bowl out of the microwave as it pinged.

Tom stifled a yawn. 'Morning.'

'Sleep OK?'

Tom nodded.

'Are you coming to watch the game today?' she asked.

'Why are you so loud and energetic?' Tom flipped the hood of his dressing gown up and over his head.

'Sorry. Are you hungover?' Lizzie asked loudly, offering him a cup of tea.

'A little.' He accepted the tea and burrowed down into the sofa. 'Thanks.'

'Well, come on!' Lizzie said, bouncing from one foot to the other. 'The game starts at nine and I've got to leave at eight so I can get there in time for the warm-up.'

'Would I be an awful friend if I just came for the second half?' Tom asked, sipping his tea and rubbing his temple.

Lizzie put her hands on her hips. 'Yes, Tom. Yes, you would.'

'I think I'm going to have to accept that then and live with the consequences. I need to assess whether or not I'm likely to throw up before I leave the house. It's just not worth the risk.' He shook his head dramatically.

'Well, maybe I can live with that. I'd rather you weren't there than distracting me by being sick on the sidelines.'

'See, I am a good friend really,' Tom said with a weak smile.

'I thought you said you were a *little* hungover,' Lizzie said, noticing his grey pallor and tufty hair.

'Potato, potaaato.' Tom stood slowly and left the room, presumably to go back to bed. The belt of his dressing gown dragged sadly behind him along the floor.

Lizzie rolled her eyes and sat at the breakfast bar to eat her porridge. Tom would be there for the end of the game. She knew she could count on him. Kirsty would be there too, so at least she'd have someone to cheer her on for the first half. Although the thought of the conversation she had to have with her sister afterwards was weighing heavily on her mind. She knew they'd talked briefly before when Kirsty had opened up after training, but nothing had been said since and somehow that was worse than if they'd not spoken at all.

The walk over to the football ground was glorious. Given the early hour, the streets were empty and so the sunshine and the birdsong were all that accompanied her as she walked across the village to the football pitch at the secondary school. She was pleased it was a home game to take away the stress of navigating somewhere new.

As always, when she arrived the warm-up was already in full swing.

'Come on, Lizzie!' cried Coach Zoe, waving her over as soon as she saw her wandering across the field.

Lizzie broke into a jog and joined in with the star jumps.

'Hi, everyone,' she mumbled.

A few smiles came her way.

She hated warm-ups. She was always exhausted afterwards and had no energy left to do what she was actually here to do. Her point was proved as Coach Zoe told them all to run a lap of the field.

The breeze as she ran was pleasant, whipping her hair away from her face and leaving her cheeks feeling fresh. The ground was perfect for playing on – no recent rain to make it slippy or squashy underfoot, but just damp enough with dew that it didn't jar her ankles as she ran.

The ladies returned to where they'd begun and stretched out under the instruction of their coach. Lizzie was pumped and ready to go, adrenaline already coursing through her veins. She watched as the opposition warmed up at the other end of the pitch. They had met before, and Lizzie squinted, trying to recognise who on the team she'd played against in the past, sizing up the competition.

A small crowd of spectators had gathered along the edge of the pitch, ready for kick-off. A few parents and partners mostly, with some children running around their legs, chasing each other.

Lizzie waved at Kirsty, who hadn't made the team, but had come to support her sister. She stood on the line down one side, in her team top, and waved back.

Coach Zoe blew her whistle. 'Right. Gather in, ladies.'

The squad huddled together for their team talk. They looked nervously around at one another, champing at the bit to get started.

'We've worked hard to get here, girls,' she said. 'It's been a tough season, but we've made it.'

There were a few nods of agreement.

'After twenty years of trying, you guys deserve to win this game. So go out there and show everyone what you're made of.'

Someone whooped, and there was a little ripple of applause.

'Do me proud. Do yourselves proud. Let's go!' Coach Zoe clapped, and the team cheered before they spread out, running to their positions on the field.

Lizzie ran to the centre spot, where she was due to kick off. The referee, from another local ladies' team, waited until everyone was ready and brought the whistle up to her lips. The players and the crowd went silent as they inhaled a collective breath.

Across the field, Lizzie looked up towards Kirsty, who gave

her a wink. Then she noticed Noah was standing next to her. She would recognise that silhouette anywhere. It threw her, her focus lapsing for a moment as a million thoughts raced through her head. She blinked hard, banishing them all from her mind, and refocused on the task at hand. It was lovely that Noah had come to watch the game – and maybe he had even come to support her – but she couldn't let that get in the way of playing a match that she had worked so hard for several years to be a part of.

The whistle blew and Lizzie kicked the ball, running forwards to chase it down, the rest of her team moving up the field with her. In a disappointing few minutes, they were down by one goal, only to equalise twenty minutes later.

After an exhilarating opening thirty minutes, the rest of the first half was tame. Boring even. The ball went back and forth, with neither team making any actual progress with it. Lizzie ran up and down the pitch, exhausted and panting when the whistle finally went for the end of the first half. She ran towards her team's end of the pitch and tucked into the traditional orange segments that Coach Zoe always prepared for half-time.

'You're doing a great job, ladies. That first goal in response to theirs was magic, but all of you, and them, seem to be lagging slightly. We just need a fraction more effort to push past their defence and we'll have this. I know you've got it in you.'

Coach Zoe paced back and forth, beating her fist into her palm and gritting her teeth. She wanted to be out there too, and had been once upon a time – Lizzie remembered her playing the last time the ladies' team had won twenty years ago, the day she and Noah had shared their first silly childhood kiss.

Coach Zoe had been a hero then, scoring the winning and only goal in the dying minutes of the game. It must be so frustrating to watch from the sidelines now and have no impact on the game itself. Lizzie felt a wave of ambition to take it home for Coach Zoe, who had been working so hard with them all season.

Taking another orange segment, Lizzie sat on the grass for a moment and drank from her water bottle. She looked over to where Noah and Kirsty were watching. Tom had joined them finally. He clearly hadn't showered and looked like he'd come straight from whatever club he'd frequented the previous evening. Lizzie was pretty sure he was still wearing last night's clothes, which he'd clearly grabbed from his floordrobe and put back on. To his credit, Lizzie was pleased to see he'd not turned up in his dressing gown at least. It wouldn't have been the first time . . .

The three of them were chatting away about something, although Tom was glazed over and just sort of looking ahead to the ground. He was much paler than usual. She was pleased that he'd made the effort – despite clearly feeling so worse for wear – to come down and support her. He really was a good egg.

As she looked on, Kirsty threw her head back dramatically, laughing at something Noah had said. Tom smiled too, although Kirsty, apparently, found it particularly hilarious. So much so that she tapped Noah playfully on the shoulder in faux disbelief at whatever he was sharing. Was she flirting? Lizzie squinted in an attempt to understand the dynamic further. Kirsty was playing with her hair now, while Noah spoke.

Lizzie didn't know why it infuriated her so much. Well,

she did actually – she still had some sort of feelings for Noah. And Kirsty was married – admittedly to Steve, but she wasn't interested in Noah, was she? She'd made her feelings about his cheating past perfectly clear when they'd spoken the other day. She'd made it very obvious that she thought Lizzie shouldn't go there. Because Kirsty was interested in him? No, Lizzie was getting annoyed about nothing. It was probably just the pressure of the game.

And as her focus moved back towards the imminent second half, a whistle sounded to signal the start of play. She pushed Noah and Kirsty out of her mind and psyched herself up for the second half.

The teams moved back to their starting positions, now at the opposite ends of the pitch, and Lizzie positioned herself, ready to receive the ball when it was kicked off by the other team's centre.

Once more, the players and spectators waited in silence as the referee brought the whistle to her lips and blew. And then they were off again. Lizzie watched as the ball headed her way. Receiving it and controlling it down to the ground, she passed it immediately to the other side of the pitch where Leanne received it and ran towards their goal end. Lizzie followed her down on the opposite side of the field, watching her closely as she ran. Leanne expertly dodged the opposing team's defence until she got close to the goal, and then their defender stole the ball, sending it up the pitch once more, both teams following.

By the eighty-sixth minute, the score line was the same. There seemed to be very little separating the two teams. Both had the gumption to attack, but both had skilled defenders waiting to stop them in their tracks, and so a game of cat-and-mouse, back and forth, had ensued.

Lizzie finally got hold of the ball and raced towards the goal. She wasn't stopping for anything this time. She was determined to make it past their back line and win the game. She'd worked too hard this season to win or lose over penalties. She raced past one defender, losing the ball for a brief moment, before knocking it through their legs and carrying on.

A second defender was flummoxed by her footwork and simply let her dribble the ball past them. Then from nowhere, she felt a player run into the side of her. Their feet and legs tangled together and they both fell to the ground. For the third time in recent history, Lizzie landed on the hard ground. She received a mouthful of mud, and grass in her eyes. For a moment, she mapped her body, searching for pain. She was shocked breathless by the fall and her front hurt where she'd hit the floor, but she was fine.

She jumped up, ready to fight her case, but the referee was already whistling and holding up a yellow card. It would be a free kick for Lizzie's team, just like they'd practised on Monday. And Lizzie would take it.

Standing in the spot where she'd been tackled to the ground, Lizzie sized up the distance to goal and analysed her best course of action. She realised quickly that her best option would be to shoot. They simply didn't have any time to waste. The clock was ticking and she didn't think there would be much injury time.

The opposing team built up their wall. She was aware of Leanne and a couple of other players to the side and considered passing to them, but they were being marked cleverly by a member of the other team – a player that had been getting in the way all game. There was nothing for it. Lizzie was going to have to shoot and hope for the best.

Seeing that both sides were ready, the referee stood next to

Lizzie, her whistle between her teeth. She looked at her watch, scanned the pitch, and blew. Lizzie wasted no time. She ran up to the ball and curved it round to the left. The players from the other team watched, gormless, as it whistled over their heads and found the top left-hand corner of the net. Even the goalkeeper didn't get a hand to it in time.

As the field erupted into screams and cheers, Lizzie let out her breath. She saw Kirsty, Tom and Noah hugging each other for a split second before she was buried underneath her teammates, roaring in her ears and knuckling her head like siblings.

Eventually, she escaped from under them for play to begin again, with only two minutes of injury time. Thankfully, nothing eventful took place and Lizzie's team had done it. They'd won the cup final 2–1. Lizzie found herself hoisted up onto the shoulders of another player in a half piggyback and suddenly she had the cup in her hand, raising it high above her head for everyone to see. She'd felt nothing like it before – sheer euphoria that they'd won, and she'd played a key part in the victory.

'How about that?' Lizzie said when she'd eventually escaped the chaos and made her way over to where Noah and Kirsty were sitting on the grass, talking. Noah stood and held a hand out for Kirsty to help her get up. She took it and joined them.

'Congratulations.' She enveloped Lizzie into an enormous hug.

'Well done,' Noah said. 'That was pretty impressive. You must have a really talented trainer,' he joked with a wink.

'The best,' she said, suddenly aware that her face was probably covered in mud and that her hair would be even crazier than normal after the game. She brushed it back from her face self-consciously.

'You were great,' he said.

'Thanks.'

'I can't wait to celebrate. Brunch?' Kirsty asked.

'Yes, please!' Lizzie was not only keen for a hugely calorific guilt-free meal, but also to get back on track with Kirsty. Things had been weird last time they'd seen each other, and she needed to talk to her about Steve.

'Let's go to Greg's coffee shop,' Kirsty suggested. 'They do the best poached eggs there.'

Lizzie held her water bottle between her legs while she redid her ponytail. 'Good idea.'

'Would you like to come, Noah?' Kirsty asked.

She'd changed her tune. He'd been the devil incarnate last time they'd spoken. Maybe she was coming round to the idea that Lizzie liked this guy and was attempting to get to know him a little better.

'No, I can't, sorry. It's a friend's birthday so I've got a day of stag-do-esque activities planned, culminating in a visit to the cocktail festival on the riverfront.' Noah didn't look totally thrilled about the prospect of his lads' day.

'Us too!' Kirsty said excitedly. 'We're out celebrating at the cocktail festival this evening. Maybe we'll see you there?'

Noah smiled politely and Lizzie felt her brow furrow slightly.

'We won't be at brunch for long anyway,' Lizzie said quickly. 'It's going to take quite a lot of effort to go from this to being presentable for socialising.' Lizzie looked down at her grass-stained football shirt.

She caught Noah's eye, and he smiled.

'How did you know you'd need celebratory drinks?' he asked.

'We didn't. We would have been going out for commiseration drinks if things hadn't gone our way,' Lizzie said.

Noah laughed. 'Lucky for you, you pulled it out of the bag in the final minutes.'

'That was always my plan,' Lizzie said with a smile. 'I didn't want you all to have got out of bed for nothing.'

Kirsty looked at her watch. 'Come on then, we'd better get going. Maybe see you later, Noah.'

'See you both,' said Noah, walking away.

'Bye,' Lizzie said.

Noah looked back briefly and smiled.

'Come on you,' Kirsty said, taking Lizzie's arm. 'Let me buy you brunch.'

'You and Noah looked like you were getting on well,' observed Lizzie, as she mopped up egg yolk from her plate with the last slice of toast.

Kirsty blushed. 'Did we?'

'You know you did,' Lizzie said. 'What's changed? He was bad news last time we spoke. You floored me because of him. And now all of a sudden—'

Kirsty had the decency to look a little embarrassed. 'I'm sorry about that,' she said, sitting back and holding her mug of tea in both hands.

Lizzie sensed her opportunity and took it. 'What's going on with you and Steve?'

'Nothing. I mean . . . what do you mean?' Kirsty tucked a stray hair behind her ear.

Lizzie didn't know how to say what she wanted to say. It was one thing asking about their relationship, or how Kirsty was, but suggesting Steve might be getting violent with her was something else. She wondered whether it was her place to say anything at all. If she was right about Steve, then it opened a Pandora's box of issues for Kirsty to work through. If she was wrong, then that could be even worse. How could she go back from accusing her sister's husband of domestic violence? What was she thinking? But of course, that wouldn't be worse. It would be a relief to know that she was wrong.

'I just . . .' Lizzie hesitated, trying to think of the right way to phrase things. 'I just get the impression that maybe things have got worse recently. That maybe it's not just unpleasant at home. That maybe things have . . .' She tailed off, not quite certain of the words.

There was a silence. Lizzie worried that Kirsty was gearing up to explode, but instead, she sat forward and placed her mug on the table in front of her.

'I'm not very happy, no. And yes, things have got worse recently.'

Lizzie breathed a sigh of relief. She'd broached the subject, and she'd been right about things being more strained between them. Now she just had to go one step further and ask the actual question.

'What happened? You know—' She glanced down at Kirsty's wrist.

Kirsty picked at a knot in the wood on the table. 'A couple of weeks ago, we had a fight.'

She swallowed, glanced briefly at Lizzie, and then back down to her lap. She wrung her hands together while she considered what to say next.

'It got pretty nasty and . . .' Kirsty hesitated, an audible lump in her throat. 'And it got—'

'Did he hit you? Grab you?' Lizzie asked, vowing right then

and there to do something positively medieval to his genitalia if she said yes.

'I think you already know the answer to that,' Kirsty said quietly. 'I know you saw it at practice.' She rolled up her sleeve to reveal a yellowing bruise in the precise shape of a handprint. It confirmed all of Lizzie's suspicions, and she was sad not to have encouraged Kirsty to talk to her about it sooner.

Lizzie looked down at Kirsty's arm and then back up at Kirsty, whose eyes were glazed with tears.

'Has he done it before?'

Kirsty shook her head. 'No, and I didn't want to hang around to find out whether it would happen again, but the boys . . . Besides, he hasn't been physical before, just hurt me in other ways over the past few years. It's been tough. The fight, it happened just before I admitted to myself that perhaps I should leave him, but I just don't know.'

Lizzie smiled. 'I'm proud of you for at least thinking about it.'

'Proud of me? I'm a forty-year-old single mother of three, who has failed to escape a loveless marriage after fifteen years of misery. It's not the first time I've thought about it and still, I've not left. I'm hardly the woman of the year.'

'Oh, Kirsty.' Lizzie shifted her chair and put an arm around her sister.

They sat for a minute in silence, periodically sipping their drinks.

Lizzie said, 'You can still leave, you know?' It was the first time Lizzie had felt sure enough to suggest it to her sister.

'I know. It's just that the consequences are so far-reaching – the boys, the house, everything. Our lives are so entwined.'

'I sometimes think that about Tom,' Lizzie joked. 'If we

ever parted ways, it'd be a huge mess.' She looked over at Kirsty, who had a half-sad smile on her face. 'Too soon?'

Kirsty shook her head. 'It's just sad, you know? That I even have to think about it. And I'm so lost. I just don't know how to take the next step and yet, I feel like if I don't do something, I'll be stuck for ever. I'm just so . . . trapped.'

'I know.' Lizzie squeezed her a little tighter and felt Kirsty's body shake as she let the tears fall.

They could have sat there all day. Lizzie wanted more than anything to hug her sister tightly and make it all go away.

'What will you do?'

'I have no idea,' Kirsty said, blowing out her cheeks at the thought of everything. She smiled weakly. 'But I'll start with enjoying tonight's cocktail festival. Steve's mum is staying over to look after the boys, so I can stay out and have a good night – let my hair down. It's what I need. I'll always have the boys to think about, though. I feel bad that in some ways they're the reason I have to stay and at times I begrudge them it. But they'll always be the most important thing.'

'That is typical of you.' Lizzie leant back into the chair.

'What do you mean?'

'Always thinking about other people. Never giving yourself a chance to be happy. You've always been mother hen, looking after me and everyone else instead of thinking about yourself. You've got an opportunity here to make a change, Kirsty. Take it.'

Kirsty smiled, the faintest hint of excitement glossing over her face. 'I might. When I'm ready.'

'I hope so,' Lizzie said, reaching for Kirsty's hand across the table and giving it a squeeze.

If there was one good thing to have come out of the hideousness of the past few years, it was how close Lizzie and

Kirsty had grown. Lizzie didn't really know why they'd been so distant when they were younger. Perhaps it was the decade's age difference, or maybe it came down to just how different they were as people. Either way, Lizzie was happy that they had grown closer over the past year or so, even if it had come at a terrible price.

Chapter Twenty-Three

Although she loved her sister dearly, Lizzie also relished a Saturday afternoon of laziness. And so, while she had a couple of hours to herself, she went back to the new flat and spent some time pottering about, arranging furniture and trinkets, and putting away clothes. Then she indulged in a hot bubble bath and painted her nails.

Lizzie was excited about going to the cocktail festival with the team. She'd not been on a big night out for a while – they seemed to get fewer and further between the older she got – but was looking forward to taking the time to do her hair and make-up properly and get dressed up.

With her unruly hair, Lizzie spent most of her chilled-out afternoon attempting to tame it. It wasn't often she wore it down naturally, but with the right amount of Frizz Ease, it could be done – on a good day. Thankfully, today was one of those days. She added a thin layer of make-up, having never been one for spending too much time or money on her face, and then opened up her wardrobe and looked at what she might wear.

'Definitely the Jessica Rabbit dress.' Tom's voice came from around the crack in the door.

'Hi,' Lizzie said.

'Congrats, you.' He came into the room and gave her a big cuddle. 'You did great.'

Tom was still in his dressing gown, his hair dishevelled and his face in shadow from the stubble he'd allowed to grow for a couple of days.

'Have you been in bed all this time?' she asked.

Tom nodded. 'I popped down to the game for a bit.'

'Yeah, I saw you.'

'And then I felt like death, so I came back for a sleep,' he explained, stretching.

'It's six o'clock,' Lizzie said in disbelief.

'Is it?' Tom looked at his wrist, where there would usually be a watch but wasn't, and then glanced at Lizzie's bedside table alarm clock. 'I'd better get ready. I'm meeting Chris soon.' He scuttled out of the room. 'Drink?' he called on his way down the corridor.

'Ooh, exciting! Yes please,' Lizzie called back.

Lizzie pulled her Jessica Rabbit dress out of the wardrobe and turned it this way and that. She'd had it for years. She'd worn it for her first official date with Noah a decade or so earlier and hadn't found the motivation to throw it away. It was also most certainly the dress of a twenty-something-year-old and not for a woman who had just turned thirty.

'You have to wear that,' Tom said, returning to the bedroom with two wine glasses full to the brim of Prosecco. Lizzie eyed the glass suspiciously as he handed her one and sat down.

'I thought we'd have to spend less time going back to the kitchen for refills,' he explained with a shrug.

'A real time saver,' Lizzie said sarcastically, taking a sip. 'I'm not sure about this dress.' She held it up again.

'Try it on before you dismiss it,' Tom said, jumping up off the bed. 'I'm going to hop in the shower and I want to see it on you when I come out.'

Lizzie looked at the dress again as Tom left the room. It was floor length, but skintight, with a slit up one side. That was how it had come to earn its Jessica Rabbit nickname, and she and Tom religiously got it out each time they had an event to attend, before Lizzie inevitably vetoed it and put it away again.

But maybe tonight was the night. She was feeling pretty good about herself, and her choice of underwear held her in in all the right places. Perhaps she could . . .

She pulled it over her head and wriggled into it, before lying back down on the bed so that she could manoeuvre into a position where she could reach the zip and do it up. She stood up again and looked in the mirror. It was tight, but it was designed that way. Lizzie had to admit, it looked OK. Maybe even better than OK.

'Looks a-maz-ing.' Tom enunciated each individual syllable. He was standing in the doorway, dripping wet with just a towel around his waist, and strangely, his wine glass still in hand. Lizzie frowned.

'Did you take that . . . ?'

'Of course – I stood it on the side so I could drink it in between shampoos.' He smiled as if that sort of behaviour were completely normal.

Lizzie shook her head sarcastically. 'Do you really think I

can get away with this?' she asked, turning this way and that one last time in front of the mirror.

'Definitely. It's gorgeous and the cocktail festival will be a better and more beautiful place for it. Besides, it's a cocktail dress by definition. It's only right that you wear it for cocktails.'

'OK,' Lizzie said, decision made.

The doorbell rang and Tom shrieked. 'He's here! And I'm not ready!'

His towel slipped in all the excitement and Lizzie covered her eyes.

'You go,' she said, a hand over her face. 'Hide in your room and I'll cover for you for a few minutes.'

'Love you!' Tom kissed her on the cheek and raced to his room, struggling to lift his towel up to an appropriate level as he went.

Lizzie shook her head and laughed to herself. She was only in a dressing gown herself, but at least it was slightly more serviceable, and she wasn't the one trying to impress Chris.

'Come on up!' she called into the buzzer. She heard a muffled thanks and footsteps climbing the stairs to the flat.

'Hi,' Chris said when Lizzie opened the door to him. He flashed his trademark smile.

'Hi, Chris. Come on in. I'm Lizzie. We met before when you showed us this place.'

'Hi, yes, I remember,' he said, following her into the flat. 'How are you?'

Chris was perfectly put together, from his perfect teeth to his perfect hair, his attractive scent and his fashionable jeans and shirt combo. Yes, Lizzie approved of Chris.

'Tom's just finishing getting ready,' she explained. 'Can I get you a drink?'

Chris accepted and Lizzie poured him a wine.

'Are you guys going somewhere nice tonight?'

'Drinks and dinner,' Chris said. He shuffled his feet and actually looked a tad nervous despite his outward confidence. 'There's a cocktail thing down by the river too, so we might pop in there afterwards.'

'That's where I'm going tonight.'

'Tom said you'd won the football earlier. Congrats,' he said, cheersing Lizzie's glass. They both drank and fell into a comfortable silence until Tom flounced in.

'Hi,' Tom said shyly.

Their eyes met across the room and Lizzie witnessed a moment. Her heart twinged and she found herself wishing she might have one of those herself. Noah's image flashed into her mind uninvited.

'I'll leave you two to it,' Lizzie said, reaching for her glass and making for the door. 'Have a great night.' But she may as well have not been there, as Tom and Chris were lost in each other already.

The whole football team crammed into a couple of booths that were smaller than their changing room at the pitch and ordered a round of drinks, each round taking so long to get right, and then make, that by the time it had all arrived, the first drinker had finished and it was time to do the whole thing all over again. But Lizzie didn't mind – they were delicious.

The cocktail festival was taking place at a pub alongside the river. Both inside and out were decorated with fairy lights and candles in mason jars. Dotted around the outside space were stalls representing different alcohol companies and small businesses that had some kind of link to cocktails. There were lots of drink options, of course, but visitors could also buy cocktail-flavoured toiletries or prints of retro alcohol signs. There was one tiny stall selling balloons in the shape of Martini and Cosmopolitan glasses.

'So, has Steve got the boys tonight, did you say?' Lizzie asked. She took a sip of her drink through a tiny straw. Her Cosmopolitan was unbelievably sweet, with the sour kick she expected at the end; she screwed up her face and shivered anyway. She hoped it wasn't too soon to bring him up again, having only finally spoken to Kirsty honestly about him earlier that day.

'Yes. He's roped his mum in too, mind,' she said, sipping her Old-Fashioned. 'He was annoyed that I was out all morning with the game and then brunch, so buggered off for a pint with the boys this afternoon. He got back about six-thirty, so I didn't have time to get as ready as I would've liked.' She pulled at her top, which Lizzie had to admit did just look like it'd been thrown on.

'Didn't he know you were going to be out this morning?' Lizzie asked, thinking how unfair of Steve that seemed to be.

'Yeah, and I knew he'd use it against me at some point. I just didn't think that it'd be today.'

'Sorry, Kirs.' Lizzie placed a sympathetic hand on her arm.

'It's OK. I've come to expect nothing less.' Kirsty smiled sadly and took another, rather larger swig of her drink.

Lizzie hoped she wouldn't have to look after Kirsty later that evening, and then felt bad. Kirsty looked exhausted. She'd thrown her hair up into a messy bun, and despite a healthy amount of make-up, the bags under her eyes were still faintly visible purple shadows.

'Would you like another drink?' Kirsty asked, moving on

from the topic, just as Lizzie had expected her to.

'I'll have another Cosmo if you're buying.'

'No problem.'

Lizzie watched Kirsty get up and squeeze her way through the crowd to the bar. Her shoulders were stooped and there was a sadness about her that Lizzie hadn't noticed before then.

Lizzie downed her drink and popped to the toilet while her sister was at the bar. She pushed her way through the throng to the toilets, which were inevitably in the furthest corner of the pub and beyond a selection of stalls selling something very popular. Catching herself in a full-length mirror on the way, she decided that the soft lighting actually didn't do too much damage to the way she looked. If anything, it actually worked well with her Jessica Rabbit dress.

In the toilets, she glanced momentarily in the mirror to make sure she'd not smudged any make-up in the hot bar. On her way back to the table, she could see that Kirsty still hadn't made it back. She decided to pass by the bar as a detour. Maybe Kirsty needed help to carry the drinks back over.

When she finally got there after a lot of 'Excuse me' and 'Sorry, can I just squeeze through?', she saw Kirsty was talking to a man. She was throwing her head back and touching him on the arm, flirting outrageously. After another, slightly closer look, she realised it was Noah.

'Hey, look who I bumped into,' Kirsty said, spotting Lizzie over Noah's shoulder.

He turned to see who she was talking to, and a smile crossed his face. After witnessing Kirsty's flirting, Lizzie was not smiling.

He really was beautiful, though. Instead of his sports kit, he was wearing jeans and a distressed-looking light-blue shirt. His hair was more styled than usual. He looked . . . different. And, for a moment, he took Lizzie's breath away.

'Wow, look at you,' he said. 'I mean . . . you scrub up well. I remember that dress . . .' He tried to take away from the fact he was commenting on her appearance, but seemed to lose himself for a minute. He reached a hand up and ran it through his hair.

'Thanks,' Lizzie said, wrinkling her nose. 'I think. So do you.'

They held each other's eye contact for a second. For Lizzie, the bustle of the bar disappeared for a moment, lost in the nostalgia of it all, but it came sharply into focus again when Kirsty passed Lizzie her drink.

'Here you go,' she said, thrusting the Cosmopolitan into her hand and spilling a large drop of it down her front. Clumsily, Lizzie reached across Noah for a napkin from the bar and mopped it up as best she could. Oddly, there was no apology from Kirsty. Had she done it on purpose?

'Great!' Lizzie rolled her eyes. She just hoped that with the heat of all the bodies in the pub, it would dry soon enough and not stain.

'And who's this?' asked a tall, bearded man, patting Noah hard on the back as he joined their little group. He was wearing a burgundy velvet suit and his hair was pulled back into a topknot.

'This is Kirsty and her sister, Lizzie.' Noah pointed to each of them as he introduced them.

'I'm Benny,' said the beardy fellow, reaching out his huge hand.

Kirsty shook it, and then so did Lizzie. It was a strong, manly handshake.

'Nice to meet you, Benny.'

'Are you guys out celebrating?' Benny asked, reaching for his pint from the bar and downing at least half of it in one swig.

'We're with the ladies' football team over there.' Lizzie gestured over towards their booths. 'We won a game today.'

'They didn't just win,' Noah said, reaching out to put an arm around Lizzie. 'This one won the ladies' cup final with a last-minute goal,' he said, releasing her.

Lizzie realised Noah was a little drunk. He would never do that if he were in his right mind. He was always so careful around her. Lizzie looked over at Kirsty to receive her judgement, which she knew would be coming. Instead, something akin to jealousy seemed to wash fleetingly over her face.

'Yes. We're celebrating this one,' Kirsty said. But something was off.

Lizzie suddenly felt self-conscious and knew her face was colouring as she spoke. 'It was a team effort.'

'Sounds impressive,' Benny said.

Noah smiled over his drink at her. 'It was.'

'We should go back and join the others,' Kirsty said, breaking up the moment, suddenly keen to return to the table.

'Yeah, we should,' Lizzie agreed and with a nod from Benny, they left.

'See you later,' Noah said, as they weaved their way back through the crowds to their seat.

'What was that?' Kirsty asked once they were sitting down again with their drinks.

'What was what?' Lizzie busied herself with her cocktail, trying not to slurp up the lemon peel that was floating on the surface. 'I could ask you the same thing!'

'I thought we'd agreed Noah was off limits because of what happened before?' Kirsty said.

'I think you said that actually, Kirs.' She was tiring of her sister now. 'Besides, nothing happened. It was a friendly thing, and he's a bit drunk, I think.'

'Then you'll need to be careful,' Kirsty warned.

It took everything she could not to lash out and accuse Kirsty of getting too involved. After all, she'd not done a great job of picking a life partner herself. Only half an hour ago, Lizzie had been talking to her about the failure of her relationship with Steve, yet for some reason, Kirsty felt like she had the authority to give her advice on her love life. But she knew it would be too unkind to say it out loud.

'I'm just going to get some water,' Lizzie said, after they'd spent a couple of minutes half-heartedly 'listening in' to some of their teammates' conversations. Perhaps she'd had a little too much to drink after all.

She shouted across the bar to the barman. 'Just a glass of water, please.'

He got a pint glass and filled it up.

'Another drink already?' came a faintly familiar voice. It was Benny, who shuffled up next to her and leant on the bar.

'Just water.' Lizzie smiled.

'You should give Noah that advice.'

They both looked over to where Noah was sitting with their other friends, depending slightly too much on the wall behind him to keep him upright.

'Is he a little worse for wear?' she asked.

'A little.'

The barman passed Lizzie her water. 'Thanks.'

'Four pints of lager, please, matey,' Benny said.

The barman went off again to make his drinks.

'Well, I'd better . . .' Lizzie tilted her head to suggest she needed to return to her friends. Hopefully, Kirsty would have cooled down by now and they could get on with having a good night.

'Wait,' Benny said, reaching for Lizzie's shoulder. She turned back to him. 'Do you want to, I mean, fancy swapping numbers? I'd really like to take you out for a drink sometime.'

Lizzie smiled, feeling pretty pleased with herself that Benny might want to take her out. The Jessica Rabbit dress had done its unintentional job, even if it had the remnants of a Cosmopolitan still drying on the front of it.

'OK,' she said.

She didn't know what she was doing, or even if she really wanted to go for a drink with Benny. She didn't even know him, but he was good-looking and he'd flattered her by asking – and it wouldn't hurt to swap numbers, would it?

'Here's mine,' she said and Benny tapped it into his phone, calling her phone so that she'd have his.

'Great. I'll text you or something in the week,' he said, flashing her an attractive smile.

'Sounds good.'

Lizzie took a moment to look at him. His face was covered in a dark brown beard and his hair was scooped up off his face. His suit was flashy and offbeat. He was tall and wide and would crush Lizzie if he even tried to hug her. But he was attractive – in a Jon-Snow-goes-to-the-Oscars kind of way.

Behind him, she noticed Noah sitting with his other friends, all slightly worse for wear after a day of birthday/stag-do activities. He was laughing at something his friend was saying and she could hear it over the bustle and chaos of the pub. His smile lit up his face and in that split second, she knew she wouldn't call Benny. He, like every other man, would never compare to Noah, so why bother trying? The feeling of being asked was still nice, though.

She rushed back over to Kirsty. 'You'll never guess what just happened,' said Lizzie excitedly, sitting down with her water. 'Benny just asked me for my number!'

'Oooh, that's exciting!' Kirsty seemed to forget her earlier grump.

Lizzie smiled. 'I know.'

'The Jessica Rabbit dress strikes again,' Kirsty said.

'It did always have that effect. Although I didn't expect it to still be quite so effective.'

Coach Zoe, who until now had been sitting down at the far end of the booths, stood up and tinged two glasses together. Despite the hubbub of the bar, the team quietened down and they could hear Zoe just above the crowd.

'Right, ladies,' she said, holding a Mojito. 'Before we all get far too drunk to say anything meaningful to each other, other than slurred "I love you"s—' She paused for a laugh, which with everyone already being a little tipsy, she got. 'I just wanted to say congratulations for today.'

There was a collective whoop, which turned the heads of the other patrons at the festival.

'You all did an amazing job, but . . .' She raised her glass in Lizzie's direction. 'We do have one special person to thank. She saved us from deadlock and won us the game. Lizzie!'

Everyone raised their glasses, 'cheers'ed and whooped in Lizzie's direction. She felt her face go the same colour as her dress and was glad when everyone went back to their own conversations and trekked over to the bar once again to buy drinks.

While there was a lull in the conversation, and the space to move through the stalls and past the bar, Lizzie popped to the toilet again. Cocktails always had that effect on her – and she'd downed a pint of water.

In the mirror, she saw herself looking a little tired. Her make-up wasn't that perfect any more and there was a faint water mark on her dress where Kirsty had spilt the Cosmopolitan. After two cocktails and the Prosecco she'd shared with Tom in the flat, she decided it was probably time to make a move while she was on a high and before she did anything to disgrace herself. She didn't want a repeat of the fundraiser.

Plus, she desperately wanted to get back and hear all about Tom's date. She'd been expecting a secret toilet text, but hadn't received one, which either meant the date was not going so well, or that it was going so brilliantly that Tom hadn't thought about Lizzie all evening – or stopped to visit the toilet. She hoped the second scenario explained it.

She put her lip gloss back in her bag and pushed the heavy door open, ready to head back over to the table – but bumped straight into Noah, who was walking past in the corridor.

Before she realised who it was, she said, 'Oh gosh, I'm so sorry!'

Noah laughed, a little more carefree than normal. 'It's OK. I'm sorry.'

He slurred his words ever so slightly, just enough for Lizzie to notice.

'Are you having a good night?' Lizzie asked, a hint of sarcasm in her voice. She stepped forward to let someone else pass and found herself suddenly very close to Noah. She breathed in his aftershave, reminiscent of their time together. It was just so him.

'Yeah, thanks.'

He looked down at her. The tips of their noses were almost

touching. Swaying, he steadied himself by holding onto Lizzie's arm.

They were too close. Her heart was racing, and she breathed deeply to get enough air into her lungs to avoid suffocation. He looked like he was going to kiss her and Lizzie realised she wanted nothing more, but not like this. Noah rarely drank to excess, or at least he never used to. She wasn't prepared for something to happen that he wouldn't remember. It would be one more thing for them to argue about. Lizzie stepped backwards, suddenly feeling claustrophobic, and Noah dropped his hand.

'I saw you talking to Benny at the bar earlier,' he said, leaning back against the wall.

Lizzie was glad of the gap between them widening.

'Yeah, he came over to say hi when I bought a drink,' Lizzie explained, suddenly feeling defensive.

'Haven't you only just met him?'

'He's *your* friend,' Lizzie said, folding her arms. 'You know that's the case, Noah. We were just talking. It was by chance that we were at the bar together.'

'But you swapped numbers,' Noah pointed out, squinting one eye to add to Lizzie's suspicions that he might, in fact, be a little drunk.

'He asked for mine. He said he would like to take me for a drink.'

The idea that Noah felt like he had the right to question her actions and even sound unhappy about them made her blood boil. How dare he?

'Are you going to go?'

Lizzie opened her mouth to answer and then closed it again, taking a moment to think about her response – or even if she was going to dignify the question with an answer.

'I don't know,' she said honestly.

'But you had to think about it.'

Noah folded his arms to mirror hers. His attitude was ruining Lizzie's night.

'Because I genuinely don't know, Noah,' she said again, her tone becoming a little clipped. 'I'm a free agent. Why shouldn't I go for a drink with him?'

Noah looked at her, his features motionless. She knew she'd hurt him with her comment.

She stared back, waiting for him to respond. He didn't. So Lizzie filled what was fast becoming an awkward silence. She couldn't help herself.

'Look Noah, I'm not with anyone. He seemed nice. I can vouch that he's normal because he's a friend of a friend . . .'

'*My* friend,' Noah pointed out.

'Yes, *your* friend,' Lizzie said. 'But he's attractive, and he asked me for his number. There are no red flags and I thought maybe it would be nice to have someone take me out.'

She didn't know quite how she'd got onto the defensive so quickly. It was something about the way Noah was looking at her, almost waiting for her to say something else. Maybe he was hoping she would talk herself out of it.

'Your decision,' he said simply after a moment.

'Yes, it is.' How had he made her feel bad about this? 'Look, I have to go.'

'See you on Monday then, I guess.' Noah pushed himself up off the wall and walked off towards the men's toilets.

God, that man was infuriating. Who the hell did he think he was? Had she done something wrong here? Was there an 'ex code' that meant she wasn't allowed to date friends of exes? It'd been ten years. Surely, even if there was an unwritten rule, it was written off after so much time.

'I'm going to head off,' Lizzie said when she finally returned to the team.

Kirsty pulled a face to show she couldn't hear over the music.

'I'm going to go home,' Lizzie shouted, inexpertly miming her sentiment at the same time to make sure Kirsty understood her.

'Really?' Kirsty shouted back.

'Yeah. I'm tired and tipsy. I need my bed.' It wasn't exactly a lie – she just needed to add 'pissed off' onto the list.

'OK.' Kirsty stood up to give Lizzie a hug. She wobbled slightly as she leant in.

'Behave, Kirsty. You know what you get like when you have too many cocktails.'

'I will.' She swayed slightly again and didn't look like she was about to follow Lizzie's advice.

Lizzie spoke more quietly now that she was so close to Kirsty's ear. 'See you on Monday.'

'Remember we're meeting at the steakhouse instead of practice to celebrate the end of the season.'

'Oh yeah.' Lizzie had genuinely forgotten that that was the plan. 'See you then.'

After saying a brief goodbye and waving around the team's table, Lizzie made her way out onto the river path, enjoying the cool evening air on her face. It really had got warm in there and she hadn't even noticed. Or perhaps an evening full of so much rage had heated her up.

Back in the hallway of the flat, Lizzie kicked off her heels and carried them up the three flights of stairs. She hoped no one would come out of their flat, because she certainly looked a lot like she was doing the walk of shame, even though it was only just 11.30 p.m.

Tom had left after Lizzie for his date with Chris, and you could tell. They'd opened another bottle of wine, left half drunk on the kitchen counter, next to two dirty glasses and the two corks Tom had popped earlier that evening. He'd been trying clothes on in the bathroom and rejected options were strewn all over the floor and the side of the bath. Lizzie picked up what she could from the bathroom and the corridor radiator, roughly folding it, before piling it onto the kitchen table for him to find, and tidy, in the morning.

'Tom?' she half whispered and half called.

Padding down the corridor to avoid waking him if he was asleep, she knocked gently on his bedroom door and listened for snoring. It was a sure-fire way to know if Tom was in the vicinity. On really awful nights, she could hear it from her bedroom.

But there wasn't a sound. She poked her head around the door and tried to make out in the dark if there was anyone there, but Tom's bed looked empty. Once her eyes had adjusted, she could see that in fact his bed, perhaps predictably, was unmade since he'd crawled out of it earlier that evening. She sneaked back out, unwilling to breathe in any more of the slightly questionable air from his bedroom.

So Tom hadn't made it home then? Lizzie hoped it was because the date had gone well and not because Chris was a mad axe murderer, which was Lizzie's number-one dating fear and why she kept away from the apps that allowed people to masquerade as normal human beings.

It had been an odd night. She'd rowed with people far more than she'd expected. It was a shame – she'd hoped to go out and enjoy the football team's success without all the drama.

At that moment, her phone buzzed. She got it out of her pocket and swiped to open the message. It was Benny.

Nice to meet you this evening. Fancy a coffee one day next week? It'd be great to catch up.

She was unsure whether she could date anyone with everything that was going on in her head – and her heart – but her encounter in the pub corridor with Noah had got her thinking. Slightly tipsy Lizzie definitely felt like there was something still there. Sobering-up Lizzie wanted to wait and see until they saw each other again on Monday at sports day. Neither Lizzie knew what to do about Benny. She marked his message as unread and went to bed.

Chapter Twenty-Four

Tom had a wonderful date with Chris, it turned out. He and Lizzie took a stroll down to Greg's coffee shop for a spot of brunch the next morning, and Tom told her all about it. She hadn't seen him this animated for a long time. She was also enjoying her own lack of hangover. She could get used to this.

'And he was such a gentleman,' Tom gushed as they walked arm in arm. 'He drove us there in his fancy car. Oh! And did I tell you he'd booked a table at that place in Sheepham village? The place with the celebrity chef? The food was divine and so was the company.' Tom had a real glint in his eye as he spoke.

They found a table outside Greg's coffee shop that looked out over the green. Tom added far too much sugar to his coffee and sat back to drink it.

'Are you feeling a little worse for wear?' Lizzie asked, basking in the glory of her own absent hangover. She sipped a green smoothie, only adding to the angelic feeling she was enjoying.

'I've been better,' Tom said, scratching his head and rubbing his temples. 'But I don't care, because I'm in love!' he announced dramatically. He flung out his arms.

Lizzie laughed. 'Tell me more.' She settled back into the wrought-iron chair to listen to his story.

'Well,' Tom began, touching Lizzie's arm gently, 'after we'd had dinner at Gusto's, we caught the bus into town to try out the new bar down Queen Street, then hit a couple more bars before we went dancing at the club down the other side of Park End Street.'

'I don't want to know where you went, silly.' She pushed his arm playfully. 'I want to know what happened with you and Chris. What's he like? What have you got in common? Are you going to see each other again?'

'Definitely yes,' Tom said decidedly. He failed to keep the smile from his face. 'We had everything in common, but he also had really interesting things to talk about, like he's learning to play the saxophone.'

Lizzie smiled at this slightly strange detail.

'And he has a tattoo in a very odd place—'

Lizzie put her fingers in her ears and sang, 'La la la!' to avoid hearing the ins and outs of that particular detail. Tom tried to move her hands away and they crumpled into fits of giggles and screams.

As Lizzie sat back upright, she noticed a familiar figure across the street – same messy bun, same casual top. It was Kirsty, and she was wearing last night's clothes.

'Kirsty!' Lizzie shouted.

Kirsty looked away at first, covering her face with her hair and upping her pace, before seeming to relent; she looked in their direction and held her hand up in a tiny wave. Lizzie and Tom shared a look – Kirsty did not look good. Her skin was grey and pale, and her hair was huge.

256

'Good night, was it?' Tom asked, laughing. He clearly didn't realise how bad this could be. Lizzie's face remained straight as she wrestled with feeling both angry with and sorry for her sister.

Kirsty's glance flickered over to Lizzie and then back to the ground as she admitted to Tom that it had been a good night. She spoke quietly as if someone might be following her or listening in.

Tom leant forward onto his elbows. 'And who's the lucky guy?'

'No one you know,' she mumbled.

'Wait,' Tom said, sitting up in realisation. 'What about Steve?'

Kirsty burst into tears and Lizzie ushered her to sit down. Kirsty continued to look around nervously.

'What happened to you?' Lizzie asked. 'Have you really come from some guy's house?'

Kirsty continued to sob uncontrollably, nodding through her tears.

'What were you thinking?' Lizzie struggled to keep the judgement from her voice. It was awful because it clearly showed Kirsty and Steve had nothing between them any more. But more concerning for Lizzie was what Steve might do if he found out. It wouldn't be the first time he'd got angry . . .

'I don't know.' Kirsty sniffed and wiped her snotty nose on her sleeve. It didn't matter that it was gross, she was a mess anyway.

'Was it someone from the pub?' Selfishly, Lizzie felt an anxiety in the pit of her stomach telling her she might just know whom Kirsty had gone home with. And if it was Noah, both relationships would be over.

'It was,' Kirsty admitted quietly, her sobs subsiding. 'But no one you know.'

'Really?' Lizzie raised an eyebrow and sat back in her chair, folding her arms. She wanted to be sympathetic to her sister's situation, but she also had her own heart to protect.

Kirsty shuffled on the chair. 'Nope.' She looked nervously at the other Sunday morning patrons. 'I have to go. Steve will need me back to look after the boys.'

'We'll arrange something so you can tell us all about it!' Tom shouted after her as she walked away from them across the green.

Lizzie thought how small she looked and felt a pang of sadness for her sister.

'So, that's exciting!' Tom said.

'It's not gossip, Tom. This could be dangerous for her. We know what Steve's capable of.'

Tom agreed, thanking the waitress as she came over and placed their brunch down on the table. But he couldn't help himself, his curiosity piqued. 'I wonder who she's been with.'

'We bumped into Noah and his friends in the bar last night,' Lizzie said. 'Maybe it was one of his mates. They were a friendly bunch.'

'Ooh!' Tom cried after a second, making Lizzie jump and poke the side of her mouth with her fork. 'Maybe it was Noah,' he said, speaking Lizzie's biggest fear out loud.

Tom said it dramatically and left the thought hanging between them. Suddenly, Lizzie didn't feel so hungry any more.

'She wouldn't do that, would she?'

'She looked pretty shifty to me. There's a walk of shame and then there's *the* walk of shame and it looked like a serious one.' Now Tom had come up with the idea, he seemed compelled to run with it.

Lizzie frowned. Surely her sister wouldn't do that to her? But then her mind flashed back to the flirting she'd seen at the football game and the bar, the way Kirsty had tackled her when they'd spoken about Lizzie's feelings for Noah and the way she always tried to push Lizzie away from him, telling her he was bad news.

Surely Kirsty wasn't trying to win him for herself? And surely she hadn't slept with him after their night out? Noah had been pretty drunk . . . and by the looks of it, Kirsty had fared little better herself. But she was married. Unhappily, admittedly. But Kirsty was always so strait-laced. No, she wouldn't . . .

Lizzie pushed her chair back, and her drink wobbled precariously. The cutlery clattered and people turned to see what the commotion was.

'Are you all right, Lizzie?'

'I have to go,' she said. 'Sorry.'

She reached for her bag and walked away from Tom, down the street, leaving him to enjoy brunch alone.

Lizzie walked down to the lake and did three laps of it before her angry, nervous energy had dissipated and she could slow down enough to sit on a bench at the edge of the water. The bench was worn and faded with the sun. In the reeds along the water's edge, a mother moorhen and her three tiny babies followed each other, weaving in and out of the grasses. It was warm and insects were providing a soundtrack to the ever-increasing heat.

Lizzie didn't know whether it was getting warmer as the day edged to noon, or whether her blood was growing warmer as it boiled. She kept trying to tell herself that she had no evidence of Kirsty doing anything wrong. But her radar told her otherwise. Over the past week or so, things had been building up to it. She just couldn't believe Kirsty and Noah would do something like that to her.

Her phone buzzed, alerting Lizzie to the fact that someone or other had uploaded some pictures from the evening before to WhatsApp. She swiped her phone open and scrolled through them, stopping when she came across a series of photos that looked as though Noah and his friends had joined the football team after Lizzie had left. There he was, sat on one side of Kirsty, with another of his friends on the other side. Benny was there too.

Benny was still quite attractive, even though Lizzie was now sober. In a split second of frustration and bitterness, she opened her messages and reread the one that Benny had sent her late last night – *Nice to meet you this evening. Fancy a coffee one day next week? It'd be great to catch up.*

Feeling uncharacteristically brave, Lizzie hit the reply button.

Hi Benny. Hope your head's not too bad after last night. It was great to meet you. Fancy a drink later?

Lizzie toyed with adding a kiss, but instead reread the message, her finger only hovering momentarily over the send button before she pressed it without a second thought.

She looked out over the lake, the water still and smooth like glass. After only a few minutes, Benny replied. He said he'd love to meet Lizzie later and suggested a bar in town. And just like that, Lizzie had got herself a date.

Chapter Twenty-Five

Lizzie raced back to the flat and scrambled through the clothes in her wardrobe, desperate to find something to wear that evening. She'd already used up the Jessica Rabbit dress and didn't really have anything else that would be likely to wow Benny. On the other hand, it was Sunday evening, so maybe she didn't need to try as hard.

'What's going on?' Tom asked, popping his head around the door.

Lizzie still had her head buried in her wardrobe, throwing item after item out of her chest of drawers as she crossed it off her mental list.

'I've got a date.' She held up a white logo T-shirt and, deciding against it, threw it onto the bed and rifled through the drawer for the next item of clothing. 'With Benny,' she added, when Tom didn't reply.

She heard him sigh behind her. 'This is because you think Kirsty hooked up with Noah last night, isn't it?'

Lizzie didn't turn around, but she could imagine him with a disapproving hand on his hip.

'Nope,' she lied. 'He asked me out last night anyway and I'm just accepting his invitation.'

'I know you, Lizzie Morris. This is a rebound-out-of-spite kind of date.'

'It really isn't,' she said, not entirely sure whom she was trying to convince.

She pulled out a white floaty top that, coupled with a pair of skinny jeans and heels, might just have potential.

'Lizzie,' Tom said gently.

She stopped and stood to face him, breathing heavily from her rush to find an outfit. Her hair was mad again and she pushed it back off her face.

'OK,' she relented. 'There is a bit of this that is in response to seeing Kirsty doing her walk of shame. And because it's likely that she was sneaking home from Noah's house. But I really can't wait around for him for ever. I'm thirty. Benny is a nice guy. And he asked me out. Noah hasn't asked me out. So I'm going on a date with Benny, because I want to. And because nobody else has asked me.' She shrugged and then pushed past Tom to get through to the living room, where the ironing board was already set up. She turned on the iron.

'As long as you're sure, Lizzie.' Tom followed her through to the living room. 'I don't want you to ruin anything with Noah because you've had a knee-jerk reaction.'

'I'm sure, Tom. There's nothing to ruin. I want to see Benny tonight. He's cute.' She ironed angrily.

'OK.' His face said he wasn't really OK with it at all.

'I have to get ready.' Lizzie turned and headed back to her bedroom.

Lizzie got dressed and tamed her crazy hair before adding a light layer of make-up. The smart-casual look was much more her, and as she slipped her heels on, ready to leave, she felt more comfortable and more confident than she had in a long time.

Benny met her on the corner at the end of her road, and they walked into town.

'I'm glad you messaged me,' he said as they walked side by side.

'Well, I had a good time last night, and I had a free evening. I thought it would be nice.' Now she was here – with Benny – her confidence waned. What was she doing?

'You look great, by the way,' Benny said, turning slightly towards her.

Lizzie smiled. Up close, Benny was very good-looking. His brown hair was tinged with red in the evening sun, and his beard was bushy but groomed. He'd risked double denim, but it looked good on him, and his musky scent stirred the butterflies that had lain dormant for anyone other than Noah for a long while.

'Thanks,' she replied. 'So do you.'

They talked about the town, their jobs and their family – just small talk, nothing deep – but it was nice and Lizzie relaxed. The large glass of wine Benny bought for her when they arrived at the pub went even further to helping her feel calm in his company.

'So how was the rest of your evening?' Lizzie asked as they settled into a corner table.

The pub was nearly empty. It was quiet because it was a Sunday, but also because people were enjoying their drinks sat outside along the riverside. There was also a good chance the entire town was still recovering from the cocktail festival.

'It was a good laugh, actually. We've not been out in a while.

Kyle – who I'm not sure you really met properly – he's pretty under the thumb at home, so it's not often we all get to hang out.'

'Same, actually. I don't get to do that nearly as often as I'd like to any more,' said Lizzie.

'Your lot got rowdy after you left,' Benny said.

'Oh yeah?' She knew they had from the photos on WhatsApp and from the state of Kirsty.

'Yeah.' He flipped the beer mat off the edge of the table and tried to catch it, missing it every time. 'We joined them later, but it had all got a bit messy by then. Did your sister get back all right?'

Lizzie tried to keep the irritation from her voice. 'She got home this morning.'

Benny smiled to himself. 'I didn't see that coming.'

'Neither did I.'

She looked at Benny, trying hard to concentrate on how nice he was, how attractive he was, how she was supposed to be on a date with him and not feeling jealous about an ex-boyfriend whom she'd split up with over a decade ago. She was pretty sure her face was betraying her, though.

'The whole end of the evening's a bit fuzzy, to be honest,' he said, flipping the beer mat again and catching it successfully. He made a little 'yess' sound. Lizzie smiled.

'Big night, was it?'

'Bigger than we intended.' Benny downed a third of his beer in one, his hand dwarfing the pint glass. 'I don't even know if Noah got back OK. I've not been able to contact him all day.'

That caught Lizzie's attention. 'Well, if Kirsty was doing the walk of shame this morning, I'm guessing Noah got back OK as well.'

Benny's brow furrowed. 'What do you mean?'

'They went back together, didn't they?'

Benny shook his head. 'No, Noah left about half an hour after you did. He said he wasn't feeling it, and to be fair, he was pretty drunk early on – he peaked too soon. Your sister left with Kyle.'

Lizzie raised her eyebrows.

'Yep, we were all shocked,' Benny said. 'Kyle is going to be in some pretty deep shit when his missus finds out.'

Lizzie pulled a face at the complexity of the situation and just how stupid Kirsty had been. Inside, she was singing. Noah and Kirsty hadn't spent the night together, and all was well in the world again.

From there, the conversation was easy. Lizzie knew she wouldn't be seeing Benny again as a date. She felt bad that she'd turned to him when she thought Noah had slept with Kirsty, but equally, she was enjoying his company and who knew? Maybe they could become friends.

At half nine, she made her excuses and left. It was a school night, after all. Benny offered to walk her back, but after a lot of protesting on her part (it turned out he was a proper gent), Benny left Lizzie to make her own way home.

She welcomed the gentle breeze as it played with her hair. It was the perfect evening to think about everything that had happened over the past few weeks and get some perspective. Mostly, she was worried about her sister. Her dysfunctional marriage had all but broken down, and she had got drunk and slept with someone who was already attached. She was flirting outrageously with everyone – well, with Noah. It just wasn't like her. Kirsty was all about the rules and boundaries. She was a lawyer, an upstanding citizen, and she just didn't do things like that.

Lizzie was just mulling over how she might need to stage an intervention, when she heard someone coming the other way.

Her guard came up slightly – it was dusk, and halfway between the pub and town, the riverside path got pretty remote. She craned her neck to see over the bushes in an attempt to assess the situation.

'Lizzie, hi.' It was Noah who stepped through the long grasses, and Lizzie breathed a sigh of relief.

'Noah.' She stopped in her path.

Neither of them said anything for a few seconds.

Lizzie cracked first and said, 'What are you doing here?'

'I could ask you the same thing,' he joked.

The sun was low in the sky and Noah was almost a silhouette. Through the dusk, Lizzie could still make out his dark eyes. He smiled.

'I asked first.' She realised she sounded flirtatious as soon as the words were out of her mouth.

'I lost my phone down here somewhere last night,' he explained, pushing his hair back from his face.

'Here? What were you doing here last night?'

'I was pretty drunk in the bar. When I left, I walked along here for a little while. I had a few things to think about.' He hesitated as he spoke.

'You *were* pretty drunk.' She couldn't resist the temptation to tease him.

Noah looked down at the floor. 'I'm sorry I was an idiot last night.'

'You weren't, don't worry.'

He smiled, sheepish. 'What are you doing here?'

Lizzie hesitated. She didn't want to tell him she'd been on a date with Benny, but what other reason did she have?

'I just came for a walk to clear my head,' she lied.

'Sounds like we've both got things we're thinking about.'

'Can I help you look for your phone?' Lizzie asked, changing the subject.

'If you want to,' he said. 'I was just heading down to the boathouse. I've got a vague recollection that I sat there for a while.'

'All right,' she replied, and they walked side by side along the river.

As dusk turned to darkness, the crickets played their discordant tunes, and the river turned silent, the surface becoming still and smooth.

'It's not like you to get that drunk,' Lizzie said as they walked. 'Or at least, it never used to be.'

'I know,' Noah said. 'I've felt crappy all day. I won't be doing it again for a while.'

They reached the clearing that opened up to the boathouse. Noah led the way. The path down to the boathouse was steep, and it was almost completely dark now. Twice, Lizzie stumbled on the uneven ground. When they reached the section of path that led down a steep drop, Noah told Lizzie to wait there. He scrambled down himself first, put a foot firmly into the earth to balance himself, and reached out his arms.

Lizzie hesitated, but put her arms on his shoulders and let him lift her down. She landed close to him, feeling the warmth of his body against hers. Once she'd regained her balance, she looked up at his face, his eyes reflecting the moonlight.

Lizzie smiled, then looked away. 'Sorry.'

'Don't be.' Noah's voice was suddenly low and quiet.

Only the nocturnal nature around them disturbed the silence. All Lizzie could really hear was her own breath and Noah's heart. Still holding her in his arms, he pulled her towards him and tilted her chin up with his finger.

'You have nothing to be sorry for, Lizzie Morris. Remember that.'

Lizzie's breath caught, and her lips parted in an attempt to breathe.

Slowly, Noah brought his lips down to hers and kissed her softly. He pulled away and looked at her.

'Was that OK?'

Lizzie nodded and stood on her tiptoes to reach up to him, to kiss him back. At that moment, there didn't seem to be any reason not to.

Lizzie brought her arms up to circle Noah's neck, her fingertips grazing his strong back and shoulders, stroking the bottom of his hair. He held her close, one hand on the bottom of her back and the other one stroking her jaw as he kissed her softly. It was like everything and nothing she remembered, both nostalgic and new all at once.

When they pulled apart, it was somehow darker. Lizzie could barely see Noah through the night, but his hands holding hers told her he was there.

She could swear her heart was audible above the hum of the crickets. She swallowed, her voice shaky as her heart did its best to slow down again.

'We should look for your phone.'

'Do we have to?'

Lizzie hesitated, and Noah leant down to kiss her gently again.

'Yes, come on,' she said once he'd pulled away.

He kept hold of her hand as he walked closer to the water's edge and looked on the ground.

'Can you phone it?' he asked.

Lizzie reached into her pocket for her own phone and swiped for his number. The sound of a phone vibrating helped Noah to locate it, a green tinge lighting up the decking of the boathouse, where Noah had clearly been sitting the previous evening.

'Thanks,' he said, wiping the screen free of condensation and putting it into his back pocket. 'Can I walk you home?'

Lizzie smiled in the darkness. 'Yes please,' she said. 'It's suddenly a lot darker than it was when I set out!'

Noah used the torch on his newly found phone to light up the path as they wound their way back to town, chatting and flirting and occasionally brushing each other's hands or finding their arms touching as they walked side by side. It was so easy, so natural. Lizzie could feel herself being drawn in further with the familiarity of it all.

At the flat, Noah walked Lizzie to the front door.

'Thank you for tonight,' he said.

'I'm glad we found your phone. I don't know what I'd do if I lost mine.'

'I don't mean thank you for that, Lizzie.' He rested an arm on the door, pinning Lizzie in with his arm resting lightly on her shoulder.

'I know.' She suddenly felt a little self-conscious. 'I'm glad I bumped into you.'

He smiled. 'Me too.' And then he bent his head again to kiss her lightly on the lips, his fingers playing with her hair.

'I'll see you tomorrow,' said Lizzie, pulling away from the kiss but holding him close with her hands on his hips. 'Big day.'

'We'll finally see if all our planning has come to anything.' Noah brushed a thumb lightly over her cheek. 'It will be brilliant, I'm sure.'

'Hope so.'

'I'll see you tomorrow.'

'See you tomorrow,' she said again, not wanting the moment

to end. She reached up on her tiptoes and kissed him, before letting herself into the hallway and closing the door behind her.

After getting a little excited dance out of her system, she went upstairs to the flat, prepared for a barrage of questions from Tom about her date with Benny, which seemed like a million years ago now.

Closing the door quietly, she tiptoed along the corridor to her room and got ready for bed. She wanted to be alone, and she wanted to relive every delicious moment of her evening before it became a distant memory. But before she could snuggle down under the covers, the doorbell rang.

With a harrumph, Lizzie shrugged off the duvet and tiptoed down the stairs to the front door. She didn't want to use the buzzer at this time of night. On the other side of the door, standing in the dark with three children and a suitcase, was Kirsty.

Chapter Twenty-Six

'What happened?' Lizzie asked as Kirsty sat down on the sofa and tucked her legs up beneath her. She curled herself up into the foetal position, looking so small, and Lizzie found herself scanning her sister for signs of Steve's violence.

The boys were already snoring quietly in Lizzie's room – two top-and-tailing on her bed and the smallest curled up in a ball on the beanbag. Tom had been in touch to say he'd be out all night with Chris and said that Lizzie and Kirsty could share his bed, so Lizzie had given the boys the run of her bedroom.

'After what happened last night, I got home this morning and I just knew,' Kirsty said quietly. 'I just knew I couldn't possibly stay there any longer.' She cupped her mug of tea in both hands and sipped at it. Her eyes darted about as if a million thoughts were running through her mind and she wasn't quite sure which problem to focus on.

'Did he . . . ?' Lizzie wanted to make sure her sister and the boys were OK, but there was no easy way to say it.

Kirsty shook her head, understanding her meaning. 'He didn't have time to do anything. I got back and he said he was going out, so I packed a suitcase and just took the boys and ran. I don't even know if he's been back to realise I'm gone yet.'

Lizzie nodded, a little worried at what might happen when Steve found out. Luckily, as far as she was aware, he had no idea where her new flat was and therefore wouldn't have a clue where to find Kirsty or the children.

'I didn't know where to go at first,' Kirsty continued, 'so we've been sitting outside at the pub in town for a while. I was worried you were angry with me after how drunk I was last night, but then, I realised I had nowhere else to go. You're all I have, Lizzie.' A tear rolled down her face and she wiped it with the back of her hand.

'I'm not angry with you,' Lizzie said. 'I can hardly talk when it comes to having the odd drunken night out now, can I?' She said it with a smile to calm her sister down as much as she could after her ordeal. Although, she thought, she had acted badly when she'd thought it was Noah whom Kirsty had spent the night with.

'But I'm such an awful person. I wouldn't blame you if you were angry with me.'

Lizzie moved over to sit alongside her sister, her misplaced anger from earlier in the day forgotten. 'Shhh,' she said. 'You are not an awful person. You've been made to feel like you're an awful person by Steve. But you are not an awful person,' she repeated. 'Remember that. None of this is your fault.'

Kirsty nodded and wiped another tear away.

'You've just taken your boys and fled an appalling situation with them. What's awful about that? You're a hero.'

Kirsty smiled and Lizzie wrapped her arms around her.

'More importantly, you're safe. And you can stay here as long as you need to.'

Kirsty swallowed and rubbed a hand over her forehead. 'I should be the one looking after you,' she said.

'Sometimes a mother hen needs to look after herself before she can look after everyone else. If you're not OK, you can't make sure that everyone else is OK, can you? Don't give yourself such a hard time.'

Kirsty nodded. 'You're right. This has been a long time coming. It needed to happen. But, oh God – what am I going to do?' Tears came again as a new wave of fear washed over her, the realisation that she was in a situation so far removed from the mundane normality of her usual existence.

'You're going to get a good night's sleep,' Lizzie said, 'and take things one step at a time. Come on.'

Kirsty nodded, biting her bottom lip and wiping away the tears from her cheeks.

Lizzie stood and reached out her hand to help Kirsty up. She took her into Tom's room, provided her with pyjamas and a toothbrush and let her have Tom's bed to herself. She tucked her in like a child, stroked her hair back and told her everything was going to be OK, even though she didn't know that it would be. In a way, she was glad that they had managed to resolve some of the bad feeling that seemed to have settled between them more recently, even if it had come from such a horrid situation.

'Night, Kirs,' she said, closing the door softly. Kirsty could have her own space for the night. Lizzie padded out to the living room and lay down on the sofa, drawing the nearby blanket up to her chin as a flurry of worried thoughts about Kirsty floated through her mind. Occasionally her thoughts cleared enough for her to wonder whether Noah was in bed on the other side of town, thinking about her too.

Chapter Twenty-Seven

Monday morning was crazier than usual. There were three boys to get ready for school and Kirsty was zombie-like, having not slept despite Lizzie's best efforts to soothe her the previous night. Lizzie, at least, was fresh from another dreamless sleep and raced around to help get everybody ready. She was worrying about her sister, but sports day was imminent too.

At school, Lizzie sat nervously through literacy and maths, helping where she could, but mostly just counting down the hours until it was time to start organising all the equipment over at the secondary school. That, and see Noah again after all that had happened at the weekend.

The morning raced by in a cycle of hope and blind panic. She glanced at the door at regular intervals, hoping that she'd glimpse him and that he'd give her a look that said everything was OK. She loved that they'd spent Sunday evening together, but she hated that now she was in a weird kind of limbo that didn't have a name. Today was going to drag.

The lunch bell made Lizzie jump, bringing her back to reality. She stood and watched the children race out to the dinner hall or the playground.

'Are you OK?' Sophie asked, joining her at the door.

Lizzie nodded. 'Of course. Why?'

'You just seem a little distracted.'

Lizzie hadn't realised that she had been preoccupied outwardly, and she blushed. 'Sorry. No, I'm fine. Just a bit anxious about this afternoon.'

'Don't be,' Sophie said. 'You've had Noah to help, and he doesn't let anyone down.' She passed by Lizzie and left, making her way down the corridor.

I hope he doesn't, thought Lizzie, a million times he'd done just that in the past racing through her mind.

Over at the secondary school field, Noah had already brought over the equipment they'd put aside ready for the afternoon's event.

He smiled when he spotted Lizzie making her way across the field. It looked like he'd maybe ironed his kit for once – a tight, navy V-neck T-shirt and shorts. His hair was definitely more coiffed than usual. Lizzie couldn't help but wonder if it was for her benefit, but then decided it was more likely because of the pressure of sports day. This was his thing, and he needed to make a good impression.

'Hi.' He ran a hand through his hair.

Was Noah a little embarrassed? Lizzie got the sense that he wasn't exactly himself. She didn't say anything though, despite it having wobbled her slightly.

'Sorry I'm a bit late,' she said.

'Are you ready for this?' Noah asked.

'I think so. Where should we start?'

They had the field to themselves, with secondary school teachers patrolling the edges to keep the students away while they set up for the afternoon.

'Would you mind taking the jump stuff and setting it up over in that corner? It's where the long jump sandpit is, but we can put the standing jump stuff over there too.'

As he spoke, he sidled up to Lizzie and pointed to a hand-drawn map, which she found terribly endearing. Their shoulders touched and Lizzie felt a spark of electricity jump between them.

'I'll set up the start/finish line and make sure the stopwatches have all got batteries and the clipboards and medals are all set out here for everything.'

'So I've got to do all the walking?' Lizzie joked, rolling her eyes.

Noah laughed. 'I'm trying to wear you out so you can't win the staff race later.'

Lizzie shook her head in mock disbelief and picked up the box labelled 'jumping', which Noah had sorted and labelled. She'd not seen this organised version of Noah before. Maybe he'd grown up a bit. The fact he was still joking with her made her relax a little. He wasn't acting oddly, so maybe, just maybe, things were going to be OK. Lizzie was desperate to get him by himself to see where they were after Sunday evening. But that would have to wait. Sports day was imminent.

The sun was scorching and high overhead. Lizzie could feel the sweat trickling down the middle of her back as she lugged the box over to the other side of the field. It seemed to get heavier the further she went. Dumping it on the floor when she finally got there, she set about putting out the tape measure and raking the sand flat so that everything was set up and ready to go once the children arrived.

'You're taking your time,' Noah said, appearing suddenly behind her.

Lizzie squeaked. 'Jeez, Noah, are you trying to give me a heart attack?' She gripped her chest dramatically.

'Sorry,' he said with a laugh. 'I just wanted to check what you were up to. I've set up everything else.'

Lizzie looked around the field and Noah had indeed finished putting out all the other equipment. She could see little stations set up all over the place.

'I was just getting the jumping zone ready.' Lizzie looked down pathetically into the sandpit at what she'd thought was her hard work. Somehow, it paled into insignificance now that she saw everything Noah had set up in the same amount of time.

Noah kept a straight face. 'Well, it is the most prepared jumping station I've ever seen.'

Lizzie poked him in the ribs and Noah wriggled away.

'I'll have you know, jumping is very important,' she said, folding her arms.

'You're right.' He held up his hands in his defence. 'Jumping is very important indeed. Come on, we're starting in a few minutes.' He picked up the empty box to bring it back to the main sports day station and walked back across the field.

Lizzie looked at her watch. Gosh, was that really the time?

Even as she thought it, the whistles blew for the end of lunch and the secondary students trudged inside the school buildings as the Cranswell Primary School children arrived, already changed and excited about sports day.

'Do you want to man the jumping station, seeing as you've taken such care over it?' Noah asked, as they walked back.

Lizzie pulled a face. 'Yes please,' she said, all faux seriousness. 'It's very important.'

'Perfect.' Noah looked down his colour-coded checklist. 'With Kate, Sophie and Ged all manning the different stations, that covers everything. I'll send groups over when it's their turn and by two-thirty, we'll all be able to come back over to the central bit and run the last races, including the staff and parent one. Sound good?'

'Sounds great,' Lizzie agreed. 'I enjoy any opportunity where there's a chance to beat you at something, Noah.' She swung round, her hair reflecting the sunlight.

'Likewise.'

She could hear the smirk in his voice.

'I'll see you back here for the race,' she said, walking away from him and back over to man her station.

Lizzie didn't realise that the afternoon would hold such a sense of occasion. Shortly after the end of lunch, parents, grandparents and younger siblings all arrived to cheer on their family and friends. There were flags and bunting, and once Noah got out the tannoy, it would have been difficult to tell the difference between Cranswell sports day and a village fete.

In her little corner, Lizzie made sure all the jumping competitors took their turn – in the perfectly prepared sandpit, she might add – and diligently wrote down their distances, awarding little medals that the Year Four class had been making all term. It was nice to meet more of the other children. The youngest ones were adorable, but Lizzie didn't relish the idea of trying to teach them anything. It was tricky enough getting them to jump in the right direction and not eat the sand.

The end of the day fast approached, and before she knew where the afternoon had gone, Noah blew his whistle and announced on the tannoy that it was time for the year group relays, and the staff and parent race. Everyone on the field gathered up any equipment that was near them and made their way over to the main set-up, ready to watch the final races.

Lizzie took her place in the Year Six zone of the spectators' area to watch the children from her class take part in the relay. Nigel, of course, was running the final leg of the race. With his long legs and love of attention, she'd have been surprised if he hadn't got involved.

'Everything OK over at the throwing station?' Lizzie asked, as Sophie sat down next to her on the grass.

The children sat and knelt on the field in front of them, cheering on their classmates.

'Well, I survived,' Sophie said, looking exhausted. 'Children under seven should not be allowed to throw things. Ever,' she added, and Lizzie laughed. 'Stacey in Year Three almost took the head off a reception kid and another one weed on the floor. Bit of a nightmare, really.'

'I definitely couldn't teach the little ones.' She looked out over the field where the competitors were lining up, playing with a long blade of grass and rolling it between her fingers.

'How are you finding it?' Sophie asked. 'Teaching, I mean. And school life. Is it what you thought it would be?'

'It's everything I thought it could be and more,' she said honestly. 'I love it. It's had a huge impact on my life. I didn't know what I was really doing before, where I was going, but now, I literally jump out of bed in the morning. It's exactly what Mum and Dad would have wanted.'

Sophie smiled. 'Jumping out of bed? Wow,' she said. 'That's great, though. We need young teachers to come and teach.'

'Young?' Lizzie said, raising an eyebrow.

'Well, fresh.' Sophie laughed. 'I have it on good authority that a job will be coming up in a year's time, you know – I can't say who, but there's going to be a teaching post opening up at the end of next year – so keep an eye out. I think you'd be perfect.'

'Wow.' Lizzie was overwhelmed by the compliment. 'Thanks. It's good to know I'm doing something right.'

'You're doing great,' Sophie said, 'which is lucky really, as from Christmas, you'll have a new mentor.'

Lizzie turned to Sophie and raised an eyebrow. 'How come? Is everything OK?'

'Yes, everything's fine.' Sophie beamed. 'But I'm pregnant, so I'll be taking some of next year off.'

Lizzie's face broke into a grin. 'Wow! Congratulations! I'm so happy for you!'

'Thank you.' Sophie placed a protective hand on her belly and smiled down at the slight bump that Lizzie hadn't noticed until now.

Lizzie could have sworn she saw the beginning of a tear in Sophie's eye. But she wiped it away as quickly as it had appeared before she said, 'Now, don't you need to go and get ready to win the staff race on behalf of Year Six?' She raised her voice so the rest of the class could hear and they cheered.

Lizzie stood up, brushed the grass off her bottom and raised her arms to elicit further cheers from the children, who had stood up and raced to the front of the spectators' area, ready to support the participants.

At the start line, rather a motley crew had assembled. There were a few parents, some of them limbering up and looking as if they were taking it very seriously. From the staff, there was Lizzie and Noah, of course. Tom had sidestepped this particular opportunity, but the caretaker and a couple of early years teachers were there too.

Miss Davies, the headteacher, was there to start the race. She had one of those joke guns that, when you pressed the trigger, fell open to reveal a flag with the word 'bang' on it.

'Are you ready to get beaten?' Noah said out of the corner of his mouth as Lizzie waited for the signal to go.

She refused to let his banter take away from her focus, and kept her eyes on the track. 'Not today, Noah.'

'ON YOUR MARKS, GET SET!' Miss Davies shouted across the field.

The children descended into a hush.

'GO!'

And they were off.

Children were jumping and screaming for their favourite teacher or parent. Lizzie could hear some of them shouting her name as she sped past. One lap of the racetrack. That was all she had to do. She definitely had this.

As she took the first bend, it was already obvious that this was a two-horse race with possible third competition from one parent who had ridiculously long legs and had come prepared, looking like a serious runner in his gym kit. Noah was the other one who hit the first corner at the same time as Lizzie.

The noise of the crowds grew faint as they raced around the far side of the track. Lizzie could hear only her heartbeat thumping in time with her feet as they hit the ground. In her peripheral vision, she could see Noah's shadow keeping in time with her, stride for stride. Whatever she did, she couldn't shake him. Typical.

As they rounded the final bend into the finishing stretch, Lizzie gave it everything she had. Her legs were powering hard and as fast as she could get them to go. Noah and the dad were neck and neck. If anything, they were slightly ahead.

The next moment fell into slow motion. Somehow, the dad tripped and crumpled into a heap on the floor. Noah, who came across the obstacle first, hurdled over him. But Lizzie, startled by the event, jumped, caught the toe of her running shoe on the fallen parent and hurtled forward into Noah. Noah skipped and then fell back into stride without a backwards glance, but Lizzie fell to the ground.

She screwed up her eyes as her face hit the hard track below. She skidded forward before coming to a stop in front of the children. She heard the spectators grow quiet and descend into a collective gasp. The race was over – for her at least. Looking up, she could see Noah crossing the finish line, his arms spread in celebration. A few feet away, the parent who had caused the pile-up was standing and brushing himself down, still in with a chance of coming fifth. All Lizzie could do was spit out the grass and dirt that had gone into her mouth as she'd fallen.

She did a quick mental sweep of her body. Maybe she could jump up, keep running and avoid coming last. But it was then that she realised she couldn't move, and the world returned to its normal speed.

'Oh my God! Lizzie, are you OK?' Sophie came bounding out from the Year Six area and crouched down to where she was lying.

'Everybody's watching, aren't they?' Lizzie was deeply embarrassed and horribly in pain. She winced as she tried to turn herself over.

Sophie looked around. 'A few people are watching, yes. But only because they're worried about you. Are you all right?'

Lizzie shook her head, scuffing her cheek on the ground. She pushed her hands against the floor to sit up, which she did slowly and with zero grace. 'I've really hurt my ankle,' she said, rubbing the area, which was already swollen to twice its usual size.

'I'll get the first aid kit.' Sophie turned to beckon over Miss Davies, who was already on her way.

'Let's get you inside,' said Miss Davies, reaching down to support Lizzie into getting up. 'I'm not sure a plaster's going to cut it.'

Suddenly Noah was there, helping her up on the other side, and she hopped between the pair of them into a staffroom.

'I'll get some ice,' Miss Davies said, 'but I'm pretty sure you'll need to get that looked at over in A&E.' She went to the freezer and took out an ice pack. 'Here.'

Noah, who still hadn't said anything, took it and placed it carefully on her ankle, that electricity jumping between them again. Except this time it made Lizzie feel pain rather than lust.

'Is that OK?' he asked.

Lizzie said nothing, but nodded once. She knew it was perfectly unreasonable, but right now, she was pissed off with Noah for tripping her, leaving her and winning. How dare he? After everything that had happened between them in the past few weeks, how could he do that to her?

'I'll phone A&E and tell them you're on your way. Do you have someone who can take you?' Miss Davies asked.

'I can,' said Noah.

Lizzie said, 'Can you get Tom? He can take me over.'

Miss Davies looked from Lizzie to Noah and back again. Thinking better of asking what on earth was going on, she nodded and left the room.

'I really don't mind taking you, you know.' Noah flipped the ice pack to the cold side and placed it back on her leg, making Lizzie wince.

'It's fine.'

'Which means you're not fine.' Noah rolled his eyes and smiled at their shared joke.

'It's not funny, Noah. Not everything is a joke.' Lizzie crossed her arms and realised that her torso ached, too.

'I'm sorry, I just . . .'

'Well, don't *just* anything,' Lizzie said, shutting him down. She knew she was having a serious sense of humour failure, but she simply didn't care. Her embarrassment at having fallen seemed to translate into completely undeserved hostility. Noah hadn't done anything wrong. Not in the last decade at least.

'I'm sorry, Lizzie. I don't know what I've done. This was an accident,' Noah said. He sounded frustrated. 'I thought after last night . . .'

'So did I, but clearly beating me is still your main aim. You got your kiss, and now you've got your win, haven't you? I hope you're happy.'

'Lizzie, you're being unreasonable. I didn't realise you'd fallen.'

'Oh, so you just assumed I'd got left behind and couldn't keep up with you, eh? Typical.' Even as she said it, she knew it sounded ridiculous, but she was hurting, in more ways than one. A decade of pent-up anger had built up inside her and now threatened to come tumbling out in one go, her sense of reason and maturity having disappeared.

'Lizzie,' Noah said, and then thought better of it. 'I . . .'

'I'm really injured here,' she said, pointing to her ankle, which was getting bigger and more purple by the minute. 'I'm not going to be able to play football either.'

'You'll be back to it in no time. It's probably just a sprain.'

'That's just so like you. You think the big things are just little and have no comprehension of how other people may feel. Well, I'm not going to let you treat me like this again.'

Noah looked understandably confused and spoke softly when he said, 'I don't know what you're talking about, Lizzie.'

'You left me,' Lizzie whispered. 'You left me for someone else.

And I know it was like a hundred years ago, but it still hurts. Last night was wonderful, but nothing's changed. You still left me.'

'You told me to go,' Noah said, his voice slightly raised. 'You were falling for someone else.'

'You were cheating on me!'

'No, I wasn't,' he said, the hurt written on his face.

'Good comeback,' said Lizzie sarcastically.

'Lizzie. You called that night and told me you couldn't be with me any more. And it wasn't a complete surprise because I already knew you'd been spending time with some guy off your course.'

'What? No! You were cheating on me.' She pronounced each individual word with the rage that had taken over her.

'Where did you even get that from?' he asked, his voice a little more even now.

'Kirsty told me she'd seen you around town with other girls while I was at university.'

'That's not true!'

'Why did she say it then?' She knew she sounded like a petulant teenager. They were arguing as though they were still at school together. She also knew that she sounded horrendously irrational and in no way sane, but she couldn't stop herself.

'She told me the same about you, about you and the guy on your course.'

Lizzie shook her head. 'It's not true. There was no guy.'

'Why would she say that then?'

Lizzie rubbed her ankle. It really was painful. She started to cry. It was too late to be embarrassed in front of Noah – she'd just embarrassed herself in front of the whole school.

'Afterwards,' began Noah, 'when you wouldn't answer my calls, I had to give up trying. You gave up on me, on us. There was only so much fighting I could do.'

Lizzie spoke through her tears in a whisper. 'My parents died that night in the fire. I didn't have any fight left. And when I think I could've been there for them. But I was too busy ignoring you.'

She didn't know whom she was angrier at – Noah or herself – or . . . Kirsty. Lizzie suddenly began to put the pieces together. Neither of them had admitted to cheating despite rumours. And the common thread was that Kirsty had been the one to speak to them. Surely she hadn't meant to . . . Now Lizzie thought about it, Kirsty had been flirting with Noah for weeks. She hadn't put it all together, until now. She opened her mouth to speak as Tom swept into the room.

'I'll take that,' he said, swiping the ice pack and nudging Noah out of the way. 'Come on, Lizzie, let's get you to the hospital. Taxi's outside.'

Without another word, Lizzie let Tom help her up. She put her arm around his shoulders and he walked her to the door. Risking a glance back at Noah, she saw him slumped with his head in his hands. What had she done? Had their break-up really been all down to Kirsty telling a lie? Had she ruined whatever it was that had started again last night? Had the last ten years all been a horrible, horrible mistake?

Chapter Twenty-Eight

The waiting room at the hospital was miserable. It was full of people who looked like they'd been waiting there for a decade, and after three hours, Lizzie realised why they looked like they did.

She adjusted her sitting position and winced as the pain shot up through her leg.

'It won't be long now,' Tom said, sensing her discomfort.

'Sorry I ruined your evening,' said Lizzie sadly.

'It's Monday night, I hardly had any epic plans.'

'I know, but even still.' Lizzie shrugged.

'Does the team know you're going to be missing the celebratory meal tonight?' asked Tom.

'I texted Zoe.'

'You didn't text Kirsty?' he asked tentatively.

Lizzie shook her head. 'Didn't you hear what Noah said?' she asked, incredulous. 'Kirsty basically broke us up, and I think it was because she had a thing for Noah.'

'It was a long time ago, though,' ventured Tom, misreading just how irrationally mad Lizzie was right now.

'I've been single and miserable for ten years, Tom, ten years, all because of her jealousy. I could've been with Noah,' she said, tears beginning to sting her eyes. 'Right now, I never want to speak to her again.'

Tom sat silently for a moment, choosing to pick up a magazine from the table rather than to push the subject any further.

Lizzie sat in silence, concentrating on her breathing and trying desperately not to cry.

A nurse came out into the corridor and addressed the waiting room. 'Miss Morris?'

'That's me.' Lizzie raised a hand and shifted her weight in preparation to stand.

'Here, let me help.' Tom lifted her up and slung her arm around his neck.

They followed the nurse slowly down the corridor and into the X-ray room.

'You look like you've been in the wars,' she said brightly. Her blue uniform was still crisp and her hair perfectly coiffed into a bun at the back of her head. She didn't look like someone who'd been in the hospital waiting for three hours. Lizzie didn't even want to think about what she looked like in comparison.

'Sports injury,' Lizzie said, which wasn't strictly true, but sounded better than what had actually happened. She shared a sly smile with Tom, momentarily letting her rage slip.

'OK, well why don't you hop onto the bench and we'll take a quick snap,' she said, taking Lizzie's free arm to help Tom get her up onto the bench.

'Right, if you get back here,' she said to Tom, gesturing to a safe space behind the wall.

Lizzie was always slightly concerned that when patients got zapped, the nurses hid behind a wall. What exactly was going on there? Surely, if it was dangerous for Tom and the nurse, Lizzie was in trouble, too. She shielded her eyes, at a loss for what else to do to protect herself. But the process was underwhelming, and she didn't even realise that the X-ray had been taken when the nurse said, 'Lovely. If you just go back out to the waiting room, the doctor will have a look at this and call you in shortly.'

The thought of waiting in the foyer any longer filled Lizzie with dread. But Tom supported her back out into the corridor and they sat down.

'I'm sorry I snapped.' Lizzie looked down at her feet, comparing her injured one to the normal one.

'Don't worry.' Tom rested his hand on hers. 'It's been a crappy day, I get it.'

Lizzie smiled at him.

The doctor called them in only thirty minutes later, which Lizzie thought might have been some kind of record, judging from the look of everyone else who was out there. He was an elderly man, with a tan that certainly didn't advocate sun safety and a spectacularly neat silver moustache.

'So it would seem that you've got a hairline fracture.' The doctor pointed to something on the X-ray that looked nothing like a hairline or a fracture to Lizzie. She nodded anyway, trying to avoid any further humiliation.

'You'll need to keep this on for the next eight to twelve weeks,' he said, pulling a very fetching navy-blue support boot out of a box. 'I'll send you home with crutches, too. You'll need to rest it, so that it has time to heal.'

'Thank you.' She was only being polite. Inside, she was raging. No football, no proper teaching, no nothing for at least eight weeks. Not to mention the fact it would eat into the summer holidays.

'It's OK,' Tom said, reading her mind. 'I can drive you to and from school. It'll be fine.'

'Any questions?' the doctor asked, shuffling the paperwork to show that despite asking, it was out of courtesy and, really, they were done here.

'No, thank you.' Lizzie used her new crutches to lift herself up and hobble out of the office.

The waiting room had since emptied, and sitting alone on a chair in the centre of the room was Kirsty. She was looking down at her hands, which she was wringing nervously in her lap.

Lizzie attempted to speed past her on her crutches, galloping like an injured horse across the room.

'I came as soon as I heard,' Kirsty said, standing between Lizzie and the door.

Tom stood awkwardly. He had no idea how this showdown was about to play out – neither did Lizzie.

Lizzie made to push past her, but was hindered by her injury.

Kirsty placed a hand on her arm. 'What's wrong?'

'I've got nothing to say to you,' Lizzie said quietly.

'What?' Kirsty narrowed her eyes, confused at the shift in their relationship. 'What's happened?'

'I spoke to Noah earlier.' She watched the change in Kirsty's expression as she guessed at where Lizzie was going.

'I wasn't walking home from his when I saw you yesterday morning, Lizzie. It was his friend. I was worried you might have thought that.'

Kirsty looked relieved, but Lizzie's expression remained stony.

'We spoke about how our relationship ended, actually,' she said, watching Kirsty's expression falter, just slightly. 'We talked about how it was your rumours, your lies, that ended it.'

Kirsty looked at Tom and then back at Lizzie. 'I don't know what you're talking about.'

'Please don't lie to me, Kirs. I've had a crappy day and I don't need you to treat me like an idiot.'

Kirsty looked down at the ground. 'OK,' she said weakly. 'I may have tried to split you two up, but you were young and you were out exploring the world. You didn't need Noah staying at home and holding you back.'

'That's not the impression I got. I don't think you split us up for our benefit.'

'Well, that's what happened,' Kirsty said flatly.

'You might like to play the role of mother hen, but this time, I think you did it for you. I think you liked Noah – still do – and that's why your broke us up. How could you?' Lizzie blinked back a couple of stray tears.

Tom suddenly seemed to find a big plastic yucca plant very interesting, and wandered over to take a closer inspection.

'Lizzie, I really don't understand what—'

'So you didn't tell me he'd cheated because you wanted him for yourself? You weren't secretly hoping that if he did cheat, it'd be with you? You didn't lie to him about my infidelity? That I'd met someone on my course that I was interested in?'

There was a stand-off for a minute, both of them silent and glaring at each other, until a tear rolled down Kirsty's face.

'You and I, we didn't have the same relationship then,' she started, her voice weak. 'I didn't think it mattered.'

'I loved him,' Lizzie said, shifting on her crutches, her wrists beginning to ache.

'I didn't know that,' Kirsty said, as if that would be an excuse somehow.

Lizzie shook her head. 'You didn't ask. You just selfishly went for it and didn't care about who you might hurt along the way.'

'I'm sorry,' Kirsty mumbled at the floor rather than to Lizzie.

'No, Kirsty. I'm sorry,' Lizzie said, getting into her stride. 'I'm sorry your marriage was so shitty. I'm sorry that you felt you needed to look elsewhere.'

'I, I . . .'

'I'm sorry that we ever grew closer after Mum and Dad died. This whole thing has been a lie.' She waved her hand between them. 'Don't even get me started about the fact it was the night of the fire. I could have . . .'

Kirsty was crying now, but Lizzie was too angry. There were no tears to cry. She knew they'd come later, when she was alone.

'Lizzie, can't we talk about this? It was so long ago.'

'Come on, Tom. Let's go,' Lizzie said, ignoring her sister's plea. 'You'll need to find somewhere else to stay. I can't have you at the flat any more.' She turned and left, horrified that it had come to this.

Tom dragged himself away from the yucca and followed Lizzie out of the hospital, giving Kirsty a look that was half apologetic and half judgemental as he passed her.

Once they were safely outside, he said, 'You can have a cry now if you like.'

'I'm sorry, Tom,' Lizzie blubbed through the tears she'd been saving up all day.

'For what?' he asked, brushing her hair back from her face like you might a small child who had fallen over and grazed their knee.

'I'm sorry you had to be there for that, and that I ruined your day.' She was almost incoherent.

Tom laughed and Lizzie joined in through her tears, her

bottom lip poking out like a cartoon.

'Can we just go home?' she asked.

'Yes, Chris is on the way and he's picked up pizza and wine already.'

'He's a keeper.' Lizzie smiled through her tears.

Tom couldn't help the grin that spread across his face. 'Yes, I think he might be.'

Chapter Twenty-Nine

Lizzie spent the next week observing lessons from a chair in the corner like a naughty child. Because of her injury, she'd been promoted from a child's chair to a full-sized one at least, but she had still been sidelined. She couldn't even get in with the children very easily to help them. She missed their conversations. Observation was dull.

And fracturing her ankle wasn't the only thing keeping Lizzie in a funk. Noah had disappeared. She'd not seen him since their argument and hadn't built up the courage to ask anyone else about where he'd gone. The more time that passed, the more she could see how stupid and angry she'd been over nothing. And she desperately wanted to talk to him and make it right.

On top of everything else, she'd been fielding calls and texts from Kirsty for days, trying her hardest not to speak to her. She was angry with her, yes; but her sister was also going through a hard time. She'd heard on the grapevine that she was staying with a work colleague, so she knew she was safe, at least. But despite avoiding her because she was angry, she also didn't know what she wanted to say to her either. She could see there would be only one opportunity to have the conversation for the first time, and she wanted to get it right.

'How long before you can take the support off?' Sophie asked as she cleared up the mess from the afternoon's lessons a week after the accident.

Lizzie had been given the demoralising task of sharpening pencils, given that she wouldn't need to walk anywhere to do it.

She sighed. 'The doctor said eight to twelve weeks, so at least seven more.'

'Hopefully by September you'll be good to go then,' Sophie said brightly.

Lizzie did some maths in her head and realised that the start of the next school year was almost exactly eight weeks away. She hoped she'd be fully recovered by then. She couldn't bear to observe any more lessons. And what would she do all summer?

'God, I hope so.' Lizzie's whole body slumped in the chair.

'It must be really frustrating.' Sophie came over and joined Lizzie at the table. 'But it's not for ever.'

'I know. I'm just not used to resting. I'm a doer, and sitting down for eight weeks just isn't me.'

'I'd struggle too.' Sophie smiled. 'Leave the rest of these colouring pencils. I'll get Nigel to do them tomorrow morning. Why don't you head off?'

Lizzie looked at her watch. Tom would be waiting to drive her home in ten minutes.

'OK, thanks.'

Sophie helped Lizzie out of the chair and made sure she was fully upright and balanced. By now, Lizzie was getting the hang of using the crutches. She hobbled out of the classroom and down the corridor to the front door of the school.

She was thankful for the friendship bench at the side of the playground. From her seat there, she could see the car park and spot Tom when he left the building. It was a sunny July day and the metal of the bench was hot on the back of her legs. She stripped off her cardigan and bent down to shove it in her bag, then sat back up again.

'Kirsty.'

Her sister had stepped out from behind the school gate, looking like she'd been waiting there for a while.

'I was hoping I'd catch you by yourself.'

'How long have you been . . .'

'Just since the end of school.'

'You know . . .' Lizzie sighed and pushed herself up from the bench. 'It's frowned upon to loiter about school gates.' She picked up her crutches and slowly moved away.

Kirsty stepped forward. 'Lizzie, wait. We really need to talk.'

Lizzie stopped and turned. 'No, Kirsty, we don't. You might need to talk, but I have nothing to say to you.'

'What, so you're never going to speak to me again?' Kirsty's tone was frustrated, and her hand moved to her hip.

Lizzie paused before she spoke, the hurt Kirsty had caused flashing through her mind. She shrugged and shook her head.

'Not right now, no.'

Walking away from a conversation was tough on crutches, but Kirsty didn't follow her and she was glad. She could feel her sister's eyes on her as she crossed the playground. She'd never been more grateful when Tom came out the school doors jangling his car keys in his hand.

'Ready?' He looked at Lizzie and his expression registered his awareness of Kirsty behind her.

Lizzie nodded, afraid to speak in case her voice cracked.

'Come on, then. Let's go home.'

He glanced at Kirsty in what Lizzie read to be sympathy, and she suddenly felt a brief flash of guilt for not speaking to her sister. She was going through a horrific time herself and Lizzie was angry about something that had happened a decade ago.

She would talk to her. She knew she would, eventually. But she wasn't ready, not quite yet.

Chapter Thirty

'Are you sure you want to do the charity thing this year?'

Tom was sitting on the floor of the living room doing up the buckle on Lizzie's sandals. A few days had passed and Lizzie was getting used to having to ask others for help.

'Of course I do. Why wouldn't I?'

'Well . . .' Tom looked down at her support brace. 'It's a long time to be out and about on your feet.'

'Tom, we go every year. It's important to the football team and you know why the collaboration with the fire service is important to me.' She looked down to her mum's ring, glinting in the light.

'No one would be annoyed if you gave it a miss this one time.'

'Thomas.' Lizzie shot him a warning look.

He held his hands up in defence. 'OK, OK. Let's go, then. So stubborn.'

Every year in the town centre, the fire service put on a

family fun day to promote fire safety and raise funds for the department. Lizzie had been helping for as long as she could remember, and her involvement had grown even more significant after everything that had happened with her family.

The green was already bustling when Lizzie arrived. The fire department had parked the fire engine in the middle of the grass; children were climbing all over it and lining up for a chance to sit in the driver's seat and turn on the siren. There were tombola stands, ice cream and popcorn, and free stickers and badges. The sun was out, and it seemed like the entire town was too.

Lizzie had signed up to sit on the information desk, given her current predicament. Tom helped her over, and she sat down next to Coach Zoe, who asked the football team to get involved every year, too.

'Lizzie! It's so good to see you.' She bent over and hugged her. 'How are you? I heard about the accident.' She looked pointedly down at Lizzie's leg.

Lizzie blushed. 'I've been better. No football for me for at least a couple of months or so.'

'That's rubbish,' Zoe said, reaching for more flyers from underneath the table and adding them to the piles.

Lizzie straightened the piles in front of her while Tom busied himself with the display behind them.

'I've been thinking, though, there might be an opportunity for you to do some coaching while you recuperate. The under-sixteens team is looking for someone if you're interested?'

She felt affronted by the suggestion. 'My football career isn't over, Zoe. This is just a hiatus.'

'I know.' She smiled. 'But I bet you'd love something to

keep you busy while you're recovering, you know, to get back out there on the pitch.'

'Maybe.' Lizzie softened and thought about how coaching might be the way forward. It might stop her from going mad over the summer holidays.

Behind Coach Zoe, Tom's expression changed and Lizzie realised there was someone walking up behind her. She turned to see Kirsty and rubbed a hand over her face. Was she ever going to give up?

Tom said, 'Maybe you should talk to her.'

'I'm not sure . . .'

He narrowed his eyes. 'It's time, Lizzie.'

She knew he was right. She'd trust Tom with everything in the world and if he thought it was time to address things with Kirsty head on, then perhaps she should.

'Why don't you go and get a drink or something,' Zoe said. 'Tom and I have got things covered here.'

Lizzie swallowed and gave a slight nod before pushing herself up out of the chair.

'Lizzie, hi.'

Lizzie didn't respond to her sister's greeting. Instead, she said, 'Do you want to get a coffee?'

Kirsty nodded. She looked dishevelled, her shirt untucked and hair sticking up at the back. She looked like maybe she'd spent the last few nights on a sofa rather than in a bed. Lizzie softened a little more.

They walked over to Greg's stall, where he'd moved the usual coffee from his shop out onto the green.

'Cappuccinos?' he asked, as Lizzie and Kirsty approached the stall.

'Yes please, Greg.'

He pushed his glasses up his nose and turned to make their coffees. Lizzie watched him intently as he measured out the coffee and turned the hot water on to filter it. Anything to ignore the ugly tension that had settled between her and Kirsty as they waited.

'Let's sit here,' Kirsty said once they had their coffees.

She led them over to a set of white plastic patio furniture and held the chair steady as Lizzie lowered herself into it.

After a further awkward minute, Kirsty said, 'So, how are you?'

Lizzie snorted and looked down at her leg. She shook her head and sipped her coffee.

'OK,' Kirsty said.

She sat back from the table and sipped her own coffee as they both looked out over the green. There were pockets of people, laughing, children screaming with delight. It felt oddly juxtaposed against their melancholy.

Kirsty suddenly sat forward. 'Look, Lizzie.' She paused until Lizzie had no choice but to meet her eye contact. 'I know that I have done awful things and I'm sorry.'

Lizzie swallowed. She didn't know what to say.

'I was in a loveless marriage, Lizzie, a toxic one. What you and Noah had was just so enviable and when you left for uni, Steve and I were going through a particularly hideous patch. I should have known then, really. The way that Noah treated you, God, even the way he looked at you! I was jealous and when I was drunk that evening, I tried to convince both of you that the other was cheating so that I might have even an ounce of what you guys had. What you guys have . . .'

Lizzie looked away, out over the field again.

'It's not just that, Kirsty,' she whispered. The images from

301

her nightmares flashed again in her mind and despite the clear summer's day, she struggled to catch her breath for a moment.

'I know. Or rather, I'll never know how much I've truly hurt you.'

She turned in her seat to face Kirsty. 'You split us up, which was bad enough, but you stopped me from being there for Mum and Dad, too. While I was wallowing in self-pity, they were dying.'

Kirsty narrowed her eyes as they glazed over with tears. 'What? I don't understand.'

'When Noah and I ended things, I was heartbroken. I turned off my phone and didn't respond to messages or phone calls for days. That night was the night of the fire. If I'd had my phone on, I might have . . .' But the words were lost in a choke, Lizzie's voice cracking beyond recognition.

'You were away at uni, Lizzie, miles away. What could you have done? I promise, they didn't phone or text you.'

Lizzie spoke through her tears. 'How can you know that?'

'They died in their sleep. It was on the reports at the end of everything.'

'I didn't know that.' Lizzie spoke quietly and ran her finger across the bumps of the reusable coffee cup.

'Nothing was your fault, Lizzie. The only person to blame here is me. And I am so, so sorry.'

'Well, you and Steve.'

'I don't want to talk about him. It's over. Since we left, me and the boys have been staying at a friend's house, but we've found a place to rent from the end of the month. I might be sleeping on a fold-out bed for a few weeks yet, but at least I know we're all safe.'

Lizzie smiled and wiped the tears from her face with her sleeve. 'I'm glad.'

'I couldn't have done any of that without your support. I may have started out as mother hen, but you're the one that's looked after me recently and I'm so grateful. I don't want that closeness to end. Not over something stupid I did years ago. I desperately want – no, need – you to forgive me. I need my sister back. More than anything.'

Lizzie sighed, relieved, not realising until now how worried she'd been about Kirsty, not understanding how much guilt she was still carrying about the fire.

They sat in silence for a long while until the sun began its descent and the smell of BBQ filled the air.

'Will you ever be able to forgive me?' Kirsty asked after a while, a tentative hope in her words.

Lizzie bit the inside of her lip. Would she?

'I know that I've ruined the last ten years of your life with my actions, but I was really hoping that by telling you now, laying everything out on the table, you and Noah might be able to reconcile something. I know that you still love him.'

Lizzie hitched in a breath. She hadn't even realised that herself.

'I think it might be too late for me and Noah.' Her mind flashed back to her ridiculous behaviour after her accident at sports day.

'No.' Kirsty shook her head. 'I've seen how you two are together. I was jealous of it, remember?'

Lizzie let out a slight laugh. 'I've not seen him since sports day. We argued and now he's gone AWOL. He's not been in school all week.'

Kirsty looked down at herself and rubbed at a stain on her

trousers. 'If there's still hope for me, then there's definitely hope for you two.'

'I'm sorry I didn't speak to you for so long.'

'You don't have to apologise. I know why you didn't. I deserved it. I just want now to be a fresh start. Can we do that?' Kirsty smiled hopefully.

Lizzie smiled. 'I think maybe we can. We can certainly try.'

Chapter Thirty-One

'Welcome, everyone, to our enrichment day,' Miss Davies said as she addressed the whole of Cranswell Primary School in the hall. The children whooped and clapped. Apparently, it was a tradition for the last couple of days of term. The children would take part in different activities during the day, all of which were loosely linked to the curriculum, but were mostly planned to enrich their education and allow them to have some well-earned fun.

After a brief assembly to welcome the children and introduce the day, Miss Davies sent them all off to find the staff member and activity they'd signed up to do for the morning session.

Lizzie was disappointed not to be involved in the mountain biking or splash pool trips that had gone out first thing that morning, but did get to take part in making cakes and selling them at lunchtime.

'Miss, have you tasted this?' Audrey said, excitedly licking the spoon and then the bowl.

'I'm not sure you're supposed to eat raw mixture.' Lizzie dipped her own finger in to taste it.

'Don't forget me,' Benjamin said. He'd found himself a huge wooden spoon to scoop up as much of the mixture as he could. 'Yum,' he said, shovelling a load of it into his mouth.

'Right, we need to tidy up,' Lizzie said. 'And as I can't stand up for long, you'll have to do the washing-up.'

There was a collective groan as they gathered up all the equipment and put it into the sink, which Audrey had already filled up with far too much Fairy liquid.

The smell of their cakes was delicious. Lizzie could see them puffing up and turning golden in the oven. She turned her attention to making the icing ready for the decoration.

'So we'll have to put the icing on after break time, otherwise the cakes will be too warm. I'll take them out when they're done. Once all that is on the draining board, you can go to break.'

Even break time was enrichment themed, with far more games and sports equipment than usual out on the field for them to enjoy. Lizzie gave it a wide berth. She'd still not seen Noah, nor had he been at school as far as she knew, but she still preferred not to risk bumping into him, especially when she was covered in flour and spots of greasy margarine.

'How are you getting on?' Tom asked when he bumped into Lizzie in the staffroom. It was going to have to be a super-fast cup of tea. It had taken her ten minutes to shuffle her way up the corridor and if she didn't get back before her group of children did, it was likely they'd make their way through the icing that she'd prepared rather than wait for her so they could decorate the cakes together. Also, she couldn't remember taking the cakes out of the oven in the first place and she couldn't risk ruining their enrichment day by burning it all.

'We're baking,' Lizzie said.

Tom pulled a face.

'I haven't burnt anything yet. You never know. This might be the start of a brand-new me. My culinary skills may just not yet have been discovered,' she added with a smug smile.

'Don't you remember Soup Gate?'

'It is not my fault that hot food expands, nor is it my fault that you didn't put the Tupperware lids on properly.'

Tom raised an eyebrow.

'All right, point taken. But that was a one-off,' she said.

'That's the only time I can ever remember you cooking,' Tom said, passing her a cool cup of tea.

'There you go, then. Definitely a one-off,' she said, taking a sip of her drink, watching him from over the top of her mug.

The staffroom was fairly full, but through the crowd, Lizzie spotted Noah coming in. She caught her breath and instantly ducked, her tea spilling everywhere. She threw a tea towel onto the floor where the tea had landed, in an attempt to clear it up.

She half whispered, 'Help get me out of here?'

'Let's go out the fire exit and round.'

They escaped as quickly as someone on crutches could, out into the summer sunshine. Laughing, they paused to catch their breath.

'Are you ever going to talk to him?' Tom asked, serious suddenly.

'Perhaps,' Lizzie said, thinking back to her conversation with Kirsty. 'Just not yet.'

'He's been asking after you, you know.'

Had he? The more Lizzie thought about it, the more

she realised that whatever had happened a decade ago, the way she'd U-turned on Monday after what they'd shared on Sunday evening had been cruel and insensitive. She would have to talk to him eventually. And she'd have to apologise, which, where Noah was concerned, was her least favourite task.

Decorating the cakes after break time was as chaotic as Lizzie had expected, but was also a lot of fun. She finally felt happy again, something she hadn't felt in the past week or so. At the lunchtime sale, the cakes went down really well, with the children raising over £50 for charity, which Audrey was particularly pleased about. Benjamin was sad, though, that everyone had paid in silver coins and they hadn't got one of those giant cheques like they get on the television. Lizzie decided she'd wait around later and see if she could steal some cardboard from the stationery cupboard and make one for him.

'What's happening this afternoon?' Lizzie asked. She looked guiltily on as Sophie tidied up the classroom. All she could do was sort out the colouring pens and pencils into their separate tubs while sitting down at the table.

'We've got a sports session, actually,' Sophie said. 'Over in the hall.'

Lizzie's heart dropped. Really? She'd gone thus far avoiding Noah and now she was going to have to spend the afternoon watching him and other people play sport. She was still pretty upset that she couldn't play football for the foreseeable future, and this would do nothing to improve her mood.

'Shall we wander over now? We can stop by the staffroom for a quick cake on the way if you like. There were loads left over from the sale,' Sophie said.

'OK.' Lizzie tried to sound excited, but ended up somewhere within mild acceptance.

They walked over together, stopping as planned in the staffroom.

'You're going to love what's going on this afternoon,' Tom said. He was in there making tea – again.

'What do you mean?' Lizzie got the distinct feeling that something was going on that she didn't know about.

'You'll see,' Tom said, wiggling his eyebrows up and down.

Lizzie furrowed her brow. 'OK,' she said uncertainly, a half-excited smile playing at the corner of her mouth.

The three of them walked together down the corridor, Tom announcing that he didn't want to miss out. Sophie let Lizzie go first and she pushed open the door to the hall before being accosted by cheering children and a hall that was covered in hand-drawn world flags.

'What's going on?' Lizzie asked once the commotion had died down.

'Well, the children knew you were feeling sad about not being able to play football any more, so they put together a table football World Cup for you to play with them this afternoon,' Sophie explained.

Looking around the hall, now that the children had dispersed somewhat, Lizzie could see that there were tables set out all over the room, each with a green pitch made of crêpe paper and teeny-tiny footballers, painted clumsily in World Cup team colours.

'Wow,' Lizzie said, speechless for perhaps the first time ever. She picked up a couple of the players and took a closer look – little cylinders of cardboard, with pipe-cleaner hair. 'You guys made these?'

'Some of us stayed in each lunchtime to make them with Mr Hatton,' Toby said.

'I helped to set up the hall this morning and made the whole of the German team,' said Nigel, stepping forward proudly.

'I made Spain.'

'I made Brazil,' said someone else.

'We did Uruguay.'

'It's been quite the mission,' Sophie said, 'but they wanted to do something to show you they cared and to make you feel better after the accident. It was all their own idea. Well, with a bit of help from Mr Hatton.'

On cue, Noah appeared from within the group of children. He smiled at Lizzie. It might have looked like an embarrassed smile to anyone from the outside, but to Lizzie, it said more than anyone else could imagine. Lizzie smiled back and held his gaze.

'Right,' he said, clapping his hands once. 'Shall we get this World Cup under way? Everybody get to a table. You too, Miss Morris.'

The children instantly moved to separate tables.

'Miss Morris, come and play with me,' Benjamin said. He had chosen the table closest to her. 'You won't have to walk too far then,' he added with a cheeky grin.

Lizzie joined him at the table. 'Thanks, Benjamin.'

'Your first game will last two minutes. On your marks, get set, go!' Noah blew his whistle, and the children flicked the tiny players, ping-pong balls cascading instantly to the floor, while chaos ensued.

Lizzie had never laughed so much in her life. She knew this differed from normal lessons, but she really did love teaching.

It was sad that these children would be off to their secondary school next term and they'd be replaced by the Year Five class, but Lizzie was excited to get to know them too and to teach properly come September.

As three o'clock approached, Noah announced the winner of the World Cup. Toby had triumphed, winning all of his games with his team, Japan. He did a lap of honour around the hall while everyone cheered him on.

'Right, back to the classroom, everyone,' Sophie announced.

As dutifully as ever, the children lined up and snaked their way back down the corridor, Lizzie hobbling at the rear.

'Miss Morris,' Noah called.

Lizzie turned.

'Have you got a minute?'

She looked back at Sophie, who gave her a nod and a smile.

'Yes,' she said and limped her way back into the hall, perching on the edge of a pile of gym mats. 'Thank you,' she said, looking around the room, the floor of which now looked like some hideous table football massacre had taken place, 'for all of this.'

'I'd love to take the credit.' He walked over to where she was sitting and perched next to her. 'But actually, it was all the children's idea. I just helped them put it together and keep it a surprise.'

'Well, thank you for doing that then,' she said, taking her arms out of her crutches and resting them against the mats.

'How's your leg?' He looked down at his keys, which he played nervously with in his hands.

'It's fine really,' said Lizzie.

Noah raised an eyebrow.

'No, actually fine,' she said, laughing. 'I've done a couple of weeks or so already. Only a few more to go.' She did a sarcastic thumbs up.

'I'm really sorry about everything,' Noah said.

'It wasn't your fault. It was that dad's. He'd better be worried if his child is in my class next year.'

'I don't mean about that,' Noah said, shifting to face her.

'Oh?'

'I'm really sorry that everything that happened . . . happened.'

Lizzie was still unclear. 'Noah, for once can you just say what you mean?' she said, exasperated.

'I'm sorry I let Kirsty break us up all those years ago,' he said quickly.

'We both let her do that. It wasn't your fault.' She looked at him. 'I shouldn't have believed her when she said that you had cheated. I knew you'd never do anything like that to me, not really. But I just took her word for it and let my silly head believe it. And afterwards, with the fire, I didn't have the emotions to think about the whole thing rationally. Who knows? If the fire hadn't happened, perhaps I'd have seen the situation for what it was and spoken to you again. But with everything that happened, it was all too much for me to deal with at the time.'

'What do you mean?' Noah asked.

'This sounds silly, but I felt for a long time that Mum and Dad . . . dying in the fire like that . . . it was sort of my fault because I'd turned my phone off to escape you.'

'Lizzie . . .'

'I realise now that there was nothing I could have done. And I know it is just a coincidence that both things happened at the same time. I guess I linked the two of them together somehow and confused all the emotions I felt – I was angry, guilty, hurt, grieving. It's taken a long time to move past them, especially when it comes to you. I thought maybe we were getting there a couple of weeks ago.'

Noah said, 'I'm sorry that after Sunday night, I let things unravel without trying harder to salvage them. I kissed you then because it's all I've wanted to do since you walked back into my life. But then Benny told me you'd been walking back from a date with him on Sunday, and I just sort of didn't know where I stood.'

'Oh God!' Lizzie rubbed a hand over her face. 'You know Benny asked me out when he was drunk on Saturday night? After you and I argued outside the toilets, and then when I saw Kirsty doing the walk of shame, I just came to the wrong conclusions and said I'd meet Benny for a drink. I was walking along the river that night because Benny had set me straight about everything and I'd left early. I'm so sorry, Noah.'

Noah looked at her and she suddenly felt very exposed.

'I guess we're both sorry then,' he said.

'You've got nothing to be sorry for, Noah.'

'I'm sorry I let you go in the first place,' he said, biting the inside of his lip.

His words took her breath away. She held it for a moment while she thought about what she was going to say next. She finally had a real chance here to tell him how she felt, and she knew she couldn't blow it.

'Me too. The thing is—'

'I love you, you know,' he said suddenly, echoing her thoughts. He studied her face for a reaction.

Lizzie looked back at him, unable to stop the smile from spreading across her face.

'I love you too, Noah. It's always been you.'

Noah brushed her hair away from her face and pulled her

towards him on the gym mats. He kissed her softly on the lips. It took Lizzie back to stolen kisses at school in the PE changing rooms. He smelt the same, held her the same way. His lips were the same. It was as though no time at all had passed, and yet so much had happened since.

He pulled away, and Lizzie opened her eyes to look at his face. His dark eyes looked right down into hers and he was smiling.

'You've made me wait weeks for that,' he said eventually.

'We kissed, Noah,' Lizzie said, poking him playfully in the ribs.

'Not that,' he said, retaliating.

'What then?' she asked, squinting.

'I fell for you again the moment I saw you at the beginning of term, Lizzie. Everything came rushing back and we've just been bickering ever since. I've not talked to you properly. I've been in love with you since the moment I saw you again. In fact, I don't know if I ever really stopped loving you at all.'

'We always did bicker, didn't we?' Lizzie said, pulling her cardigan around her.

'It was what I loved most about you, what I still love most about you. You're never afraid to say how you feel, Lizzie Morris.'

He held her hand in his and stroked his thumb across her palm. Lustful feelings shot through Lizzie's body and made her stomach flip. She bit her lip.

'Have you spoken to Kirsty since?' he asked.

'Sort of,' Lizzie admitted, taking her hand away.

Since their conversation at the charity event, things had been better, but they weren't quite there yet.

Noah took her hand back and said, 'She's your sister and

she's had a crappy time of it recently. You need to make up with her properly. I think it's important to you.'

She wasn't prepared to get into an argument about this one. She knew he was right.

'I know,' said Lizzie. 'And we're working on it. It'll just take some time.'

'Well, whatever you need, I'll be here for you,' he said, wrapping his arm around her and kissing her on the top of her head.

And she knew that he would be. She embraced his warmth and breathed in that familiar woody scent, and Lizzie knew she was right where she wanted to be. She was home.

Acknowledgements

As always, I have to begin my thank yous with everyone who has championed my writing and helped me in the process of getting *A Match to Remember* to publication. So, firstly, thank you to Saskia Leach and everyone at Kate Nash Literary Agency for your support, and to everyone at Allison & Busby for once again guiding me through the publishing process. A special shoutout goes to my editor, Sara Magness, for ironing out my timeline and making sure everything happened where it should.

I also want to thank readers and friends who supported me with my first novel, *A Concert for Christmas*; all of which means I've been given the opportunity to publish a second book. So, huge thanks to all the friends, family, colleagues, book bloggers and social media followers who shared, retweeted, followed, liked, reviewed and engaged with me on social media, helping to make it all so special – and ultimately, a success! Thank you also, to the wonderful Romantic Novelists' Association, Yolly Colucci, Jennifer Page and Kimberley Adams for all sorts of support in various forms – you are all brilliant!

Thank you to Mum and Dad, Aunty Heather and Aunty Linda who have been my cheerleaders throughout.

And to Matt and Audrey as always. Thank you for giving me an extra hour on weekend mornings to get the words down. I love you both so much.

HELEN HAWKINS is a writer, editor and English teacher. Her first novel, *A Concert for Christmas*, was shortlisted for Penguin's Christmas Love Story Competition and highly commended in the I Am In Print Romance Competition in 2022. When she is not writing, Helen can be found editing, singing and dancing with her local operatic society in Oxfordshire.

helenhawkins-author.com

D